An Unexpected Suitor

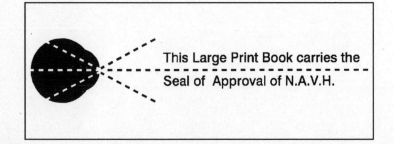

This Large Print Book carries the
Seal of Approval of N.A.V.H.

An Unexpected Suitor

Anna Schmidt

THORNDIKE PRESS
A part of Gale, Cengage Learning

GALE
CENGAGE Learning·

Detroit • New York • San Francisco • New Haven, Conn • Waterville, Maine • London

GALE
CENGAGE Learning™

LIBRARY OF CONGRESS CATALOGING-IN-PUBLICATION DATA

Schmidt, Anna, 1943–
    An unexpected suitor / by Anna Schmidt. — Large print ed.
        p. cm. — (Thorndike Press large print Christian historical fiction)
    ISBN-13: 978-1-4104-2490-7 (alk. paper)
    ISBN-10: 1-4104-2490-1 (alk. paper)
    1. Businesswomen—Fiction. 2. Tearooms—Fiction. 3. Threats of violence—Fiction. 4. Nantucket Island (Mass.)—Fiction.
5. Religious fiction. 6. Large type books. I. Title.
PS3569.C51527U54 2010
813'.6—dc22   2010002603

Published in 2010 by arrangement with Harlequin Books S.A.

Printed in the United States of America
1 2 3 4 5 6 7 14 13 12 11 10

Let me sing to Yahweh
for his generosity to me.
Let me sing in the name of
Yahweh, the most high.
                              — *Psalms* 13:6

In celebration of our differences
as well as our similarities.
To friends, family and passing
acquaintances.

Just a sandy windswept island!
What more would you have it be,
With a turquoise sky above it,
Around a sapphire sea?
— Mary Eliza Starbuck,
Nantucket and Other Verses

CHAPTER ONE

Nantucket Island
May 1899

"Mail must be in," the barber said as he slapped lime cologne onto Harrison Starbuck's freshly shaved cheeks. "There goes Miss Nola. Set your watch by that woman." He spoke of her as if she were some island institution or a bit of a legend. By Harry's calculations she couldn't be more than thirty. He'd gone to school with the Burns brothers, two boisterous lads who were incredible athletes but not very good students as he recalled. Was she older than the boys or younger? He couldn't remember. The day after he'd graduated Starbuck had left for New York and he'd lost touch with her brothers.

He paid the barber and stepped outside, taking shelter from the drizzle under the awning over the bookstore. Down the street, her face hidden by the large black umbrella but her no-nonsense stride unmistakable, Nola Burns continued on her way like a crusader on a mission.

Harry considered his next move. He'd had his eye on the property that housed Miss Nola's Tearoom. With the owner out, maybe he could get Judy Lang, who did the baking for the tearoom, to show him around. The truth was Nola Burns intimidated him — always had. Judy Lang, on the other hand, was a talker and even at age sixty or more, still a bit of a flirt. She would no doubt let slip problems the tearoom had suffered, perhaps a leaky roof or faulty plumbing. All fodder for giving Starbuck the upper hand when it came to negotiating. He strolled across the street and tried the door.

Locked. Harry stared at the silver door handle then scratched his jaw. No one in 'Sconset ever locked a door, not even shopkeepers out on an errand. They might post a Back in Five Minutes sign, but they did not lock up except at night. He frowned and walked the length of the wide front porch that overlooked the town's main street. Then he followed the porch around to the side of the mansion. On a clear day, the vista now obscured by fog and mist was the best view of the Atlantic on the island. The thud of the waves hitting the beach several feet below the bluff reminded him that if the sun were out, he'd be looking beyond the horizon toward the next land any sailor would see — the coast of Spain.

As the new century approached, tourism had firmly established itself as Nantucket's economic bread and butter. Below stood the railroad station where vacationers fresh off the steamer in Nantucket Town would soon arrive in droves for their holiday in 'Sconset. They could either walk to the stairway that climbed up to the top of the bluff or hire one of the surreys or drays waiting at the station. Either way, when they got to the top, the first major structure they saw was Miss Nola's Tearoom. He took a moment to light his cigar, shielding the match from the salty sea breeze and slackening rain. Yes, this was the perfect location.

"May I help you?"

There was not an ounce of warmth in the female voice that came unexpectedly from behind Starbuck. When he turned — a smile firmly planted on his face — Nola Burns stood as stiff and rigid as a marble lawn statue not two steps from him.

Starbuck was pretty sure that in all the time he'd spent in 'Sconset, he'd never been this close to her. They had little in common beyond attending the same church where she played the organ and he sang in the choir. And while he was sure he had acknowledged her in passing, she rarely hung around long enough after services to socialize. Had he ever engaged her in casual conversation surely he would have noticed the skin like alabaster, the full mouth that she appeared to be an expert at taming into a precise thin line, and those eyes — fiery, dramatic, and black as a starless Nantucket night. It occurred to him that onstage her features would be quite an asset in communicating the drama of any production.

But he suspected that Nola Burns, like many in the small village, disapproved of the growing presence of a colony of actors and musicians who had discovered the pleasures of summer in 'Sconset. Since Starbuck was also a summer resident and involved in a variety of theatrical enterprises, he was used to being cast in the same mode by some of the locals. On the other hand, he'd always had some success in winning over dissenters with his charm and wit, so he removed his hat and widened his grin. "Caught me," he admitted with a smile, the true power of which he'd discovered at age fifteen. More than once he'd been told that his smile — a little shy with a touch of cockiness — could send any woman's heart into the kind of palpitations that had her thinking she had laced her corset far too tight that morning.

Nola Burns's breathing did not change one iota. "Well?" she demanded.

Starbuck decided to take another path. He thrust out his hand. "Harrison Starbuck, ma'am, although everybody calls me Harry or just Starbuck. I knew your . . ."

His hand hung there in midair, ignored and rejected. "I know who you are. What is it that you want, Mr. Starbuck?"

Strike two.

He withdrew his hand and straightened to his full height, a head and then some taller than the petite Miss Burns. From what he could see of her hair beneath the ugly little bonnet, it was not the premature gray he had thought. It was platinum — almost like spun silver. Fascinated at the contrast of the onyx eyes and the pale hair, he had to resist the urge to touch the wisp that fell against one ear. Instead he rolled his cigar between his fingers, dropping ash onto the floorboards of the porch as he placed it back in his mouth and drew on it. He lifted his chin and slowly exhaled so that the smoke formed a halo over her head. "I've heard that you're a shrewd businesswoman, Miss

Burns, and I came to discuss a proposition that may interest you."

"My business is not for sale," she snapped.

"Well, now, ma'am, I'm not exactly cut out for operating a tearoom." He chuckled. Nothing.

Since she appeared to have a lot in common with every spinster schoolmarm he'd ever encountered, he tried the tactic that had worked on teachers preparing to thrash him when he was in school. He ducked his head and murmured, "If you'll just give me a moment of your time, I . . ."

"It's a small town, Mr. Starbuck. Everyone knows that you have your sights set on my property. Apparently you plan to tear it down or completely renovate it to accommodate some fancy inn for entertaining your business associates and their wives. My late father, Captain Elijah Burns, personally designed this house. Our family has lived here for decades. For these last several years, it has not only been my home, but also my livelihood. It is not for sale."

Harry fought his irritation at her presumptuous attitude. "You might at least want to hear me out," he said, clamping down hard on his cigar.

"Let me be perfectly clear about this, Mr. Starbuck. I do not approve of games of chance or other frivolous entertainment that has people spending money they cannot afford in order to —"

"Games of chance?" He studied her for any hint that she might be joking, then the light dawned and he laughed — a sound that clearly irritated her. "You think the cabaret we're putting up down the road there will offer gambling?"

For the very first time she looked a bit flustered. Starbuck realized that Nola Burns prided herself on having her facts straight and filed that bit of insight away for future reference.

"Well, won't it?" she demanded. "Gambling and alcoholic beverages?"

"No, ma'am." He leaned a bit closer and continued to puff on his cigar. "I'm surprised your sources haven't set you straight well before this. The town fathers have been quite clear on that point. The cabaret is a kind of a clubhouse where the locals and tourists can enjoy family entertainment and sporting events such as tennis and badminton and croquet. In the evenings they can take in a lecture, recital or variety show. In fact, the opening night program will be the debut of a new play. Wholesome entertainment for all ages." He turned so that they were standing side by side looking out toward the shore. "Think of it, Miss Nola," he said, lowering his voice as he extended his arm to encompass the span of coast before them. "It's going to attract a whole new class of tourists beyond those who come for their health or with their families. It's going to bring in folks with money, Miss Burns, lots of money and they are going to want a place to stay that will give them the kind of privacy and charm they expect when they travel."

He could see that he had piqued her interest although she was waging a mighty battle to squelch that curiosity. She eyed him warily. "There are already hotels."

"Perhaps if you knew me . . ." he said at the same moment.

Big mistake. He had broken the mood he had so carefully created. Nola pursed her lips. "I have already said that I know exactly who and what you are, Mr. Starbuck." She took a step back and looked him square in the eye. "You are related — quite distantly, but conveniently — to John Starbuck, one of the island's founding fathers. You turned your back on the island as a youth and began visiting around the same time several others connected with the theater discovered our island. Now those short visits have stretched to stays of the entire season and you have established an entire enclave of . . ."

"Why, Miss Burns, other than Alistair Gillenwater, I wasn't aware that 'Sconset had an established enclave of businessmen and entrepreneurs like me. Please do go on."

Her lips tightened until they nearly disappeared altogether. "I am speaking of your dealings with the theater, Mr. Starbuck. Rumor has it that you have written a new play that you are anxious to preview in a reading for the opening of your cabaret."

"Well, now, miss, it's not really *my* cabaret. I've just had the privilege of putting the deal together for a number of investors and community leaders who . . ."

"Yes. No doubt you saw an opportunity to trade on that family name and enhance your fortune, which is rumored to be impressive."

Starbuck chuckled. "People tend to exaggerate such . . ."

"At the moment, the town fathers have entrusted you with the construction of this place you refer to as the cabaret down there at the end of town. But they have not to my knowledge given you carte blanche to concoct a way to further enhance your own fortune by purchasing my property."

"Are you done?" Starbuck was rapidly losing patience with this prim little . . .

"I also know you are quite fond of the ladies and they of you, if local gossip can be believed. And furthermore you are quite used to charming your way into whatever strikes you as the most interesting business or social 'proposition.' " She pulled the cigar from his fingers and stamped it out in a concrete urn filled with sand at the corner of the porch. "What more should I know, Mr. Starbuck?" she asked.

Starbuck couldn't help feeling a twinge of respect mixed with annoyance. "Well, now, I should point out that I have put a considerable amount of my own money into the construction of the cabaret, which has cut into my adequate but hardly impressive finances. And that was an expensive cigar, Miss Burns."

"You can surely afford another cigar. I, on the other hand, cannot afford to have my home and business burn down." She made her point by using the toe of her shoe to grind out an already dead ash that had fallen to the porch floor. "Now if you'll excuse me, this is my time to go through my mail before I attend to the marketing for the day."

In spite of his annoyance with her, he had to fight to hide his smile. "Your time? The market appoints times? I never knew that."

"I appoint the time, sir. I am a busy woman and I really don't wish to waste any more of *your* time." She stepped aside, indicating that she was waiting for him to leave the premises.

As he started to take his leave, Starbuck had a moment's pity for the woman. He was quite sure he'd never in his life met a woman more in need of a real friend and confidante than this one. And he was immediately stupefied by the very notion that befriending this little prude should occur to him at all. "You have a good day, ma'am," he said, fighting hard to hang on to the last vestiges of his charm as he brushed past her.

That's when he caught a whiff of his favorite flower, lily of the valley.

He paused and glanced around for the source of the small white bell-like blossoms hidden beneath draped green leaves, but the flowerbeds running the length of the porch featured only hydrangea bushes not yet in bloom. The scent was coming from her. Starbuck pulled out a fresh cigar from his pocket. So the lady had at least one vanity. "Enjoy your day, Miss Nola," he murmured as he moved closer than necessary to get past her. She stiffened and this time her breathing definitely changed. Starbuck tipped his hat and bathed her in the full radiance of his triumphant smile.

Nola was well aware of the stunts a much younger Harry Starbuck had pulled in order to get around his parents and his teachers whenever he wanted something. He could be downright innocent when he chose. Her older brothers had thought the sun rose and set on him and her younger sister had hoped to attract his notice, like just about every other single female on the island. Now as a businessman, Harrison Starbuck had returned and was using those very same charms to acquire the village's backing for his various enterprises. The proposed cabaret was just the latest of a long list of ventures he had persuaded others were necessary. "We have to be able to hold our own with Nantucket Town," one merchant had told her. "Starbuck has connections. According to him, 'Sconset could be the place folks go for entertainment on the island and that means money coming into town." She, on the other hand, was perfectly content with the way things were. Men like Harry Starbuck were always looking for ways to turn an even greater profit.

Such arrogance, Nola thought.

On the other hand, no one — even those

who disapproved of his plans to stage plays and other entertainment in the village — ever seemed to question his ability to do it all and do it well. Nola could not deny that the growing population of summer guests had been good for her business. Still, it was one thing when tourists came for health reasons or even to take a short respite from the sweltering heat of summer in a large city. But how could theater people who were dependent on seasonal work afford such a luxury? She had to admit that the actors who had summered in 'Sconset so far seemed nice enough whenever Nola saw them on the street, and since not one of them had ever frequented her tearoom, there had been no real reason for concern. Still, Nola had been raised to believe that people who worked in the theater were not the sort of people one associated with on a regular basis.

"It's a question of upbringing and lifestyle," town matriarch, Rose Gillenwater, had stated earlier that spring as she held court in the tearoom. "It's unseemly the way they rent those cottages all clustered together and move freely between them as if they are all part of some larger family. The very fact they have coined the term 'the colony' to label their living quarters must be held up to question. These people often tour the country — traveling together, staying in hotels — all without proper supervision. Well, one must assume there are certain temptations."

"But, Mother, surely you can't condemn an entire group by the actions of a few," Rose's daughter, Violet, had protested.

"I am not condemning anyone, Violet," Rose had replied. "I am entirely sympathetic to the fact that circumstances beyond their control led these gifted young people down the wrong path."

"They want to perform and use their talents," Violet had started to protest, but her mother had silenced her with one raised finger.

"There are other avenues, respectable avenues, for making use of such talents. Nola here is a shining example of that. As a girl I recall she had a notion to study music in Boston, no doubt with an eye toward performing concerts and such."

"Classical music," Nola had interjected.

"It's no more than crossing the street to make the shift from respectable classical entertainment to the kind of vaudevillian and melodramatic fare that Harry Starbuck puts together and that these people invading our little village are only too eager to perform. Thank goodness, Nola, that you had the good sense to see your duty to your dear mother and siblings and turned your God-given talents toward something as necessary and respectable as providing the music for Sunday services."

Nola flinched now at the memory. It had hurt to have her dream dismissed in such a cavalier manner. Yet she could not deny that the actors' colony had doubled over the last two seasons and now there was rumor that Starbuck planned to enhance the local population of actors by bringing in his own troupe of handpicked performers from New York. In fact, everything Harrison Starbuck was doing seemed designed to encourage that population to frequent the island.

"They'll drive out the regular summer families," Rose had warned. "Mark my words. Once that cabaret opens, there will be an increase in the level of rowdiness and respectable visitors will look for other places to vacation."

Nola had never had reason to question Rose's authority on such topics. The woman had been raised in the high society of Boston. Rose had often talked of their houseguests, an impressive parade of the rich and famous that had included at least one European duke and his duchess. And the very fact that Starbuck had now set his sights on Nola's home and tearoom to expand his empire seemed further proof that Rose's warnings should be heeded.

"Well, you have met your match, Harry Starbuck," she muttered as she watched him pause outside her gate to light a fresh cigar before crossing the street. Oh, he was handsome, all right, in that insolent manner that set her teeth on edge. Everything about the man, including the way he dressed, seemed deliberately calculated to affect an image of nonchalance. The sable-brown hair was straight and a little too long, and it blew across his forehead whenever he removed his hat. And those eyes — blue as a summer sky — and the mouth that always seemed just a breath away from bursting into laughter.

His clothing was yet another affectation in Nola's view. Above the perfectly tailored trousers his attire evoked a kind of careless aplomb. Especially the battered straw fedora that he always wore at a rakish angle. Then there was his preference for a red bandanna scarf tied at the open neck of his shirt in place of a proper tie. Nola's inventory continued as she watched him. He usually preferred a vest but no jacket. On those occasions such as today when he deigned to wear an unstructured — never tailored — jacket, he left it unbuttoned, loosely hanging from his broad shoulders and revealing a gleaming white shirt with no collar and no starch.

Nola could not help wondering who did his laundry. Those shirts were always so pristine, even lacking the proper appearance of a good dose of starch. On the other hand, that softness linked to the faint scent of lime that clung to his clean-shaven jaw and the wide-brimmed fedora indeed gave him an exotic air that even she had difficulty dismissing entirely.

Not that Nola made a habit of assessing men's apparel. It was just that clothing on Harry Starbuck seemed one more detail of the man's determination to stand apart from others. Shaking herself back to the reality of the moment, she realized she was still standing where he had left her. She'd come back to the tearoom before going on to the market for some reason, but at the moment she could not recall what. She tapped the day's mail against her skirt as she tried to gather her thoughts. She refused to move until she had determined her destination, lest Starbuck see her go into the tearoom and immediately out again and believe he had achieved his purpose of befuddling her. If only he would go on about his business.

But he'd paused in the middle of the street to help a visitor with directions. Then he passed old Mrs. Jacobs hobbling along and fighting to keep her umbrella upright against the wind. He relieved her of the umbrella, held it steady over them both and took her elbow as he escorted her safely to McAllister's general store before heading up the side stairway to the office he'd rented in addition to his cottage. Halfway up he paused just long enough to look back at Nola, catch her watching him, and give her a slight bow before entering his office.

CHAPTER TWO

"He's always been a handsome rascal, that one," Judy Lang noted as she came out onto the porch, broom in hand.

"You're half-right," Nola agreed.

"Which half?" Judy actually winked.

"Oh, Judy, surely I can give you more credit than to be taken in by a man who is more charm than substance," Nola said as she brushed past the woman who had become like a surrogate mother to Nola and her siblings after their mother died.

"Word has it that he has plenty of substance, if you catch my meaning," Judy said, following her inside and rubbing two fingers together in the ageless symbol for money.

"Well, if he continues to buy everything not nailed down in 'Sconset, he won't have it for long." Nola opened the first of the stack of envelopes. "Now then, if we are finished discussing Mr. Starbuck for the day, the mail is here."

Judy set the broom aside and picked up the feather duster, running it over the railing that separated the seating area near the windows from the one closer to the fireplace. "You didn't get to the pharmacy?"

Of course, the headache powder Judy had wanted, Nola thought. She'd been on her way to the druggist when she'd caught sight of Starbuck standing on her side porch and altered her route. "I'll go back for it right away," she promised as she sifted through the mail and focused on the envelope marked with the return address of the employment agency she relied upon to provide her a full staff for the season. She'd been anxiously awaiting word from them since she had written several times with no response. She sliced through the envelope with the whalebone letter opener her father had carved for her on one of his voyages and quickly scanned the contents.

"What is it, child? You've gone white as a sheet." Judy thrust a chair under Nola. "Sit," she ordered and Nola did. "Now tell me what's got you so upset that you'd follow my direction without question. That letter spells trouble from the look of you, but we can weather it. We've been through hard times before, right?"

Nola waited for the always excitable

woman to calm herself, making use of the moment to collect her own wits. "The employment agency has closed. They are out of business." Nola swallowed around an enormous lump that threatened to block her breathing. "The first of the summer visitors will soon begin arriving and we have no help, Judy."

"People still need jobs," Judy argued, taking the single sheet of paper from Nola's fingers and reading it carefully. "Why, they've not only closed, they've taken your deposit as well." She handed the paper back to Nola, pressed her palm to Nola's forehead and cheek and added, "I'll go for that headache powder. Looks like we both could use some." Then she grabbed her shawl and hurried out the door.

It did not take long for the news to spread through the small community. If there had been an electric current running from business to business and from one vine covered cottage to the next, word could not have traveled faster. Starbuck was the third person to hear once Judy had told her husband, Jonah.

Jonah Lang often did odd jobs for Starbuck and when he showed up at the office just before lunch, he was clearly downcast about something. "Everything okay?" Star-buck asked nonchalantly, knowing the older man would tell him the real problem sooner or later.

"Aye."

"You feeling okay?"

"Aye."

"How's Mrs. Lang?"

"She's holding her own under the circum-stances."

There it was, the invitation to probe deeper. "She got some bad news, I take it. Anything I can do to help?"

Jonah stared at his scuffed work boots for a long moment. "She might be looking for work." And then it came, the entire tale of the arrival of the letter, the stunned Miss Nola, the handwriting on the wall.

"I see," Starbuck said once the older man had finished his tale.

"Of course, this might be good news for you," Jonah added, eyeing Harry closely. "If she can't keep the place open, I mean."

"The failure of another person's business is never something to be celebrated, Mr. Lang," Harry replied as he saw Jonah to the door. "You go on now and tell Mrs. Lang not to worry. You'll both always have em-ployment with me."

But the truth was that Harry couldn't help

wondering if Nola's apparent misfortune wasn't actually a sign. God's signal that Harry was on the right track and should pursue his idea of buying Nola out.

It had always amazed Harry how prayer worked. It had always stunned others to discover that Harrison Starbuck was a deeply religious man. He was well aware that most people simply assumed there was some ulterior motive to his singing in the choir or volunteering to help with the annual church clambake, but the fact was that Starbuck believed in God. How could anyone not? All a person had to do was get up every day and face the rainbow of possibilities each rising sun brought with it. It would appear that this day had brought opportunity for him in the form of misfortune for Nola Burns.

On the other hand, he had always taken bad news for others as something of a challenge. In this situation, he had no doubt that God would expect him to realize that he had to help Nola Burns find an equally satisfying outcome. But with someone like Nola, simply throwing money at the problem was not going to be the solution. He stood at his office window and studied the house down the street.

"Okay, so if not just money, what else?"

31

He prayed in the casual manner he had adopted as a boy when talking to God. "Nola Burns is a devout woman so I can't believe You've sent her this trouble without something else good behind it. Question is, am I the one who needs to help her discover that good?"

Surely a woman like her who had endured hard times would likely have a stash of cash put away for just such an emergency. Judging by her choice in fashion — plain unadorned sturdy cotton or wool dresses of gray or blue — she certainly didn't spend much on herself, and if the vendors around town could be believed she drove a hard bargain when it came to getting the best price for what she did buy.

So, what else?

He could offer her a partnership where he would own the premises and she would manage the inn he hoped to open there. *Work together?* The idea was laughable even if there was the slightest chance she would go for such a thing. He turned back to his desk and rolled out the plans he'd had drawn up for putting up a new luxury inn on the site.

"She'll never go for it. Not with me," he argued as he rolled up the blueprints, closed up the office and headed down the outside stairs to retrieve his bicycle.

Not with me. Not with me. The words matched the rhythm of his pedaling as he rode the rutted grassy road past the old pump and trough in the town center then turned down Rosemary Lane to the cottage that had become his 'Sconset home.

He needed to talk to someone who not only knew Nola, but could be trusted not to go running all over town with the news he'd been asking questions. *Rachel!* The image of his mother's first cousin, Rachel Williams, popped into his mind as he sat alone at his kitchen table cracking open the clams he'd prepared for his noon meal. Everyone liked and respected Rachel. More to the point, the woman knew everyone and every detail of their lives. And like Nola, Rachel had never married. Had chosen not to marry. Yes, Rachel would understand a woman like Nola and know the best approach to take with the tearoom proprietress. Harry flicked the last of the clamshells into a bucket just outside his cottage door and mounted his bicycle for the short ride into Nantucket.

"Well, if it isn't my long lost cousin," Rachel Williams exclaimed when she opened the door to her house on New Street and saw him standing there. "I thought you'd been lost at sea or some such disaster.

Surely nothing short of that would keep you from calling on your mother's poor old relation."

Harry laughed. "You are neither poor nor old, Rachel," he replied as she ushered him inside and took his hat. Harry glanced into the dining room where the table was piled high with an odd assortment of items. Rachel was a dedicated historian and charter member of the island's historical association, and she had made no secret of her disappointment in her cousin once she realized that Harry was far more interested in Nantucket's future than its past.

"What's all this?" he asked, fingering one of a pile of carved ivory pipes.

"Members of the historical association have been collecting all sorts of these thousand-year boxes and depositing them here for me to sort through and catalog." She sighed. "It's amazing how people simply assume that a single woman has all the time in the world for such projects. Not that I mind. There are treasures to be found in these collections of clutter."

"Thousand-year boxes?"

"Now, Harry, you are not so young that you never heard the term. Your own mother must have had just such a box — a depository for all the odds and ends of the household. Odd doorknobs or keys that no longer fit a lock or the heads of walking sticks?" She fingered each item as she named it. "Stuff she probably wouldn't use for a thousand years but kept just in case the need arose?"

"And of what possible use is all this junk?"

"This 'junk' provides a tangible portrait of daily life here on Nantucket in years past. It can be used to create living history for the younger generations, and actually being able to see and touch the things once used in daily life is ever so much more exciting than reading about them in some book. You might want to think about that when you write your next play." She pulled out a chair and sat, then indicated that he should do the same. "Now, why have you come?"

"You make it sound as if I need some pretense to call upon my favorite cousin," Harry replied with mock hurt as he began following her lead in sorting the miscellany into more organized categories.

"You've been back here for a good month already and this is the first I've seen of you other than the day you arrived."

"I've been busy."

They worked in comfortable silence for several minutes. Then Rachel rested her elbows on the table and studied his face.

"Gossip has it that you're interested in buying Nola Burns's place. Turn it into some kind of fancy inn for your rich friends from Boston and New York."

"That's fact, not gossip," Harry replied, continuing to sort the knobs and watch parts and keys.

"Save yourself the time and trouble and find another site — maybe out by the golf course. Those businessmen seem to enjoy their golf and their ladies like puttering around." She cackled at her play on words. It was well known that the wives of men who played golf often entertained themselves by putting on the large green set up for practicing putting below the veranda of the clubhouse.

"The Burns place has the best location."

"Why?"

"The view. The proximity to everything. Even the dwelling itself has a certain aura of nostalgia that guests will appreciate."

"Harrison, take it from me, you cannot simply ask a woman who has spent her entire life in one place to walk away from it just because you can afford to offer her a boatload of money."

Harry felt a flush of embarrassment creep up his neck. Of course Rachel would see things that way. She'd spent her entire life in this house. She grew up here, buried both her parents, and continued to live in the same house. Some said she never married because she was married to this house.

"It's not the same thing," he replied quietly.

"It's precisely the same thing," Rachel countered. "Nola Burns and I may be fifteen years apart in age but we share a great deal in common. And it's high time men like you stopped thinking that you are doing us some favor by creating a situation that will force us to go off and 'live' in the larger world. I have no desire to live in that world and from what I know of Nola Burns, neither does she."

"I am not trying to force her to do anything," Harry protested. "I don't even know the woman."

"More's the pity," Rachel muttered as she stood and headed for the kitchen. "I've just received a keg of lime juice from South America. Would you like some limeade? We can sit in the garden. Now that the rain has passed, it's turned into such a lovely day."

She did not wait for a reply and Harry could hear her bustling around the kitchen preparing the beverage. When he heard her chipping ice for the pitcher he dropped a ring of odd keys into the assigned box and dusted off his hands. "I was thinking perhaps that Miss Burns and I might work together — in a kind of partnership," he explained as he carried the tray out to the garden and set it on a small cast iron table.

"And what did she say to that idea?"

"I haven't suggested it yet. I wanted to get your advice on the best approach. As you said, you and Miss Nola have much in common."

Rachel focused on pouring the limeade. "If you're determined to give your guests an ocean view, then why don't you just buy some beach property like everyone else is doing?"

"Two reasons, the best parcels are gone and precisely because everyone else is doing it, I don't want to."

Rachel handed him his drink, then leaned back in her chair and sipped her own. "That's the Starbuck piece of you, I suppose. This not wanting to follow the crowd." She sighed. "Very well. I can see that you are set on this course regardless of what I may think."

"So you will talk to Nola? Miss Burns?"

"I will not. What I will do is offer you two pieces of information about that young woman that may possibly keep you from making an incredible fool of yourself and losing any chance you may have of working with her."

Harry grinned. "You know, cousin, it's been said that I do know a thing or two about charming the ladies."

Rachel spewed limeade in the air as her laughter exploded. "Ah, yes, I had forgotten to calculate that famous male arrogance into the equation. Very well, first piece of advice — you cannot charm Nola, especially when it comes to business. That young woman has had a lifetime of hardship. She knows how to take care of herself and frankly does not trust anyone else to do so for her."

"And the second piece of advice?"

Rachel sobered. "Find another property to buy — leave the woman in peace. She's earned it."

"Can't do that," Harry said as he drained the last of his limeade and stood up.

"Then tread lightly, Harry. Nola is a good woman, and she'll be good for Nantucket long after you've moved on to your next venture."

Business in the tearoom was already slower than usual for May. The current trade was mostly locals, but that generally set the tone for what Nola might expect over the summer. Even so, Nola recognized that she and

Judy could become quickly overwhelmed if the signs were wrong.

After getting past the initial shock of the news from the employment agency, her first move had been to contact her attorney to get her deposit refunded. Then she had asked him to wire other agencies on the mainland to ask what they might offer in the way of help.

"I hate to be the bearer of more bad news, Miss Nola," her attorney, John Humboldt, had told her the day before.

"Just tell me the worst of it so I can decide what to do," Nola had replied.

Humboldt had folded his fingers and stared up at the tin ceiling of his office. Nola realized he was avoiding having to look directly at her as he delivered his news. "The agency has not simply closed its doors," he began, and Nola stiffened her spine as if about to receive a blow. "The owners have disappeared. I'm afraid there are a number of other creditors in addition to yourself who have been left empty-handed."

"And the other agencies you contacted?"

Humboldt sighed and leaned back in his cracked leather chair. "The other agencies sent responses that barely concealed their mirth at the very idea that they might have help available at such a late date."

"I see," Nola had replied as she pulled on her gloves and stood. "Thank you, Mr. Humboldt."

The attorney had walked her to the door offering ideas Nola was well aware were his desperate attempts to help.

"I understand Harry Starbuck has some interest in your property, Nola. Perhaps this would be a good time to give that some serious consideration."

"Never."

"Be careful about rejecting the idea, Nola. You need to consider not only your future, but Mrs. Lang's as well. She's not getting any younger, you know."

"There just has to be another way." But the truth was that at the moment she couldn't think of a single solution.

When she returned to the tearoom and gave Judy the news, Judy suggested asking the owner of the Beach Hotel to lend her three or four members of his staff until she could find her own. It was a good idea, but Nola really hated asking people she knew for favors. Since her mother's death, she had taken on the mantle of "the strong one" in her family, in the community and certainly in her business. But the truth was that she often longed for the kinds of close friendships her siblings had enjoyed while living on the island. True, she had Judy and there was Rachel Williams in Nantucket. She had even thought of stopping to see Rachel in order to seek her advice after leaving the attorney's office.

But Rachel was Harrison Starbuck's cousin and surely her loyalty to him as family would color any advice she might offer Nola. She stood at the kitchen window staring out and seeing nothing. She was so tired of shouldering the entire burden of the business. Her siblings would send money if she needed it, but they could not leave their busy lives to return to 'Sconset for a summer and help out.

Sometimes, Father, it just gets so hard. And so lonely.

"Nola?"

She turned her attention back to Judy and smiled. "We'll get through this," she assured the older woman. "We've been through worse, haven't we?"

Harry stared at the scattered pages of the script for his new play. If he was going to stage a reading of this for opening night at the cabaret, it was going to need work. A lot of work. His investors were not convinced that this particular play would attract enough of an audience to recoup their investment and bring them a profit. The reading would be his one opportunity to convince them of its merits.

The theme of the play was getting back to the very foundations that had made America great. Over the last several years Harry had become increasingly alarmed at the growing gap between those who had vast sums of riches and those who struggled to get by. The same scenario was playing out around the globe. Surely God's plan had always been that the rich would share their wealth so that no one had to suffer. How to bring that message home through a play? How to touch the hearts and minds of those very people he hoped to reach? How to deliver a play based on a message of charity and interconnection without having it come across as "preaching"?

He forced his concentration back to the script. When he'd first thought of the concept, the lines had practically written themselves. Never before had he written an entire script so quickly. Surely God had been guiding his imagination, his thoughts, his fingers around the pen. But now the words seemed stale and lifeless and he was glad for the interruption of Jonah Lang's slow heavy tread on the steps outside his office.

"Got some bad news, boss."

Starbuck removed the wire-rimmed glasses he always wore when he was working. Jonah Lang was a glass-half empty kind of a fellow and his definition of bad news usually wasn't that bad at all. "On a glorious day like this?" Starbuck said with a smile.

"Roofing materials got held up in New Bedford," Jonah reported.

Starbuck's smile froze. "Because?"

"Well, now, the skipper of the *Maximus* took another job and left 'em high and dry, as they say. Shipment's been loaded but there's nobody to captain the boat."

"So what's wrong with moving the shipment to a vessel with a captain and crew ready to sail?"

Jonah shrugged. "Busy time, boss. Everybody's got winter repairs to get done before the season gets going and things are tight."

Starbuck placed his glasses carefully on the desk. "Any idea how long before the materials arrive?"

"Week — maybe two."

Starbuck stood and braced his hands on the table that served as his desk. "Two weeks?"

"That's the company talking. Ask me, you're looking at maybe three weeks —

maybe a month."

"The acting troupe I hired arrives on Monday. They won't have lodgings until that shipment arrives," Starbuck muttered, thinking out loud.

They could move in with those performers already in 'Sconset for the summer, he thought. Hardly room enough in those cottages for the families already there, though. He paced his office. Hotel? It'd cost him but it was early in the season and just maybe . . .

He was aware that Jonah was still talking but he'd stopped listening.

". . . little chance that Miss Nola would put them up. She's got the rooms just sitting there," Jonah continued and chuckled. "I must be clutching at straws, boss. The very thought that Nola Burns would put a bunch of New York theater folks up there at her place?" Now he was laughing out loud and shaking his head. "Oh, the ladies at the church wouldn't like that."

He certainly had Starbuck's attention now. "Say that again," he said quietly.

Jonah stopped laughing and blinked. "About the ladies of the church?"

"About Miss Nola having rooms to let. Are you saying that Nola Burns has enough space above her tearoom to house a company of six actors?"

Jonah scratched his balding head. "Well now, there's four rooms on the second floor and probably another two or three on the third. Haven't been up there in some time myself. You've been keeping me pretty busy and Miss Nola hasn't called for repairs in a while, but yep, I'm thinking she's got the space. But, boss . . ."

Starbuck pulled on his jacket and slammed on his hat as he headed for the door. "Let me know the minute that shipment sails," he said. "I'll pull a crew of workers from the cabaret project so you can get the roofs on and the interiors painted as soon as possible."

"Will do," Jonah replied as he followed him out the door and down the stairs. "Anything else?"

"See if you can get enough tarps to cover the open roofs on the cottages and get going on the inside work."

"They might have extras down there at the cabaret construction site. You headed there now?"

"Later. Right now, I'm going to have a little chat with Miss Nola."

Harry headed straight for the tearoom and this time, the fact the place was closed for the day did not stop him. He knocked on the frosted etched glass of the double front door and, because he was impatient to get this matter settled, rapped again louder.

CHAPTER THREE

"What on earth?" Judy huffed as she opened the door, but the minute she saw Harry she smiled. "Why, Harry Starbuck, did you come for tea?"

Harry grinned and sniffed the air. "Why, Mrs. Lang, is that your sweet lemon bread I smell?"

"Fresh from the oven," she replied. "Come on back to the kitchen and I'll cut you a slice."

"Maybe later," Starbuck replied, then glanced at the wide circular staircase that wound its way up to the vacant rooms Jonah had mentioned. "Is Miss Nola here?"

On cue, as if she'd been standing just offstage awaiting her entrance, pocket doors leading to the parlor slid open to his right and there stood the woman herself. As usual her lips were pursed as if she had just been sucking a lemon and not yet quite gotten past the startling sourness of it to enjoy the unique tart flavor. Her spine was as stiff as her starched apron, and her hair was pulled so tight he wondered how she could work up the frown that creased her forehead. "May I help you, Mr. Starbuck?"

"I've come to discuss a business proposition. A *different* proposition," he added with a grin. "Truth is, I need to ask a favor."

Instead of replying, Nola turned to Judy. "Thank you, Mrs. Lang. Mr. Starbuck and I will continue this conversation in my office."

How could Starbuck have momentarily forgotten Judy Lang's love of gossip? She stood there looking first at him and then at Nola, curiosity making her eyes fairly dance as she sopped up every nuance of the exchange.

"Sorry, Miz Lang," he said, ducking his head and looking at her with eyes that both apologized and flirted with a single blink. "Could I take you up on the offer of lemon bread another time?"

Her eyes narrowed. "Now, don't you go causing trouble for Miss Nola here, Harry Starbuck," she warned. "She's already given you her answer about selling this place so just see to it that you mind your manners, young man." And with that she turned on her heel and marched back to the kitchen.

Harry faced Nola. She indicated the room beyond the pocket doors. "Won't you come in?" she invited, her voice cool. "I have a few minutes."

Starbuck took heart. At least she hadn't thrown him out. Yet. "Yes, ma'am. Thank you," he said and stepped into the inner sanctum of her private quarters.

The parlor that doubled as her office was surprisingly spare in its furnishings. Despite the preference many women had for filling every square inch with doodads and furniture, Nola's place was light, airy, inviting. The sea breeze stirred the lace curtains that covered open windows. The wood floors were polished to a high sheen with only a single, pastel-colored Oriental rug interrupting their flow. There were library bookcases to each side of the Carrara marble fireplace. Instead of being crammed with volumes they featured a selection of books interspersed with a few of the most impressive seashell specimens Harry had seen on the island. Her desk was positioned near the large bay window, carefully placed at an angle to take maximum advantage of the view. In front of the fireplace were two matching chairs, their armrests covered with dainty lace doilies that matched the curtains, and a single large ottoman.

In spite of its sparse furnishings, the room was cozy and welcoming. It felt peaceful, nothing at all like what he would have expected from the very prim Nola Burns.

She took the chair at her desk, leaving him little choice but to stand, hat in hand, the inviting chairs being turned away from her position at the desk.

"Now then, what is this all about?" she asked.

"Jonah Lang tells me that you have rooms upstairs to let."

"Exactly how is that your concern?"

"I'd like to rent them."

He could not help but be fascinated by the range of emotions that flashed across Nola's features at that simple admission. Surprise was followed by wariness, followed by the sheer will to maintain control and reveal nothing. "It's true that on occasion I rent out the upstairs rooms, but I only do so at the height of the season when the hotel is fully booked and then only to people of unimpeachable character," she replied evenly.

Starbuck saw a potential opening. "I would only need the rooms for a short time now at the start of the season, before the real crowds arrive."

Nola frowned and her eyes narrowed. "If

this is a ploy to offer your city friends a preview of the luxury inn you hope to create here . . ."

"I wish to rent the rooms to house my troupe of performers until such time as the cottages I secured for them can be repaired. A month — perhaps less."

"I'm afraid, Mr. Starbuck, that you . . ."

"Will you stop with the Mr. Starbuck? It's me — Harry. I went to school with your brothers. You were no more than what? Two years behind me?"

"Three," she replied.

"Exactly. We grew up on this island and as you pointed out the other day, you know exactly who I am, Nola."

"But you have little knowledge of who I am," Nola said as she rose and came around the desk. "I am sorry that you have run into a problem of housing your company, but I'm quite sure with your considerable resources you can find a solution."

"I'll pay you well, Nola, and in light of recent developments with the employment agency going out of business and all . . ."

She arched one eyebrow as she passed him on her way to the door. "This is not about money," she said. "Besides, I should think that having heard about my staffing shortage, you would see an opportunity to acquire my property."

"I'm not following you, Miss Nola. I simply need to rent some rooms. You have rooms to rent. I'd pay you, which adds to your business income. How exactly does that help me in getting you to sell?"

"I should think it's obvious. You would have your people here in residence, watching, listening, snooping about."

"I'm not that devious and my friends don't stoop to such tactics, either. Now will you rent me the rooms or not?"

"No. And I will not be selling you this property. Now, may I suggest that we both get on with finding alternate solutions to our business difficulties?"

"This isn't over, Nola," he murmured as he headed for the door.

"Yes, it is. Have a good day, Mr. Starbuck."

On Sunday, as always, Nola was up with the sun but she could not seem to decide on her costume for church. She was well aware that Harry Starbuck was the reason for her hesitation. The man made her painfully conscious of her plainness, although why she should care one iota what his opinion might be, she had no idea. Well, she had some idea.

After his visit a few days earlier, it had dawned on her that Harrison Starbuck was not going away any time soon and for the time being the two of them were locked in battle. In her view he could afford any piece of land he wanted, so why set his sights on her property? The answer was as clear as the cloudless sky and calm sea outside her bedroom window. He didn't give one minute's thought to the fact that this had been her family's home for decades. Well, if Harry Starbuck wanted a fight, then she was prepared to give him one.

After finally settling on her standard Sunday garb, Nola took one last look at herself in the gilded mirror that dominated the entrance to the tearoom. You look fine, she thought to herself. Now go to church.

It was her habit to arrive at the church a full hour before services were scheduled to begin. She liked having the time to run through the hymns and her prelude on the temperamental pump organ before the congregation began to gather. But on this morning, as soon as she approached the church, she realized that she was not to have that quiet time to herself.

There was no mistaking the sound of Harrison Starbuck's laughter as it rolled up the center aisle and out through the open church doors to greet her. His obvious good humor rumbled from the depths of him, like a wave building power before finally exploding onto the beach. In the environment of the church with its high beamed ceiling and echoing acoustics, the sound reverberated, hanging on the morning air.

Nola stepped into the small vestibule and considered her options. He had not yet spotted her. She could take a walk through the church cemetery until he had vacated the premises, or she could refuse to abandon her normal routine. She chose the latter, squaring her shoulders as she marched into the sanctuary.

"Ah, here she is now," Oliver Franks, the choir director, announced.

Nola walked straight to the pump organ across from the choir loft at the front of the chapel. "Good morning, Oliver. Mr. Starbuck." She removed her gloves and set them down along with her purse as she slid onto the polished organ bench and positioned her music for the prelude.

"Harry has agreed to favor the congregation with a solo this morning," Oliver said. "And not a minute too soon since Minnie has come down with laryngitis and won't be in church today." Oliver's wife, Minnie, often sang a solo while the ushers accepted the offering.

"I'm so sorry to hear that Minnie is ill," Nola said and meant it. Minnie Franks was a good neighbor and friend. The two women shared a great deal in common, including their concern over the influence of the actors' colony on the young people in the village. "Is there anything I can do for her?"

"Not a thing. She'll come around," Oliver assured her. "Now then, Harry here has suggested 'Holy, Holy, Holy,' and I completely agree that the hymn was made for a rich baritone like his." Oliver opened the hymnal and set it on the organ in front of Nola. "Shall we give it a try?"

During this entire exchange, Harrison Starbuck had said nothing, but Nola was keenly aware that his eyes had never left her face. She adjusted the hymnal and pulled out several of the organ's stops. Then she raised her hands high over the keys and struck the opening chords. But when Starbuck touched her shoulder, she missed the timing and the organ screeched to a halt. She glanced first at his hand still resting on her shoulder and then up at him.

The scoundrel was smiling jubilantly. "Perhaps a bit less pomp and circumstance?"

"It is a hymn of praise," she reminded him stiffly.

"Sometimes praise can be whispered as effectively," he countered.

"Perhaps you would prefer no accompaniment at all." She could see Oliver nervously wringing his hands as he observed the exchange.

"Interesting idea," Starbuck said as he leaned past her and struck a key, his face close enough that she could see the smoothness of his freshly shaved jaw. He hummed the note, then stood straight and tall and faced the empty pews.

"Holy. Holy. Holy." He sang each word as if it stood alone, allowing the sound to build without increasing the volume. And then he paused as the third *holy* echoed across the rafters. When all was silent, he continued. "Lord God Almighty." This he held as if sending up a plea for God's attention.

Nola could not help it. His fresh interpretation of the old standard was mesmerizing and for that moment she completely forgot who was offering the hymn. Her fingers found the notes and ever so softly, she began to play as he sang, "Early in the morning, our song shall rise to Thee."

Starbuck looked back at her and nodded and indicated with hand gestures how the rest of the hymn should build. When they came to the final phrase, instinctively, Nola lifted her fingers from the organ keys, allowing his voice to carry the final words without accompaniment.

"God in three persons," he sang softly, his inflection filled with wonder, and then "Blessed trinity" with the emphasis on *blessed.*

"Oh, my," Oliver gasped as the last note died away. "Oh, that was just splendid."

And hard as she tried not to take pleasure in the moment, Nola found herself beaming up at Harrison Starbuck.

But her smile faded when his eyes locked on hers for he wasn't smiling at all. He was studying her as if she'd suddenly turned into a completely different person. And then it was as if he tore his gaze from hers as he accepted Oliver's compliments.

"In the theater, the actors are well aware that often they are made to look better than they are by those who support them." He gave Nola a little bow. "We make a fine team, Miss Nola. Are you satisfied with the arrangement or shall we try it your way?"

Was Starbuck mocking her? He knew very well that what he had done was magnificent. Nola stiffened. "I doubt there's time for testing other arrangements," she said, deliberately looking at the gold brooch watch she had pinned to her jacket lapel. "And if you'll forgive me, gentlemen, I should like to run through the prelude and review today's congregational hymns before people begin arriving."

"Of course," Oliver said. "Nola always uses this hour to rehearse. She's so busy during the week. I'm afraid we have intruded on your time, my dear."

"Not at all," Nola assured Oliver. "The prelude today is a standard that I've done many times before. Mostly," she added for Starbuck's benefit, "I rely on this time to make sure the organ is working well and to warm up for the service." And not waiting for a response, she turned her attention to the music and began to play.

To her relief the two men moved up the aisle and she assumed they had gone outside to give her privacy while they enjoyed the warm spring morning. Reverend Diggs arrived and nodded to her as he went through his own preliminary preparations for the service. He placed his notes on the pulpit, marked each hymn page with a bookmark and then headed into the small side room where she knew he would don the black robe he wore for services.

She sounded the final chords of the prelude and then leaned back, stretching her shoulders and splaying her fingers as she lifted her arms high above her head.

"I never appreciated how gifted a musician you are," Starbuck said.

Nola whipped around to find him sitting alone in the last pew, one long leg crossed over the other and his arms stretched along the back of the pew in a posture that seemed to announce ownership over his domain.

"Thank you," she replied rigidly and scanned for some way to occupy herself as a means of escape. In her peripheral vision, she saw the long legs unfold, saw the polished shoes beneath the tailored black trousers move down the aisle, and felt her breath grow shallow.

"Seriously," he continued as he propped one foot on the platform that held the organ and rested his elbow on his knee, "you should think of doing a concert — classical music."

"I do not perform for profit," Nola said and was surprised when instead of being rebuffed Starbuck leaned even closer and grinned.

"Who said anything about paying you?" Then he pushed himself upright and turned to join other members of the choir who were beginning to fill the pews across from the organ.

As she walked back to the tearoom after church, Nola was still trying to work through the range of emotions that had come with the morning's service. It was not the sermon that had touched her. The truth was she had barely heard Reverend Diggs's lesson for that day and during the closing prayer she had asked God's forgiveness for her inattention.

No, her consternation came from the fact that in spite of her reservations about Harry Starbuck, she could not help but relish the experience they had just shared with the entire congregation. She had been thrilled by the silence that had filled the little chapel as his last note floated to the rafters and out the open windows. And yes, she took some pride in the way she had improvised the hymn to complement his voice and style.

She was humming softly to herself when Harrison Starbuck fell into step beside her.

"Lovely day," he acknowledged as if they had been conversing already. "Weather like this will bring out the tourists earlier than usual."

Ah, so he was taking a circuitous approach to bringing up the subject closest to his heart — the idea of buying her property. Well, he wasn't fooling her.

"Yes. I'm looking forward to quite a profitable season," she assured him. "I might even consider expanding the services of the tearoom."

To her surprise he nodded thoughtfully. "That's an idea," he said almost absentmindedly.

They walked along in silence for several more steps and Nola was keenly aware of others taking note of Starbuck appearing to walk her home.

"Was there something you wanted?" she asked finally.

He glanced down at her as if he'd quite forgotten she was at his side. "Yes, as a matter of fact. May I come in for a bit, Nola?"

It was the last thing she had expected. Her mouth opened but nothing came out.

"I'd like to ask a favor," he added.

"As I have said repeatedly, my rooms are not available to rent to your actors and my home and tearoom are not for sale. Nothing is going to change that."

He blinked down at her and then grinned. "I can see where you might think that's what this is about, Nola, but actually it's something altogether different."

Nola could not help wondering if there

might not be charm schools for men like Harry Starbuck. That smile, that twinkle in his eye, the dimples that punctuated each cheek. No wonder half the women in town were constantly on the lookout for him.

"So, please may I come inside?" he asked.

"I have another engagement." It was only partially true, for Nola had no other plan than to make herself a cold lunch and eat it while she went over the latest batch of bills for the tearoom. She mounted the steps of her house and realized with relief that Starbuck was no longer with her.

"Pretty please?"

She turned and saw that he had swept off his hat, placed it over his heart and was on bended knee at the foot of the porch steps. Across the street two women from the church had stopped, their gloved hands covering their mouths as they obviously placed their own interpretation on the scene playing out before them.

"Get up, Harry," Nola ordered. "This is not one of your plays. People are staring."

Starbuck got to his feet but he was grinning as he turned and bowed toward the women across the street. When he turned back to Nola, he gave her a boyish shrug. "Might as well let me speak my piece, Nola. That way you can put to rest the rumors that we've started."

We've? Nola was speechless. "You, sir, are no gentleman," she muttered.

"Never took credit for being one," he agreed amicably as he mounted the steps and indicated one of the wicker rockers that lined the wide veranda. "Shall we sit out here or go inside?"

"You will state your business and be on your way," Nola muttered as she plopped herself down in the first rocker, forcing him to take one that was hidden from the street by a trellis lush with rosebuds ready to burst into bloom.

"Well?" She sat on the edge of her seat, back ramrod straight, gloved hands folded on knees pressed together under the smooth challis of her skirt.

He lounged, one ankle crossed over his knee, straw hat pushed back to fully reveal his clean-shaven face. "You are a talented musician," he began.

Nola sighed. "I told you I do not play except at church."

He ignored this. "I was chatting with some folks after services and Oliver mentioned that you've done some composing." When her eyebrows shot up in surprise, he added, "Oliver also said you had planned to attend the conservatory in Boston but then your father died."

"There was a time when I had thought . . ." Nola stopped herself in mid-sentence, horrified at what she had almost revealed to this man.

"You had hoped for a career in music," he guessed and leaned forward, elbows resting on knees as he searched for more. "You were going to but then your father . . ."

"My family's history is none of your business," she said tightly as she focused all of her attention on her clenched hands to avoid meeting his eyes.

"I remember now, Nola. Even after the whaling industry collapsed your father refused to give up. He made one last run but his ship was caught in a storm and all were lost at sea. That left your mother — and you — to manage the family. When she died you took over that parenting role even though your brothers were older by three years. You see? I know a great deal about you. Yes, now as I recall . . ." He frowned as if trying to retrieve a long-buried memory.

She looked up at him, curious in spite of herself. "What?"

"Well, it's just coming back to me how your brothers were always at every school or church function. And your younger sister as well."

Nola brushed the memory aside. "As was I. What's your point?"

"They were there with the rest of us — the young people, the children. You were always with the adults."

Nola fidgeted uncomfortably. "As usual you have moved us away from the topic at hand."

Again he continued as if she had not spoken. "You gave up your dreams and ambitions for them."

Someone had to take responsibility, she wanted to shout at him. What did he think? That it was easy? Keeping them all together? Making sure there was some money coming in so the others could get through school and find lives of their own?

To her utter dismay, Nola felt the grief over her own lost youth that she had effectively stuffed inside for years threaten to explode.

"Nola?"

Starbuck leaned even closer, his hand hovering an inch from hers, his eyes watching her with concern.

"Please do not presume to understand anything about the choices I have made in my life. And now I must ask you to please leave," Nola whispered.

He stood up but did not make a move to

leave. "I'm sorry for upsetting you," he said quietly. "Here's what I came to say. You know the play I'm working on for the opening of the cabaret? Well, today during church it came to me that the message of the play would be more powerful if it were told in the form of an operetta. Time is short but I think if I set the lines to old classics — even some old hymns — it might just work, at least for the preview at the cabaret. Would you be willing to read over what I've written and see if you can perhaps suggest some classics that might work?"

She drew in a breath but said nothing. Did he truly think he could win her trust by asking her advice on his play?

"I'm not trying to pull anything over on you here, Nola, by flattering you. I was genuinely impressed with the way you adapted the accompaniment to fit my solo this morning. You have a natural gift — in the business we often refer to it as a natural 'ear.' "

She soaked in his words, examining each for any hint of trickery.

He stood up and when she heard the creak of the top porch step, she risked looking at him. "Hey." He half turned then added with that trademark boyish smile, "What could it hurt to have a look at it?"

Nola sat stone still.

"Okay," he said, putting on his hat. "How about this? I'll drop off a copy tomorrow. You take your time, but I'd be grateful for any thoughts you might have."

And then he was gone.

CHAPTER FOUR

Try as she might to make sense of the bills, the orders and how she could possibly stay open for business with no staff, Nola's mind kept wandering back to the church service that morning and to Harry's request that she take a look at his play. Under other circumstances she would have been flattered. But how could she possibly trust him? He had one agenda and that was to acquire her property. She had to keep her wits about her and realize that everything Starbuck did or said was somehow tied to business.

"Hello? Nola?"

Nola's spirits lifted at the call of her friend, Rachel Williams. With everything else on her mind, she had forgotten that Rachel was stopping by. "In here," she called as she hastily stacked the business papers and set them aside, realizing she'd been so disconcerted by Starbuck's request that she'd left her front door wide open.

"More rain coming," Rachel said as she entered the parlor and accepted Nola's hug. "My hip is acting up again." Using her cane she limped over to a chair.

"Have you had lunch?" Nola asked.

Rachel eyed the untouched tray on Nola's desk. It had enough food on it to serve three people. "Perhaps I could just share yours?" Rachel suggested.

Nola laughed. "I'll get an extra place setting. We can eat there by the fireplace. No need for you to move," she assured her friend.

Rachel watched as Nola bustled about setting places, bringing the laden tray over so Rachel could make selections from its contents of small sandwiches, sweetbreads, fruits and cheeses. After Nola had poured glasses of iced tea for each of them she hovered, trying to decide if there was anything else she could do to make her guest welcome.

"Stop fussing about, Nola, and sit," Rachel said as she spread a linen napkin over her knees and reached for a cube of cheese. "Now tell me what the trouble is." Nola started to protest but Rachel held up one finger. "A woman does not prepare mounds of food for herself if there isn't something troubling her. It's that cousin of mine, isn't it?"

"No. Yes. Not really. Actually he has the perfect solution to my troubles. He is willing to buy me out."

"So I heard. Ridiculous idea. The man has his finger in far too many pies if you ask me. Of course, no one did, least of all him." She studied Nola closely. "You aren't seriously thinking of selling to him, are you?"

"I don't want to — I don't want to sell at all. I mean, what on earth would I do?"

"You could travel?"

"I suppose," Nola replied without much conviction.

"But the truth is this is your home — not just the building itself, but 'Sconset. So don't sell."

"If only it were that simple. You must have heard by now that I'm short staffed?"

Rachel nodded.

"Well, even with business being as slow as it is now, Judy Lang and I can't manage alone. Anyone locally who might be available is already employed for the season."

Rachel popped a finger sandwich into her mouth and chewed it slowly. "John Humboldt and I shared a lovely dinner just the other evening," she said.

Nola was used to Rachel's flights of fancy

71

that seemingly had little to do with the subject at hand. She knew that Rachel was mulling over an idea that she would share in time.

"Our server was a lovely young man — a musician. He and his young family rent one of the cottages here in 'Sconset." She glanced at Nola.

Nola understood that there was a point to all of this, one she was not yet grasping. "That's nice," she ventured.

"How large is your summer staff, Nola? Normally, I mean."

"Five or six people — two to help in the kitchen, two to serve and one or two to clear and set up the tables."

"What a coincidence. I believe Harrison mentioned he was hiring an additional six performers to complement the talent already in residence for the opening of the cabaret."

"He didn't mention a specific number when he inquired about renting my upstairs rooms for his group but yes, I believe that Jonah mentioned there were six."

Rachel grinned. "Then it's perfect. His performers stay here and work in the tearoom for the interim."

"That's not possible, Rachel. People of the theater? I'm already losing local business. If I actually employ actors? And that doesn't even begin to address the eyebrows that would be raised if I were to house them as well."

"Yes, you have a point. On the other hand, it is my understanding that people of the theater are quite used to supplementing their spotty incomes by waiting tables or performing kitchen duty, and it isn't as if it's for the entire season."

"Even so . . ."

"And it would give you the upper hand with Harry. He needs your rooms, Nola. Everything else is booked solid. You can set terms to suit your needs, such as offering the rooms on one condition."

"That his performers staff the tearoom for as long as they reside in my upstairs rooms," Nola murmured.

"Precisely. It buys you the time you need to secure a more suitable staff."

"But what of their rehearsals and . . ."

"There are twenty-four hours in every day, Nola, and this place is open — what — seven of those hours? Harry is a resourceful man. He can surely figure out a rehearsal schedule around that."

"It might just work," Nola said, warming to the idea as she devoured a slice of melon.

"Of course it will work and you mustn't

delay. First thing tomorrow you should march yourself over to that office my cousin keeps above McAllister's store and present the offer. If he has any sense at all, Harry will leap at this opportunity and your problems will be solved as well as his." Rachel dusted crumbs off her lap and reached for a cluster of grapes. "Now, how else can I improve your day, my dear?"

The following morning Nola made a detour from her normal routine. She walked to the post office and then she climbed the stairs outside the general store to Starbuck's office. She saw his bicycle parked in its usual place under the stairway and forced herself to take several deep breaths to calm her nerves at confronting Starbuck on his own territory. After all, up to now, he had always come to the tearoom. Somehow the shift in venue gave Nola pause.

At the top of the stairs, she knocked lightly on the door. It surprised her that there was no sign or lettering on the frosted glass panel in the door. She would have thought a man like Harry Starbuck would be inclined to exclaim his accomplishments to the stars. She rapped again.

"He left early this morning for town," Ian McAllister shouted up at her as he stood on the landing outside the back of his shop below her. For people on the island, town meant the larger community of Nantucket Town. "Said he'd be back by noon."

"Thank you," Nola said and prepared to leave.

"If you like, you could leave him a note. He never locks up," Ian said.

Nola considered the appropriateness of entering the office when Harry was gone. If she left the note, he would come to the tearoom and she could state her case and she would lose no more time. She waved at Ian and stepped inside.

Harry's presence was everywhere in the small room. The swivel desk chair was pushed back and turned to one side as if he'd just stepped downstairs for a moment. Next to the window stood a wooden hall tree with four metal hooks. Two held the familiar sack jackets — one a light fawn linen and the other a charcoal serge. On the third hook hung the black woolen scarf he often wore on cooler days, one fringed end thrown casually over his shoulder. And on the very top hook was a straw hat, battered and shaped to the imprint of Harrison Starbuck's head. But it was his desk that drew her closer, or rather the contents of that desk.

The first thing she noticed was that everything was in perfect alignment. The blotter was precisely even with the edge of the desk. The lamp centered on the blotter's back edge stood behind a brass inkwell, a matching tray holding three pens and a letter opener. She wondered why he chose to use the old-fashioned pen and ink rather than the more popular self-filling fountain pen and found it charming that he did.

To the right was a stack of clean white paper and to the left a smaller stack of the same paper filled with a masculine scrawl. Nola picked up the top sheet.

SIMPLE FAITH
An Operetta

For the next hour Nola sat on the edge of Harry's chair and read. The pages laid out the story of a family living on Nantucket and then moving to the city where they faced a life like none they had ever known or could have imagined. It was the story of how that family faced their fears and opened their hearts to what they came to accept as God's will. It was a play about differences between people. By the final page the members of that family found love and purpose away from the safe surroundings of life on Nantucket by simply remaining true to the traditions and the faith with which they had been raised.

When Nola reached the last page, the handwritten margin notes trailed off after several lines that had been scratched through. This was Harry's first attempt at converting the lines to lyrics, she realized.

She leaned back in his chair, still holding the last page. In so many ways this was her story. She had lived her entire life on Nantucket. As a child she had dreamed the same dreams other children dreamed. She had thought she would go to Boston and study classical music. She had even imagined that one day she would give concerts in recital halls across America — perhaps in Europe.

But everything had changed for her. She had promised herself that once her siblings were off on their own, there would be time enough for her to . . . what?

Follow dreams? Find love?

Hearing footsteps outside and the muffled voice of Ian calling out to Harry, Nola hastily stacked the pages of the play and placed them on the side of the desk. Then she pulled a clean sheet from the other stack of papers and picked up the pen just as Harry stepped through the door.

"Well now, this is indeed a surprise, Miss Nola," he said. "To what do I owe the pleasure of your visit at an hour I believe you usually reserve for marketing?"

Nola's hand shook slightly and a blob of ink splashed onto the paper. She quickly wadded the soiled paper and replaced the pen in its holder, buying the time she needed to steady her nerves now that Starbuck himself was standing before her.

"I was going to leave you a note," she said. "Mr. McAllister suggested it. I . . ."

"And the note would say?"

"I was asking you to stop by the tearoom at your earliest convenience."

Harry grinned and tossed his hat expertly onto a rung of the hall tree. "My earliest convenience is now, so shall we take a walk back to the tearoom or conduct your business here?"

"This is fine," Nola said and she stood up as Harry sat down in the other chair in the room.

He crossed one ankle over the other as he stretched his long legs out in front of him, then folded his arms over his chest and cocked one eyebrow. "I'm listening."

Nola had rehearsed what she would say at least two dozen times and yet now her throat closed and her mouth felt as if it had suddenly been filled with sand. She cleared her throat and looked at him, then away. Part of the problem was that he was sitting with his back to the window. The sun was streaming in and his face was completely in shadow. She moved around the desk and out of the glare of the sun and faced him.

"Your company of performers may occupy the rooms on my upper floors," she began. "With several conditions."

Starbuck slowly uncrossed his feet and arms and sat taller in the chair, his attention riveted on her. "You do have a way of getting my attention, Nola. Okay, what are your terms?"

"One, this is a temporary arrangement until I can hire the staffing I need for the tearoom or you can complete repairs on the housing you rented — whichever comes first."

"Seems fair. What's number two?"

"I will not tolerate raucous behavior, spirits or card playing under my roof."

Harry nodded. "Goes without saying. Three?"

"You will need to arrange whatever rehearsal schedule you have planned around the open hours of my tearoom." Nola took some pleasure in seeing that she had managed to surprise him once again.

"And that would be because?" he asked.

"That would be because in exchange for their room and board your performers will be staffing my tearoom."

Starbuck burst out laughing and Nola's heart sank. She steeled herself for his derision and for his rejection of the entire idea. But to her amazement he stood up and stuck out his hand.

"You've got yourself a deal, Nola."

Unsure of what to say in response to that, she placed her hand in his and fought against the awareness that his was twice the size of hers and yet his grasp was gentle but firm. "Very well, then," she managed. "I'll ask Mr. Humboldt to draw up an agreement."

Starbuck frowned. He was still holding her hand. "Is that really necessary? I mean a gentleman's — and lady's — agreement surely . . ."

"This is business, Harry," she replied and withdrew her hand from his, then headed for the door. "If you'll just let me know when you are expecting the company?"

"Day after tomorrow," he replied as he moved around his desk.

"Then I'll get in touch with Mr. Humboldt right away. Good day, Harry."

She had opened the door and stepped out onto the landing when she heard the rustle of papers followed by his voice.

"Nola?" He handed her the copy of his play. "So, what did you think of it?"

"It's quite good," she replied primly as she pulled the door closed behind her. It's going to be brilliant, she thought and as she descended the stairs she could not help but marvel at the many talents God had seen fit to bestow upon Harrison Starbuck.

Two days later Nola could not seem to control her curiosity. Judy had reported that Starbuck had sent Jonah to the railway station to meet the performers and bring them up the hill to Nola's place.

"I would think Mr. Starbuck would meet them himself," Nola said.

"Oh, he'll stop by later, I'm sure, but something came up with the cabaret construction so he's had to go over there for the time being. Perhaps you should go on down there and greet them," Judy suggested.

"I hardly think that appropriate," Nola replied and yet she seemed incapable of moving away from the bay window of her parlor as the little train chugged into the station. With a swoosh of its brakes, the two open railway cars came to a stop and what she observed next gave her pause.

The first passengers to appear were a couple of dandies — young men in boater hats, striped jackets and vanilla-colored flannel trousers. They did a little tap dance when Jonah greeted them and ended it with a bow. Next they took positions to either side of the platform and appeared to announce the arrival of three women, each of them flamboyantly garbed. The first was a tall stately woman of indeterminate age. She wore a violet gown fitted to every curve of her full-bodied figure down to her knees where the skirt flared. She wore a ridiculously large plumed hat with a veil and twirled a small lavender parasol over one shoulder.

The next two women were slim and also tall. Dressed identically in bright green gowns more suited to evening wear than traveling, they seemed to be talking in unison and nonstop. The fabric of their colorful clothing glinted in the sun and while their arms and necks were covered in white lace, the effect was somehow far too dramatic for proper daytime attire. They also wore hats — smaller than the purple monstrosity the first woman wore but every bit as overdone with plumes and tulle.

Nola sighed. What had she let herself in for?

She was about to turn away when she caught the shadow of yet another passenger. A petite elegant woman dressed in a fashionable canary-yellow suit with a wide-brimmed straw hat banded in yellow tulle stepped into the sunlight. She was holding a small white dog.

Fascinated, Nola watched as the woman stepped from the train and started walking down the platform where a porter was unloading several large steamer trunks onto the dray Jonah had hired. The others trailed behind her forming an unlikely little parade of characters. To Nola's surprise, the woman in yellow stepped up to have a word with Jonah as he pulled the carriage and waited for the actors to climb aboard. She saw Jonah indicate the tearoom at the top of the bluff and then the stairway that was the only way other than the beach road to get there.

The actress appeared to thank him profusely and then she headed directly for the stairs while her fellow performers paused, appeared to consider the climb and then trailed after her.

"Well, they're here," Nola said to Judy, who had also watched the arrival by pretending to sweep the side porch and steps.

"Let's hope I haven't made the gravest of errors in judgment," she murmured.

As Nola stepped out onto the porch to greet them, Judy joined her, smoothing her hair back and setting her broom aside.

The woman in yellow was a good ten steps ahead of the others, who appeared to be struggling to catch their breath after the steep climb.

"Miss Burns? I am Eleanore Chambliss. Harrison tells me you have quite literally rescued our little band from homelessness." She offered Nola her hand and Nola could not help noticing that the actress's fawn leather gloves were the finest she had ever seen.

"This is Mrs. Lang," Nola said, turning to Judy, who curtsied to the actress.

"Ah, the chef," Eleanore said and Judy blushed scarlet. "And this is Sir Lancelot," she said, introducing the white ball of fur that might have been taken for a muff if the season were different. "Not to worry," she assured Nola, "he's quite housebroken and well-behaved. He was born backstage during a matinee."

"I hadn't expected to have . . ." Nola began but the actress interrupted.

"Come along, darlings," she called over her shoulder. "Miss Burns has a business to run here and we are delaying her."

"I'll just show you to your rooms," Judy offered.

"Lead on," Eleanore instructed with a dramatic wave of one hand.

The rest of the introductions were hastily made as the remainder of the troupe followed Eleanore through the doors and up the main stairway. "Of course, we shall use the back stairs when we are working," Nola heard Eleanore instruct the others.

"There was no mention of a dog," she muttered, wondering what else Starbuck might have failed to tell her. "Interviews will begin promptly at eleven," she called up the stairs. "And I assume you will wish to change."

"Your traveling attire simply will not do for serving here at Miss Nola's," she heard Judy explain.

Just half an hour later Nola was pleased to see all six members of the group seated on the twin tufted benches that lined the foyer between her parlor and the tearoom. They had all changed into clothing that, while still a bit colorful for her taste, was at least more subdued than the garb they had arrived in.

"Very well," she said, "shall we begin with the gentlemen?"

The two young men leaped to their feet and smiled at her with confidence. "Jasper March," the one announced.

"William Andrews," chimed in the second, "but everyone calls me Billy."

Nola glanced at their hands — smooth as the inside of an oyster shell. She sighed. "Have you gentlemen ever washed dishes?" she asked as she waited for them to precede her into the parlor and then shut the doors.

The interviews went far better than Nola might have expected. Jasper and Billy assured her that kitchen duty was just fine with them. In fact, they relished the opportunity to work with Mrs. Lang and learn from her. "After all, Billy here will be pulling double duty cooking for the rest of us once we get settled into our real digs," Jasper informed her. "See, he's new and as the new guy he gets the bottom-of-the-barrel assignments — and parts." He chuckled and nudged Billy with his elbow. "Not that I'm saying working in your kitchen is bottom of the barrel or anything," he hastened to add.

"Stop talking now," Billy muttered under his breath and Nola repressed a smile.

"We'll see how things go," she said, ushering them to the door. "Please go see Mrs. Lang and ask her for further directions. Next," she called and the two identically dressed females stood up. They were girls really, surely no more than eighteen, if that.

"Deedee and Mimi Kowalski, ma'am," they chorused.

A bit nonplussed that the two of them not only dressed alike but seemed to speak in unison as well, Nola turned to the third woman — still wearing purple although now it was a plainer skirt and blouse ensemble. Nevertheless it was still fitted to show off her large chest, tiny waist and curvaceous hips. Her face was heavily made up in what Nola realized was an attempt to hide her true age. "And you are?"

"Olga Romanoff — Countess Olga Romanoff," the woman intoned in a deep throaty accented voice as she brushed past Nola and entered the parlor.

Nola saw Eleanore roll her eyes and heard Sir Lancelot give a low growl as the countess passed.

The Kowalski twins were eager to please and seemed to look upon this entire business as some grand adventure. The Romanoff woman, on the other hand, appeared bored and dismissive and Nola was trying hard to decide how best to handle her when the interview was interrupted by a loud shriek and repeated yaps from the dog outside the door.

"What on earth?" Nola muttered as she got up from her desk and slid open the pocket doors. The sight that greeted her explained a lot.

Harrison Starbuck and Eleanore were clasping hands, laughing and talking over each other while the dog danced excitedly at their feet.

Nola's first thought was that there was more between Harry and the actress than simple friendship. "Oh, Harry," Eleanore crooned in that light musical voice of hers, "it's been too long, darling. And what a wonder Miss Burns is," she gushed, widening the circle to include Nola. "Why, she has made us all feel so welcome and at home and we've barely just arrived. I have to believe that it's her innate sense of hospitality that has made her so successful in business."

"So I've heard," he said, a half grin playing at the corners of his mouth. "I'd like to add my appreciation for your kindness, Miss Nola." He stepped toward her and instinctively Nola moved a step away, her back coming up against the frame of the open parlor door.

This was a mistake, she thought. This entire idea of having them stay here and work for her. Up to now it had been Nola versus Starbuck, but she could see that she had played right into his hands. How could she possibly ever explain her reasoning to Minnie and Rose and the others? Perhaps Rachel Williams could pull off something so bold in Nantucket, but this was 'Sconset and things were different here.

The sound of Judy's high-pitched laugh rolled down the hall from the kitchen and behind it came the voices of the two young male actors. The unmistakable sounds of pots clanging and the fragrant scent of Judy's cinnamon bread fresh from the oven accompanied their chatter.

"Oh, Mrs. Lang, that's lovely," Nola heard one of the men exclaim.

"Oh, Billy," Judy mocked with a laugh, "don't be charming me now. That pot needs more scrubbing."

Nola recalled the interview with the young men. They certainly had experience working in restaurant kitchens and Judy was clearly in need of some immediate help she could count on. The exchange from the kitchen had caught everyone's attention — except Harry's. He was watching her. The reality was she needed these people to work the kitchen and tearoom if she had any hope of staying in business at the prime opening of the summer season. She glared up at

Harry and it had the expected effect of making him retreat half a step.

"You have lip rouge on your face," she said as she opened the console where she kept a fresh supply of folded linen napkins and handed one to him. Before he could react she moved back into the parlor where Olga and the Kowalski sisters were waiting and deftly slid closed the doors.

CHAPTER FIVE

As soon as Nola shut the door, Harry turned to Eleanore, his eyes wide with confusion. Eleanore was no help at all. She practically had her fist crammed into her mouth as she tried to stem what he realized was laughter.

"What?" he barked irritably as he scrubbed at his face with the napkin.

"Oh, darling, I do believe that we've gotten off to a poor beginning with Miss Nola." She glanced at her reflection in the mirror next to the hall tree and checked her hair. "Perhaps I should try and smooth things over," she said, stepping to the door prepared to knock.

But from behind the closed doors they heard Olga's raised voice. "I do not do menial tasks," she declared.

Nola's more modulated reply was difficult to hear without actually pressing closer to the door. There was no sound from the twins.

Harry sighed. "The countess is overacting as usual," he muttered. At auditions he had sized up the potential for each of the actors to add to the success of the season or be a problem. Olga would be a problem, but she was perfect for the role of the matriarch.

At the audition she had been introduced as Olga Romanoff — an introduction she had quickly corrected to *Countess* Olga Romanoff.

"Ah, Countess," Harry had said almost reverently as he bent over her hand and kissed it lightly. "It is always a delight to have royalty on the bill."

Now Harry couldn't help wondering if he'd made a mistake hiring the temperamental actress.

"Perhaps Olga would be happier in the role of hostess," Eleanore mused, turning his attention back to the situation at hand.

"Perhaps," he replied. "She does bring a certain mystique to her performances and what is serving the public but another performance?"

Behind them the doors opened and Nola emerged with Olga and the twins. "Ladies," she said, "if you would all be so kind as to see Judy in the kitchen. She can supply each of you with an apron and give you the tour of the pantry and cupboards. We open in half an hour."

Harry saw that Olga was about to protest but Eleanore took her firmly by the arm and ushered everyone down the hall to the kitchen.

"You're still here," Nola said, her eyes settling on Harry.

"Just leaving," he assured her. He took his hat from the hall tree and clamped it onto his head at the usual jaunty angle. "Could I ask a question?" he asked.

As usual Nola blanched as if he'd insulted her but she gave him her full attention.

"Just what was it you thought you saw when you opened those doors and saw me with Eleanore?"

Nola looked down. "Your relationship with Mrs. Chambliss is none of my business as long as it does not affect her work — or her stay here."

Harry sighed. "Look, I realize I don't owe you an explanation, but Ellie and I are old friends. Her late husband was a gifted actor. Ever since he died unexpectedly, she's had a difficult time of it and it was just so nice to see . . ."

"As you said, you do not owe me an explanation," Nola interrupted. "At least not about your relationships with the female population."

He saw her wrestle with the facts he had given her. She wanted to believe him but something prevented her from fully giving her trust. *Could it be that Nola Burns's hard exterior was no more than a facade behind which she hid the truth — that she was every bit as afraid, unsure and insecure of herself as the next person?*

Harry took a step closer and placed his hand lightly on her shoulder as she stood with her arms crossed protectively over her chest. "Nola, I've never been anything but forthright when it comes to my intentions. I would like to buy you out, but that doesn't mean we have to be adversaries. You can trust me."

The look that flashed across her dark eyes mixed weariness with resignation. "It hardly matters at this point, does it? Your actors are here and that was completely my doing. As one of your fellow playwrights once noted, 'The die is cast.' "

Ah, Nola, don't give up so easily. I haven't won yet. He felt the urge to tighten his grip on her, to reassure her. But instinct told him that she would either take the gesture as too forward or worse, as pity, and she would not allow him to view her as weak.

She pulled free of him and all trace of

defeat evaporated with a flash of her eyes. "If there's nothing more?"

"Going now," he said with a grin as he fumbled for the doorknob and made his escape.

Nola forced herself to take a long steadying breath. When Starbuck had touched her shoulder she'd suddenly remembered another encounter they'd shared the summer when she'd been sixteen. As usual her brothers had abandoned their chores in favor of fishing. It wasn't unusual for them to disappear like that on a summer's evening. The fish in Tom Nevers Pond held far more appeal for them than scrubbing baking pans in the hot kitchen of the tearoom did. But on this night Mama had become dizzy and almost fainted. Nola had persuaded her to lie down while she went to find help.

As she approached the pond, she'd heard laughter and the splash of the water. The merriment had only served to make her more annoyed with her brothers. But the first person she'd run into that evening was Harry. He'd been laughing and calling back some insult to his friends as he strode up the path from the pond.

"Nola?" He had touched her then, his

hand damp on her wrist. "Are you all right?" He had not waited for an answer. Instead he had shouted for her brothers and they had come running. What happened after that was hazy. Nola knew that she and her brothers had hurried back home to attend their mother while Harry ran to get the doctor. But the only clear memory was of his hand, gentle and concerned, touching her lightly as he assured her everything would be all right.

He was wrong. Her mother had died a few weeks later.

Did he remember?

Of course he doesn't remember. By that time he'd been off to the mainland to seek his fortune. Stop this foolishness, she mentally ordered herself. She rarely indulged in such romantic nonsense, but now realized that ever since Harry Starbuck had first stepped onto her front porch just two weeks earlier, something had changed.

It's only because he's — what? Suddenly where you are so often? Or is it because someone like him is beyond attainable for someone like you? Nola glanced toward the mirror and her image shocked her. The woman in the mirror looked wistful, almost sad.

She pressed her hands over the starched

96

bodice of her shirtwaist. You're pathetic, she thought and turned resolutely away from the mirror.

"Judy, it's time," she called as she stepped outside to post the sign proclaiming the tearoom open for business.

When she returned to the foyer, she was pleasantly surprised when the Kowalski twins presented themselves promptly for duty, their crisp white aprons properly tied. More to the point, the bibbed aprons went a long way toward downplaying a bit of the actresses' natural flare for overstatement especially when it came to their hair and makeup. When Nola asked why the countess had not put on an apron, Eleanore explained that, if Nola agreed, Olga would be greeting the guests while the Kowalski sisters waited tables and the two young actors helped Judy in the kitchen.

"And you?" Nola asked.

The actress smiled and gave a small bow. "I am here to serve at your pleasure wherever I may be needed," she said. "However, I did have a thought." She cast her gaze toward the piano that filled one corner of the large room. "What would you say to a bit of the light classics — background music?"

For years now the piano had just sat there

in the corner of the tearoom, a relic of the future she'd once imagined for herself. Nola immediately saw the potential in Eleanore's suggestion and wondered why she'd never thought of it herself. On the other hand, she was reluctant to give the actress too much control over things. "We could try it," she said. "Business won't really pick up until next week. So if our current guests find the music intrusive or annoying . . ."

"Exactly," Eleanore agreed. "Thank you, Miss Burns, for everything."

"You're welcome, and you may call me Nola." She could give the woman that, at least. No need to let Eleanore think she was a complete stick-in-the-mud.

The actress's smile was radiant. "And I am Ellie. *Eleanor-a* is so pretentious, don't you think?" She placed the back of her hand to her forehead and struck a melodramatic pose, then shrugged and giggled. "But then, that's the point of stage names," she explained. "I'll just run up to my room and get some music."

"Ellie?"

The actress paused on the third stair.

"Mr. Starbuck mentioned the passing of your husband — I'm sorry for your loss."

Ellie's lovely face flushed as she fought against her grief. "Thank you, Nola. I think the summer here may help. Performing always takes me back to the happier days before Phillip became so ill."

"You performed together?"

Ellie nodded. "It's how we first met and from that day until he died we were never apart. Have you lost someone dear to you, Nola?"

Nola thought of her mother and father and nodded.

"Then it's no wonder you are so understanding," Ellie said and hurried on up the stairs.

Not really, Nola thought. She'd never known that kind of loss. That kind of love.

"Miss Nola?"

Nola turned to face the countess, who was actually smiling. "Yes?"

"I hate to raise the matter, but the room I'm to share with the Misses Kowalski is quite — cozy. Forgive me, but I could not help but notice a more spacious room just across the hall."

"You would prefer the larger room?"

"Not at all," Olga replied quickly. "I was thinking that it would be more comfortable for the girls. I would happily remain in the smaller room."

"And share the bath?"

Olga's smile cracked slightly but she

recovered by lowering her lashes. "If it would suit you," she said.

Why not? It's not as if you plan on renting the rooms to others. And it may well make for smoother sailing with the countess.

Nola gave the actress a warm smile. "I think the idea is quite a good one," she said. "Have the Kowalski sisters ask Judy for linens for the beds."

Olga dipped into a curtsy worthy of greeting a queen. "Thank you," she whispered huskily. Nola was relieved when the tinkle of the bell above the front door announced the arrival of customers. Olga glided forward. "Good afternoon and welcome, ladies," she said. "We have a lovely table by the window if you'll follow me."

Nola knew from the expression on Rose Gillenwater's face that she and her constant companions, Lucille Dobbs and Dorothy Bosworth, had not come for tea. Rose ignored Olga as she stepped forward and mouthed to Nola, "A word in private?"

Nola indicated the parlor and waited for the three stalwarts of the church to sail through the doors. "Please don't hesitate to interrupt should there be anything you cannot handle alone," she told Olga.

The countess seemed offended. "There is little that could occur that I would not be able to 'handle,' as you so quaintly put it," she said.

Just then Ellie came down the stairs, a music book clutched in one arm. She glanced from Olga to Nola and said, "Shall I just begin playing or introduce the music?"

"It's background," Nola reminded her, and Ellie nodded.

"Right. Just strike up the band, then," she said and headed for the piano.

Now it was Olga's turn to give Nola her full attention. "She is to perform?" Clearly she was offended by this change in assignments.

"Yes, well, the job of greeting our guests was taken — and I must admit you are doing it beautifully, Countess," she added hurriedly and realized it was exactly what Harry Starbuck would have said to soothe the actress's ruffled ego. "Ellie — Eleanore — is simply going to provide a bit of soft classical music to further enhance the mood you have already begun to set for our patrons."

She saw Olga process this information even as Nola heard the impatient tapping of Rose Gillenwater's leather shoe on the bare wood floor behind her. "Carry on, then," she said with a weak smile at Olga as she once again closed the doors to her inner sanctum and turned to face yet another problem.

"Actors, my dear?" Rose said the moment they were behind closed doors. She clicked her tongue against her teeth and shook her head slowly. "I can possibly understand employing such people since you are admittedly in a bind regarding keeping your tearoom in operation. But putting them up in your home? Has it come to this?"

As the wife of Alistair Gillenwater, Starbuck's business partner and a successful attorney as well as 'Sconset's self-appointed keeper of the standard for decorum, Rose Gillenwater had a well-defined and equally well-known code of conduct she expected others to follow. Those who did not risked not only her disapproval but her considerable influence in the community to impact the individual's social standing, and in Nola's case, her business.

But from the moment news of her father's death at sea had reached them, Nola's mother had drummed one lesson into her children's heads — survival. "Whatever it takes as long as no one is harmed and you aren't breaking the law," she had lectured.

And now as Nola faced Rose and her cohorts, she couldn't help thinking that these women had never once had to even consider what they might do under adverse conditions. The greatest problem any one of them had ever had to face to Nola's knowledge was whether or not the fabric they had ordered for a new gown had arrived.

She remembered what Harry had told her about Ellie's devastating loss and felt sympathy for the actress. The truth was that, in spite of her concern about the theater people coming to 'Sconset, more than once she had questioned the underlying prejudice with which many had treated the resident actors. And suddenly she had to fight her inclination to tell Mrs. Gillenwater that who she chose to hire — and house — was no one's business but hers. Instead she drew in a breath and smiled. "Ladies, please," she said, "let's sit for a moment. Shall I ask Mrs. Lang to bring us some tea and a plate of her delicious cucumber sandwiches?"

"We won't be staying," Rose replied haughtily even as the other two women nodded eagerly at the prospect of tea and treats. "Imagine my surprise earlier when I was calling on poor Mrs. Hogan down the lane and we observed this little band of minstrels approach your door. Well, I was quite certain that I would soon see them on their way to Ina Matthews's boardinghouse. I never imagined . . ."

"They have fallen on some difficulties that are not of their own making," Nola explained. She mentioned the damaged cottages and the delay in getting materials. Encouraged by the sympathetic expressions on the faces of Mrs. Dobbs and Mrs. Bosworth, she continued. "And then, as you know the help I had hired for the season became unavailable."

Rose glared at her, unmoved. "I would remind you, Nola, that the Devil often waits for just such coincidence. It is a form of pure temptation, putting you in circumstances of distress and then seeming to offer the perfect solution when in fact you are putting not only your position in the community but perhaps your very soul in peril."

The other two women rearranged their features to support this position, frowning at Nola as they nodded in agreement with their leader's point of view.

Nola was well aware that Mrs. Gillenwater believed every word of her sermon. This was hardly the first time she had felt compelled to deliver similar warnings. But outside the closed parlor doors, Nola could hear the sounds of sterling on fine china, accompanied by quiet conversation and the soft underpinnings of a Viennese waltz.

Experience told her the tearoom was filled for the first time in months and she believed she knew why. Rose and her companions were not the only ones who were curious about Nola's decision to staff the tearoom with traveling entertainers. If she stepped across the hall she suspected she would see her tables filled with locals.

"It appears that business is quite good for this early in the season," she noted.

Rose waved a dismissive hand. "We are all well aware that what you have attracted are curiosity seekers. They will not return. And so, my dear, although one does not like to broach the subject of finances," Rose continued, "your mother was a dear friend and I would be remiss were I not to keep an eye out for your well-being — a task I might add that has been unnecessary until now. Still, if you have had to resort to hiring unsuitable staff, I can only assume . . ."

"I do not need money," Nola said softly, even as she clenched her fists against the sides of her skirt. "Money is not the issue. After all, one cannot serve customers with dollars and cents. It takes actual people to pour and serve and clean up after."

Rose's eyes widened and the shocked expressions of her companions told Nola that she had crossed a line in daring to challenge the matriarch. She smiled apologetically and added, "But I appreciate your concern, Rose. Mama always said that I could count on you to watch over me."

Actually what Mama said was that Rose would watch my every move, expecting me to fail. But Nola had spent many long hours making sure that she did everything by the book, from raising her siblings to running her business, so that she found favor with people like Rose Gillenwater. Now she was surprised to feel a bubble of rebellion rising from within. She had worked hard and proved herself first as the sole support of her family after their parents had passed and then as a successful businesswoman. She was no longer the girl she had been when she took on such responsibility. She was a grown woman and had long since earned the right to the respect of these women.

She was on the verge of saying just that when her pragmatic side prevailed. "Forgive me," she said. "It's been a stressful time as you've so rightly observed. Please understand that this arrangement is temporary. Surely you can see that I must be able to keep the tearoom open while I seek the proper staffing. By the time the season is fully underway, I have little doubt that everything will once again be quite back to normal."

Somewhat mollified, Rose stretched the fingers of her gloves more tightly over her stubby fingers. "It's just that appearances, especially for a woman alone like yourself, simply cannot be underestimated."

"Absolutely, and thank you so much for your concern." Nola made a move toward herding the three toward the door, but Rose headed off in the opposite direction toward the window.

"And speaking of appearances, Nola dear, there's the matter of Harrison Starbuck."

Nola opened her mouth to protest, but Rose held up a restraining hand. "He has been reported calling here with some frequency in recent days. Mrs. Dobbs observed a most unsettling scene just recently as she was on her way home after church."

Lucille Dobbs made a detailed study of the pattern on the rug as Rose continued. "Really, child, a man on his knees outside your door and then you invite him onto the side porch where your interactions are concealed by foliage?" Once again she clicked her tongue in disapproval.

"It was a business matter," Nola said quietly. "Surely having seen Mr. Starbuck in church, all of you are well aware of his penchant for the dramatic? He was putting on an act to —"

"Harrison Starbuck was a rogue as a youth and I am sad to report that he does not seem to have matured much in that facet of his personality. He quite devastated our daughter, Violet, just last summer. And my dear boys looked up to him — so impressionable. So young and trusting. Vulnerable even in spite of their size and age." She shook her head and her companions nodded sympathetically.

Rose's sons, Edgar and Albert, were now fifteen and sixteen respectively. They were hardly children. The truth was that although they were quite pious and innocent-looking whenever their mother was around, there had been some rumors that they were at the center of a group of mischief makers on the island. In fact Nola had heard more than one local resident compare them to a younger Harry Starbuck.

"My interactions with Mr. Starbuck are purely business," Nola repeated.

"Sadly we were forced to send dear Violet off to Europe to recover," Rose continued as if Nola had not spoken. "Alistair insists that the man is very shrewd in business, but, if you ask me, people do have a tendency to give him far more leeway than is usual. You would be well advised to watch your step, my dear."

"I . . ."

"All of which brings us back to the main point," Rose interrupted as she moved to the door and slid it open. "These people are not our sort, Nola," she said. "As my dear Alistair is quick to remind me, they provide a service in enhancing the appeal of our little community to the tourists to be sure, but one crosses the line in actually forming alliances — business or otherwise. Lucille, Dorothy," she commanded as the two hurried to follow her out into the foyer.

Harry Starbuck and your husband are partners in numerous business ventures that include theatrical productions, Nola wanted to shout as the three women descended the porch stairs and set off down the street. Maybe you should speak to your precious Alistair about interacting with "that sort."

When she turned away from the door, biting her lip, Olga was waiting. "These women are bourgeois," she huffed, and Nola realized that she had heard Rose's last comment.

Nola could not hide her surprise at what she realized was Olga's expression of sympathy and support. "Nevertheless, they are quite powerful here in 'Sconset," she warned.

Olga shrugged. "And history has taught us that those who think themselves invincible are the easiest to topple," she said as she glided across the hall to greet the latest customer.

CHAPTER SIX

Although Nola agreed with Rose that once the locals had satisfied their curiosity business would slacken, at the moment the tearoom was quite busy, and the afternoon flew by. Nola barely had time to dwell on the encounter with Mrs. Gillenwater as she circulated among tables occupied by townspeople and even a few early arriving tourists. A mother and daughter visiting from New Bedford seemed so taken by the ambience of the place that they asked if Nola had ever considered renting the tearoom out for weddings or receptions. She was pleased to receive compliments on the fare, the service and the addition of the background music. She did not want to take credit for Ellie's idea but at the same time did not wish to get into a long explanation of how Ellie and the others had come to work for her.

By the time the last customer had left,

Nola had all but put the encounter with Rose Gillenwater behind her. She gathered the remaining cups and plates on a tray and pushed the swinging door to the kitchen open with one foot then paused.

". . . so then what happened?" Jasper March asked as he stood at the sink, shirtsleeves rolled back and forearms buried in sudsy water.

"They left," Olga reported. "But people like that, they will be back. They will bring trouble," she added ominously.

"Well, I don't see how they could cause any trouble," Mimi Kowalski replied. "Everyone was so impressed. Why, they'll be talking to all their friends and neighbors about this place. You mark my words."

"They loved the music, Ellie," her twin sister Deedee added. "That gave the whole place such class. It was like one of those elegant tearooms in New York."

"And just what would you know about such a place?" Billy teased.

"My gentleman friend took me to one once," Deedee countered.

"You mean that old guy who came to see you at the Majestic five nights in a row?" Billy asked and everyone laughed.

But as soon as Nola entered the room, they all sobered and focused on their work.

The two men gave their attention to washing and drying the china while Deedee and Mimi put the dishes in their assigned cupboards. Olga sat half reclining on a kitchen chair, a cup of tea without a saucer at hand while Ellie sat across from her, folding napkins.

"Where's Mrs. Lang?" Nola asked as if she had not overheard any of their discussion.

"We told her we would clean up," Jasper replied. "Hope that was all right?"

"Yes. Thank you. It was a busy day, especially for this time of year."

"Curiosity seekers," Ellie said with a smile. "Don't worry. In our business you get used to people wanting a look."

"Yes, well, it was good practice for you all. Next week when the season begins in earnest we are likely to see this kind of business daily — especially if the weather turns damp."

"Speaking of practice," Billy said. "Mrs. Lang said that Mr. Starbuck stopped by earlier and dropped off copies of the script. I took a peek and it looks to me like he's making the play into a musical and I've got the opening number. Ellie, he said to tell you to have me try it to the tune of Clare and the loon?"

" 'Clair de Lune,' " Ellie corrected. "I know it."

"So, could you give me a hand with it? I could come by your room later and . . ."

"Absolutely not," Nola interrupted and all six actors turned to her. "There will be no visiting between rooms," she said. "At least not between those who are residing on the third floor and those on the second."

"Between men and women," Ellie translated when the others looked a bit mystified.

"But we have to learn our parts — and now there's music as well," Billy protested.

"How about if we use the piano in the tearoom, Miss Nola?" Jasper suggested.

Nola hadn't even considered that the actors might expect to make use of her home for rehearsing during their off time. She had simply assumed that they would gather at the cabaret. Of course, that building was still under construction.

As usual her first thought was how holding rehearsals on the premises in addition to the transgressions she had already committed might set with Rose and her group. On the other hand, it was a sight better than the idea of working together in their bedrooms. And really, where was the harm? The tearoom was closed at six with clean-up usually taking another hour. It was now seven and if the actors were rehearsing at least she knew where they were. They wouldn't be out getting into trouble. "I suppose we could see how that goes."

"You're sure?" Ellie asked. "Maybe we should just wait until tomorrow and see if Harry has found another rehearsal space."

Nola was tempted to reconsider as she itemized the events of the day. There had been the arrival of the actors, followed by her encounter with Starbuck, and the confrontation with Rose Gillenwater close on the heels of that. For a moment, she was so taken aback with the enormity of what she had gotten herself into that she was speechless. Instead she gave the company a curt nod and before she knew it Billy had taken off for upstairs while Jasper and the others began pulling drapes closed and arranging chairs in a semicircle near the piano.

When Billy came pounding down the stairs waving a sheaf of music, Ellie took a seat at the piano and waited while Billy passed out scripts to the others. "Thank you," she mouthed to Nola as she played the introduction while the others found their places.

"You won't be long at this," Nola instructed, checking her watch for emphasis.

"Eight o'clock at the very outset."

Ellie stopped playing and nodded. "Not a minute past," she assured her.

"Why don't you join us, Miss Nola?" Jasper called.

"Yes, do," the twins chorused.

"Thank you for asking, but I have work of my own to attend. I'll be just across the hall should you need me." She locked the front door as she crossed the foyer. "Eight o'clock," she said firmly just before closing the parlor doors, but not quite all the way.

"And then what?" she heard one of the Kowalski twins ask in a stage whisper. "Are we to go to bed? I mean, what is there to do in this town?"

The others mumbled their agreement.

"I don't know about all of you," Nola heard Ellie say in her normal voice, "but after a full day of performing for customers — or waiting tables or cleaning up — and now trying to work our way through these new lyrics, I for one will welcome a good night's sleep. Remember, dear ones, we are doing double duty for the time being. We not only have day jobs, we have music to learn. And unless I miss my guess, there are going to be several rounds of revisions before this show is ready for even a preview performance. There will undoubtedly come a time when we long for a few early nights and some extra sleep."

Thank you, Nola thought. She had already moved to the parlor door, prepared to step forward and offer further rules for conduct to the group. Horrified at the very idea that they might yet go looking for some non-existent nightlife and finding none, would come up with their own version, she had been prepared to nip such ideas in the bud. And yet she hated always being the one to throw cold water on the enthusiasm of others. It had been her role with her siblings and after they had moved on to lives of their own, it had transferred onto the hired help she brought in every summer to cater to her guests.

She turned to her desk and prepared to tackle the pile of bills she had put aside while handling the staffing crisis. But her attention was drawn to the tearoom where the cast had moved on to other numbers. Ellie played an introduction and then she heard Jasper and Billy stumble through a chorus.

"No, no, no!" Olga cried. "Forte! Forte," she commanded and Nola heard Ellie play the introduction again.

This time the two actors boomed out the words. Then the women joined in and after several starts and restarts, Nola found herself keeping time with the music as she made short work of the bills and prepared the menu for the coming week.

It was after seven by the time Harry finished his work for the day, but instead of heading directly home to his cottage, he pedaled his bicycle aimlessly through the village. He reasoned that it was a fine spring evening, redolent with the scent of the sea and the hint of flowers on the verge of bursting into full bloom. He rode past Rest Haven, the group of cottages run as a spa and homeopathic health facility. It was owned by two doctors from New York who specialized in "Nervous Diseases and Diseases of Women and Children."

Harry couldn't help smiling every time he passed the place. To his way of thinking, a person didn't need some doctor to tell him that time spent in a quiet seaside village was good for the nerves — not to mention the soul. In Harry's view, God had given every human certain ingrained instincts and one of them was that when a person was feeling stressed and tense, a few moments communing with nature and the wonders that God had created was all that was called for.

He considered riding out Milestone Road

to the golf moors. Harry had invested money in the nine-hole course and he took some pride in looking at the finished product. But he rejected the idea of walking the links as pointless on a moonless night. Perhaps he should check on what progress workers had made on construction of the cabaret.

But instead he turned in the opposite direction and coasted past yet another landmark of the community — the large dwelling with the modest sign announcing Miss Nola's Tearoom in gold script and in smaller block lettering below, Serving the Public Daily in Season Except the Sabbath. The windows on the second and third floors were dark as usual. Light from what he now knew to be Nola's private quarters spilled onto the porch and a muted glow found its way around the closed drapes of the tearoom and out through the fanlight over the front door. He paused and heard the unmistakable tinkle of a piano accompanied by a chorus of voices.

So she has given them permission to make use of her piano after hours. Harry couldn't help but be impressed that the actors had somehow managed to get past that wall Nola had built around herself and persuade her to allow such a thing. He'd seen the trio of women from the church headed to the tearoom earlier as if on a crusade of utmost urgency. Harry was well aware of Rose Gillenwater's poor opinion of him since he'd ignored her thinly veiled attempts to match him up with her daughter, Violet. On the other hand, the fact that Alistair Gillenwater owed at least a part of his financial success to some profitable business ventures that Harry had brought his way left the woman in a bit of a quandary. It amused Harry to see that she had decided to deal with this matter by avoiding him whenever possible and lavishing him with compliments when a public encounter forced her to keep up appearances of civility.

Frankly he didn't care either way. It was her husband he felt sorry for. The man was a walking definition of the term *henpecked*. And truth be told, it was partly out of a desire to bolster Alistair's self-confidence that Harry had hired him as his solicitor and included him in his business dealings.

Rose and her ladies-in-waiting had not been at Nola's longer than a quarter of an hour when Harry saw them march back down the front stairs of the tearoom and board the surrey, driven by the eldest Gillenwater boy. As the lad navigated the carriage full of chattering women past his office, Harry couldn't help wondering what had transpired in that meeting. He was a keen observer of people and everything about Rose Gillenwater's expression and posture screamed that she was less than pleased with whatever had taken place. He was certain that the three women had not had time to stay for tea and yet what would have set them off? Rose Gillenwater had more than once made a point of praising Nola's conduct and comportment. He'd even heard her hold Nola up as a model for her own daughters to emulate. In fact, until recently, when he had thought about Nola Burns at all it had been as a younger version of Rose Gillenwater.

Until recently. In his encounters with her these last couple of weeks, Nola had shown a surprising amount of spunk — an independent streak he'd never anticipated. Was it possible that Nola had broken ranks with the matriarch?

He leaned his bike against the natural stone fence that surrounded Nola's property and considered stepping up the front walk and ringing the doorbell. He could say he'd stopped by to drop off his copy of the agreement Nola had insisted on.

Since when does Harry Starbuck need to plan an excuse? What if he was in the mood to call on Ellie? She was a dear friend. It was a free country.

Unbidden came the memory of the shocked look on Nola's face when she'd opened her parlor door and seen him with Ellie. In the moment it had taken for her to recover he had registered something in the way she looked at them. Jealousy? No, Harry had had enough experience with competing females to know that look all too well. No, it was something else, something more poignant and unexpected.

Longing.

Well, and why not? A spinster like Nola? He shook off the notion of going in. He wasn't in the mood for another debate with her tonight. The truth was that the woman confounded him. What was it about this uptight female, his adversary in business, that drew him to her like a moth to a flame? That was it, he realized. She was a woman and he was used to doing business with men and charming the ladies. This was business — pure and simple.

Relieved that he had solved the mystery of his fascination with the tearoom proprietress, Harry strolled out onto the footbridge that led to the stairway down to the beach and looked back at the impressive home with its mansard roof and dormer windows. Nola had done a fine job with the grounds. They were inviting and made good use of traditional 'Sconset plantings — climbing roses that lay heavy on the low stone walls marking the boundaries of the property. They would make an instant positive impression on city types who'd come with a preconceived and romantic notion of what an island resort town should look like. Those carefully pruned hydrangea bushes that lined the foundation of the porch, and the lush ferns in ceramic planters on high plant stands stood sentry among the several rocking chairs that aligned the front porch. In back near the carriage house, he was sure he'd seen a small herb garden surrounded by a picket fence. Beyond that was a small windmill for pumping water for the kitchen and bathrooms, and climbing the trellis at the side of the carriage house was a thick vine of morning glories.

The whole place was dignified and uncompromising in its propriety and yet with a certain aura of unexpected charm. *Like Nola herself.*

Harry frowned. "Not at all like Nola," he muttered and wondered where such a ridiculous thought had originated. He left his bike by the stone wall and headed up the walk. Light from Nola's office and parlor spilled onto the porch. He hesitated. If she was working he didn't want to disturb her. He could certainly deliver the agreement the following morning.

He stepped onto the porch and up to the window, expecting to see Nola bent over her paperwork. But she wasn't there, although the random stacks of paper and open ledger and pushed back chair gave the impression she had just stepped away. He was about to leave when a movement on the far side of the parlor caught his attention.

Harry blinked and wiped his eyes with the back of one hand, certain that the salty air had impaired his vision. Nola Burns was standing in the open doorway of the parlor. She was tapping one foot in time to the music and as she leaned against the doorway he caught a glimpse of her profile. She was smiling.

Seeing that, Harry rethought his notion of holding off until morning. "No time like the present," he said as he rapped lightly on the front door.

Nola had given up trying to concentrate on making the monthly entries in her ledger. The activity going on across the hall was too intriguing. She eased the parlor door open and leaned against it. Ellie played through a passage they'd been working on for the last quarter of an hour. This time she slowed the beat just a touch. Billy sang the words and the entire troupe murmured their agreement that it was better.

Yes, it is. And perhaps if . . .

A light rapping on the etched glass of the front door startled Nola, but went unnoticed by the group in the tearoom. She felt the familiar twinge of guilt as if she'd been caught again and wondered if Rose Gillenwater had been passing the house and somehow known she was neglecting her work. The clock on the mantel chimed eight, the piano fell silent and the actors began gathering their scripts and moving into the foyer on their way up to their rooms.

"Who could be calling at this hour?" she said to herself. In the shadows of the porch she could see the figure of a tall man wearing a telltale hat. She sighed. "Mr. Starbuck," she greeted as she opened the door.

"Good evening," he said, sweeping off his hat and giving her a grin and a little bow. "I was bicycling home and happened to hear the music and I —"

"Your cottage is in the opposite direction," Nola pointed out, making no move to step

125

aside and invite him inside. "But to put your mind at ease, you did not imagine the music. Your acting company has been rehearsing."

"I see." He lowered his voice for her ears only as he added, "And did I imagine you enjoying the music, Miss Nola?"

She was so stunned that she took a step back, opening the way for him to greet the others. "Well, now, it sounds as if you've all gotten off to a fine start."

"Miss Nola was kind enough to let us try some of the music here tonight," Ellie explained.

"And speaking of that," Nola said, stepping forward to face Starbuck, "I assume you've stopped by at this hour to announce the rehearsal schedule — and venue?"

"Why, Miss Nola, I had no idea you were taking such an interest. I stopped to bring you this." He handed her the agreement and then moved past her to the tearoom. "You know I had thought to hold rehearsals at the hotel until the cabaret is completed, but this might work quite well. Nice high ceiling, private, and everyone's already here, so . . ."

"I . . . That is. . . ." Nola was astounded at the way this man seemed to enter any door and take ownership of the situation.

She stepped around him and pointedly closed the lid of the piano. "The hotel would be a far more appropriate choice. And now, if you don't mind, it's late and these people have had a rather arduous day already."

Harry laughed. "Nola Burns, you are a force to be reckoned with. I will give you that. Still, you might want to give my idea some thought. You could keep your eye on things." He turned to the assembled group. "Rehearsals start in earnest tomorrow — venue and time to be determined." He stepped onto the darkened porch. "Have a good evening, all," he called to the actors and then he focused on Nola. "Miss Nola . . ."

Nola shut the door before he could say anything more.

"He's so . . . so . . ." Deedee Kowalski sighed, hugging herself.

"Beautiful," Mimi sighed.

"He's impossible," Ellie said with a laugh. "Always has been. Come on, girls. Bedtime." She herded the twins up the stairs as Olga trailed behind, leaving Jasper and Billy standing in the foyer.

"Miss Nola?"

Nola forced her thoughts away from the sheer audacity that Harry Starbuck seemed

127

to wear as easily as he wore that hat and focused on Billy Andrews. "Is there something you young men need?"

"No, ma'am, but, well, Jasper and I were talking earlier about how well Ellie's playing went over today. And well, maybe you might want to think about expanding on that. Offering the occasional recital or reading . . . I mean, I write poetry and Jasper sings opera. If we did something here — maybe one evening or something — it would not only be a way of promoting the theatrical season. It would also be a way of promoting the tearoom. Not to mention that Jasper and I can always use the extra money."

Nola stared at the two young men. They were barely out of their teens and yet in many ways they were more worldly than men Nola knew who were a decade or more older. "Well, Billy, I believe that Mr. Starbuck might intend to take up a great deal of your time with rehearsals for the gala opening," she said. And yet they had a point. Her customers had loved the music. Why not let the others entertain her guests as well? "Let me give your suggestion some thought," she told them.

Billy grinned and elbowed Jasper as the two raced up the stairs and to their room on the third floor.

Nola had barely gotten to sleep when she was awakened by a noise. She listened carefully and realized it was coming from the kitchen. As quietly as possible she got up, put on her robe and slippers and tiptoed out into the foyer. On her way through the tearoom, she picked up the brass poker from the fireplace, pushed open the swinging door to the kitchen and raised her weapon.

Ellie Chambliss nearly dropped the dish of water she was about to offer her dog as both of them froze and stared up at Nola. "It's just me," Ellie said, holding up her hands. "And Lancelot. Sometimes at night I have trouble sleeping and a little warm milk helps." Her voice betrayed nervousness as she slowly stood and backed away from Nola. "I'm so sorry. It's not my place to . . . I should have asked permission . . . I should . . ."

Nola lowered the poker and released a long breath. "No, I'm the one who should apologize. I cannot tell you the last time there's been a burglar or cause for alarm in this town. I have no idea why I imagined the worst. Please, have your milk."

"Join us," Ellie invited, setting the bowl down for the dog and then turning back to the stove. "I made enough for two."

Nola hesitated, then propped the poker by the door and reached for a cup from the sideboard. "Do you often have trouble sleeping?"

Ellie shrugged. "Mostly since Phil died. I wake up and he's not there and sometimes I forget." She gave Nola a weak smile even as her eyes brimmed with tears.

"I'm so sorry," Nola said. "It must be very difficult for you."

"The days are so full of other things and of course, Lancelot here is a comfort, but at night . . . But of course, you know," she added.

"Not really," Nola admitted. "I lost my parents and it was tragic in both cases but I've never lost — never been in love."

"Not once? Even as a girl?"

Nola shook her head and concentrated on her milk. But when Ellie chuckled, she looked up at the actress. "It's hardly a laughing matter," she said.

"Oh, honey, I'm not laughing at you. I'm thinking about the day when you finally are in love and how it's going to be like the Fourth of July with fireworks and all."

"Because I've waited so long," Nola

guessed.

"Because when the right man comes along you will know it — likely given your inexperience you will fight it, but there will be no way you can not love this man."

"That's how it was for you and Mr. Chambliss?"

Ellie smiled. "Exactly. We met when we were both hired to do a Shakespearean comedy. Are you familiar with *The Taming of the Shrew*?"

Nola nodded.

"Talk about your fireworks," Ellie recalled. "We were at one another's throats from day one. I thought to play it one way but Phil had quite different ideas. And as the weeks passed we found ourselves fighting the attraction that was practically palpable in the room. Everyone else knew we were meant for each other."

"Apparently it all worked out," Nola prompted.

"It did. By the end of the run we were mad for one another. The night the show closed we persuaded a local minister to perform the ceremony and from that day until Phil's death we were never apart again." Ellie drank the last of her milk and got up to wash out her cup.

"How did you know?" Nola asked softly.

"You just do," Ellie said, scooping Lancelot into her arms. "A woman like you, Nola, was not meant to go her whole life without love — the love of a man, a partner, a husband. I refuse to believe that God meant for you to be alone."

"You believe in God?"

This time Ellie laughed out loud. "Oh, Nola, honey, how could I not? A country girl like me who grew up on a farm in the mountains of Tennessee? How could someone like that make it to the city and have the opportunity, the sheer joy, of performing for others? How could someone like that meet and marry a man from a family of high social standing who was just as drawn to the stage as I was?"

"Fate?"

"What is fate but God in action?" Ellie asked.

Nola could not have been more surprised and she realized that she had been guilty of pigeonholing Ellie and the others. They were actors, therefore . . .

"Well, I should get some rest if not sleep," Ellie said, putting Lancelot down so he could take one last lap of his water. "Thanks, Nola — for the milk and conversation and most of all for opening your home to us."

"It was nothing," Nola said.

Ellie wagged a finger at her. "It was something, Nola. Don't think for one minute that we don't know how some people feel about our being here. You've gone out on a limb for us when you didn't have to. We won't forget that."

Nola felt a rush of pleasure at Ellie's compliment. "It's quite nice having people in the house again," she admitted.

"We'd be here every evening if you changed your mind about letting us rehearse here."

You and Harry Starbuck.

Ellie took her hesitation for rejection. "Not a problem. Harry will figure something out. Still, maybe we could still get together for tea or coffee?" Ellie indicated the pan of warm milk on the stove and Nola's half-filled cup. "A midnight chat now and then?"

"I'd like that."

"Lovely," Ellie said as she tiptoed up the back stairs with Lancelot in tow. "Say good night, Lancie," she murmured, burrowing her face in the dog's fur.

Lancelot gave a yap and Nola smiled. "Good night," she replied.

What a day! Nola thought, but she was smiling as she returned to her bedroom and that night she slept better than she had in weeks.

CHAPTER SEVEN

Harry had lain awake most of the night thinking about how Nola's place was a far better venue for rehearsals than the hotel. The play was not yet in good enough shape to risk hotel staffers hearing the clunks and clinkers of it. At Nola's they could work through all of that in privacy. But he hated asking Nola Burns for anything. It just gave her the upper hand.

He was lost in thought as he rounded the corner of McAllister's store and nearly collided with a young woman coming out of the bookstore.

"Why, Harrison Starbuck," Violet Gillenwater trilled as she raised her parasol against the late morning sun and spun it flirtatiously. "How lovely to see you."

Two summers earlier when Harry had first returned to 'Sconset, Violet's mother had done her best to foster a romance between the two of them. Her efforts had escalated once she had assessed his wealth and connections to influential people on the mainland. There had been repeated invitations to join the family for Sunday dinner or to attend gatherings. These invitations came with the unspoken understanding that he would be Violet's escort for the occasion.

"Miss Violet," he said, tipping his hat and buying the time he needed to gauge her mood. Things had ended badly between them the previous summer just before he'd returned to New York. "It's a pleasure to see you looking so well."

"I've been on holiday," she replied with a bright smile. "In Europe."

"Ah, an adventure," he replied.

"Now, Harry, you know very well that I left because you broke my heart." She looked up at him from under lowered lashes.

"Apparently Europe was the remedy then, for you are looking quite lovely."

She laughed. "Mother always said you were a rogue and a charmer."

"Did she, now?"

"Well, of course that was only after we parted ways. Before that she was quite fond of you. In fact there were times when I thought she was more fond of you than I was."

It was Harry's turn to laugh. "Why, Miss

Gillenwater, and here I was feeling guilty about any heartache I might have caused you."

She shrugged. "I'm not a fool, Harry. I knew exactly what my mother was trying to do. Frankly, you did me the greatest favor when you refused to go along with her plan. I suspect we both would have been quite miserable."

Harry's respect for the young woman escalated. "Obviously Europe has made you a very wise woman indeed," he said.

"I have matured, yes, but more to the point I have seen the world beyond this island. The world is far too grand and exciting and our time on this earth far too short to waste."

"Shall I take that to mean that you have not come home to stay?"

Violet actually shuddered at the thought and then she smiled up at him. "I shall stay for the opening of your grand new venture, Harry. I presume, knowing you, that it will be a spectacular occasion. I've invited my fiancé and his family for that week."

"We'll do our best not to disappoint," Harry promised. "You're to be married, then?"

Violet beamed. "Over the holidays. In Boston. To Charles Edgemont Carrington."

"The shipping heir? Your parents must be so pleased."

"Ah, Harry, we're on the brink of a new century. The important detail in this is that I am pleased and so is my darling Charlie. And now I really must be going. You know how Mother can be about tardiness."

"It's very nice to see you, Violet," Harry said as he stepped aside to allow her to continue on her way. She crossed the street, and at the same time he saw Nola making her return trip from her morning errands.

He watched as she marched down the grass-covered street without so much as a glance in his direction. A delivery wagon rumbled by, blocking Starbuck's view as it splashed its way through the rain-soaked ruts of the street. The wagon passed and there she stood looking down at her mud-spattered skirt. In spring the Nantucket weather could sometimes be as gray as the high-necked cotton dress Miss Nola Burns wore. Starbuck couldn't help noticing that the solemn color of her dress found little relief in the black three-quarter cape she'd donned for protection against the damp morning fog. Her straight-backed posture and perennially pursed lips only added to the impression of a woman who took life seriously and had little time or patience for the frivolity of others.

And yet she had risked the considerable ire of Rose Gillenwater and others by taking in Ellie and the rest of the troupe.

She spoke to Violet who hurried on as she offered the same excuse of needing to meet her mother. Then Nola looked across the street at him. For one instant her step faltered. Harry smiled and tipped his hat, but Nola did not acknowledge his greeting. Instead she made an abrupt detour into the notions store.

It's a small village, Nola. Hard to avoid me if I set my sights on seeing you. And he set off down the street to wait for her return to the tearoom.

In spite of her deliberate stop at the notions store where she had purchased a length of ribbon she certainly did not need, Nola saw that she had failed in her attempt to avoid Starbuck. He was perched on the porch rail talking to Billy Andrews.

"If you think you can handle the role, then it's yours," he said as Nola unlatched the gate and started up the walk.

"Yes, sir," Billy replied and he seemed ready to burst with glee. "You can count on me, sir. Mind if I tell the others?"

"Might as well. They'll figure it out when

we start rehearsals in earnest tonight."

Billy took off and Harry stepped to the edge of the porch and relieved Nola of her parcels. "You know, you can send one of the actors to the market, Nola."

"I like to make my own selections and besides, they won't be here that long. Now, how can I help you?"

"Came to ask another favor." He grinned as he headed down the side porch and into the kitchen.

Nola had little choice but to follow him.

"Lovely day, Mrs. Lang," he said as he set the packages on the table.

"Judy, Mr. Starbuck and I will be in my office if you need anything," Nola said without breaking stride as she continued through the pantry and into the front hallway. She waited for Harry to follow, then busied herself removing her hat and gloves and hanging up her cape. "Well?"

He glanced toward the parlor, but Nola remained where she was.

"I want to rehearse here until we get this thing converted to music," he said, all evidence of lightheartedness gone.

"And why would you think I might agree to that?" She realized from his expression that he hadn't expected her to agree at all, which made his asking all the more intriguing.

"Because," he began, then rejected whatever he'd been about to say and started again. "Because I think when you read my play you saw something in it — some real potential."

"I have already said that it is quite good."

"And would be even more powerful in musical form?"

"Perhaps."

He ran his hand through his hair and it fell right back over his forehead. "Look, I know it's asking a lot and I assure you this has nothing to do with the business of buying you out. I need some time to get the music in place and the lines changed to lyrics. If we work at the hotel, people are bound to get the idea that it's not going well and that could affect ticket sales for the opening which could affect the pocketbooks of my investors which affects their willingness to invest in this play down the road. Are you following me?"

"Not entirely, but go on."

"If we could rehearse here for the duration of the time my lead performers are in residence and working for you, then . . ."

"And if I refuse?"

Harry scowled. "You know, Nola, I can

141

find another place for them to stay. It might not be as convenient, but . . ."

"Don't threaten me, Harry."

"I'm not. I'm just pointing out that a smart businesswoman like you must understand that the bargain we've struck works both ways. I mean you can back out of it any time and so can I."

"You signed an agreement."

Harry sighed. "To satisfy you. Just help me out here, Nola."

"There will be no more threats to remove the actors until I have found replacements. Are we quite clear on that?"

"Yes, ma'am."

"And . . ."

Harry rolled his eyes.

"And rehearsals may run from five until eight."

"Nine," he bargained.

"Eight-thirty," she countered.

"Done."

After just a couple of days, Nola realized that any concerns she might have had about the actors causing her trouble or embarrassment were unfounded. They were courteous to her patrons and any visitors who might stop by, and seemed to have a sixth sense about whether or not their company

142

might be welcomed. By the end of the week, they had settled into a daily routine of helping Judy prepare for the day's business in the mornings, serving tearoom guests in the afternoon and rehearsing in the evenings. After Harry left, they would sometimes gather on the porch or in the kitchen to unwind before going up to their rooms.

Although they always invited Nola to join them, she felt it was important that she not become overly involved in their lives. Instead she would plead the need to finish some paperwork or tell them that she usually reserved this time for reading. That was true, but, of course, that had been before these lively people had come under her roof. On the evenings they chose to sit on the porch, she could not help listening in as they shared stories. What interesting experiences they had all had, and not just in the theater. Their personal lives were as diverse as they were. Every one of them had been through difficult times — disapproving families, money woes, times when they couldn't find work — and yet they told their stories without an ounce of pity. Indeed it seemed to Nola that they saw their experiences as fodder for their ability to understand a character they might be called upon to play.

Nola was thinking about that as she made her morning walk to the post office, picked up her mail and then started back down the street toward the market.

What if one morning I failed to pick up the mail at this hour? What if I decided to do the marketing first and then pick up the mail?

Of course, then she would need to stop at the house to drop off her parcels from the market before coming on to the post office, but was that a problem?

"Nola, wait a minute." Essie Crusenberry, 'Sconset's postmistress, had left the post office and followed Nola up the street, waving an envelope. "There's this one other piece of mail," she shouted as she rushed up the street and handed Nola a blue sealed envelope. "It was just there on the counter. Someone must have dropped it off while I was sorting. You'd have thought that whoever it was would have said something to get my attention, but not a sound. I turned around and there it was." Essie made no pretense of her curiosity about all the secrecy. "Aren't you going to open it?" she asked outright when Nola placed the envelope on the bottom of the stack she carried.

"It will keep," Nola assured her, although her own curiosity was piqued by the unfamiliar printing of her name. "Thank you, Essie." She tucked the envelope in with the rest of the mail and continued on her way. She was well aware of Essie's disappointment and equally aware that within the hour half the village would know she had received a mysterious envelope.

And yet by the time she'd completed the rest of her errands and chatted with Judy in the kitchen, Nola had put the blue envelope completely out of her mind. It was only later that morning as she was going through the day's mail and the blue envelope floated to the floor that Nola remembered the odd circumstances surrounding its delivery.

"What's this?" Judy asked, bending to retrieve the envelope and turning it over to examine the address. "Looks like an invitation." She handed it to Nola and moved a little behind Nola so she would be able to see. "Wonder who's having a party this time of year when everyone's so busy."

"Let's see." Nola set the rest of the mail down as she slid her letter opener under the thick flap of the vellum envelope.

An odd assortment of words in a variety of print fonts and sizes had been cut from newspapers and magazines and glued to the expensive paper.

God-fearing residents of 'Sconset do not
  bind
With actors, musicians and their kind;
Remove them from your circle now
Or suffer consequences you will find
  most foul!

A friend

"What kind of invitation is that?" Judy asked, squinting down at the page. "Makes no sense at all."

"It's not an invitation," Nola said as she scanned the words once more and then crumpled the paper into a ball and flung it onto the table. She picked up the envelope and examined it closely as Judy sat down opposite her and smoothed out the crumpled letter.

"Why, Nola, this is like a warning. Somebody is trying to warn you to stay away from the actors."

But Nola ignored Judy's rising concern. "Found it just lying there on the counter indeed," Nola grumbled under her breath as she stormed out the back door, muttering all the way back toward the post office. "As if Essie Crusenberry doesn't hear that squeaky door every time someone comes in or out. As if she doesn't stop whatever she's doing to see who it is."

Calm down. You'll only make matters worse.

She slowed her step and even smiled and nodded at the few people she passed. But her thoughts were on the note. Judy was right. Someone meant to warn her — to scare her. It wasn't a question of why someone had sent the note. That was clear enough. But who would stoop to such tactics?

Starbuck?

Certainly he had the most to gain. After all, if his actors did not staff her tearoom she would be once again without the help she needed to remain open now that the tourists were beginning to arrive in earnest. And certainly the blue stationery was close at hand. The bookstore just across the street from his office kept a ready stock of it in a selection of cream and blue.

So, you are still playing pranks, Harry, she said silently, recalling all the times he and her brothers had pulled some trick or hoax in their youth. *And what if I simply ignore your little stunt?*

"Yes, that's the best course," she decided, reversing her direction and walking slowly back to the tearoom as if she'd only been out for a bit of fresh air. "I will simply ignore your childish prank. In fact, I will ignore you, Harrison Starbuck." For the rest of the day she was in unusually high spirits.

Promptly at five that evening Harry arrived for rehearsal and so, promptly at quarter to the hour, Nola shut herself away in the parlor. This continued every day after the note arrived. Whenever she could she would leave the premises altogether on the excuse of visiting a friend or attending a church meeting. But on those evenings when she had nowhere to go, she couldn't help pulling her chair closer to the closed doors and eavesdropping as Harry and the company slowly worked their way through his script.

The process of building the show fascinated her. The changes the cast suggested for the lyrics or tempo or sometimes even the music itself opened her eyes to the fact that putting together a theatrical performance was a collaborative effort. She had imagined that once Harry began directing the rehearsals, he would simply state what he wanted and the others would do their best to comply. To her surprise, he would ask for their ideas and listen to their suggestions. Sometimes Nola would hear all of them talking over the top of one another as they called out new ideas for how a particular lyric or song should go.

And sometimes Nola would long to add

her own ideas to the mix. A chord that was half a key off for Olga's rich contralto. A little known madrigal melody that would perfectly fit the lyrics for the number at the close of the first act. Once or twice she had scribbled some notes and even made one or two offhand suggestions to Ellie as they sat with their tea late in the evening. And a couple of nights later she heard Ellie offer those same suggestions to Harry and when he took them, Nola had felt a sense of pride and accomplishment that she hadn't known in some time.

But every time she caught herself concentrating more on the operetta than on the business of running her tearoom, Nola would remind herself of the note. Then she would drag her chair back to its proper place at her desk and force herself to get back to work. The tearoom was struggling, but Harry Starbuck would not defeat her.

Still, Nola had to face facts. Business had not improved much even with the arrival of the first seasonal visitors and it wasn't only Rose Gillenwater and her crowd who had shunned the tearoom since Nola put the actors to work. She was no closer to finding more permanent — and more suitable — help, and she resented the prejudice against the actors. They were doing a fine job and their behavior was above reproach. If only she could come up with some way to attract new customers, the loss of local business would not be so critical.

She kept coming back to the suggestion Billy had made that first night. Why not expand background piano music to include the occasional solo or reading? The more she thought about it, the more the idea grew into something grander — perhaps a recital or poetry series. She studied the figures on the ledger. If she extended the hours of the tearoom to include just two evenings a week, she could potentially increase her gross income by at least ten percent. "And over the course of the entire season," she muttered aloud as she did the math, "that could possibly amount to an extra . . ." She stared at the number and released a long breath. But the actors needed their rehearsal time. Extending hours would have to wait until she could find permanent staff.

Still, she decided to discuss the idea with Ellie.

"And what would you do with all that extra, anyway?" Ellie wanted to know when Nola broached the idea to her later that night as they sat together in the parlor for what had become their regular late night talk. "No, don't tell me. You'd put it all right back into this place — fixing up the grounds or buying a new stove for Judy. Not that she wouldn't love that. It's just that for once in your life wouldn't it be nice to think about getting something for yourself?"

Nola laughed uncertainly. "I don't know what you mean. It's all for me. This is my livelihood . . . my home . . . my . . ."

"Life," Ellie replied firmly. "I may not know you all that well, Nola. But from what you have told me about your family and growing up on the island here, I have to believe that your blessed mother would want more for you than working from dawn to dusk and finding adventure in those books you read after I go off to bed."

"Oh, Ellie, my mother certainly understood hard work."

"No doubt. Judy told me that when your father died, your mother said that if it was the last thing she did she was going to make sure that none of you ever had to worry. Well, she didn't get the chance to see it through, but you made sure that her dream was realized, at least for the others. And speaking of the others, where are your siblings? Why aren't they helping out?"

Nola frowned and folded her arms tightly across her chest. Ellie's innate bluntness could be unsettling when her questions

151

raised doubts in Nola's head about decisions she had made.

"Oh, Nola, I apologize. It's none of my business, but it's hard for me to understand and I feel as if you deserve so much more."

Ellie had touched a nerve without realizing it or meaning to. "After Mama died," Nola admitted quietly, "everyone assured us that we would be better off if we each went to live with a family elsewhere on the island."

"Split up?" Ellie was clearly horrified at the very idea. "After all you'd already lost, they would have you lose each other?"

"They meant well. The minister at the time and others — including Rose Gillenwater — tried reasoning with us. 'It's not as if you'll never see each other again, Nola,' she said. She told us we could visit one another at these foster homes."

"And what did you say?"

"I asked where *our* home would be. No one had an answer for that."

"So what happened?"

Nola shrugged. "I struck a bargain with the elders. If we could all stay in the house we had inherited, then we would run the tearoom in the summer and I, as the responsible one, would make sure the others completed their schooling."

152

"This is like a drama," Ellie said. "What happened?"

"The minister and a woman from the office of social services agreed to check on us regularly and the Langs agreed to move in with us until we were old enough to be on our own."

"How old were you then?"

"Sixteen." Nola smiled at the memory. "The minister told me that he was certain that I was acting purely out of grief and shock. He said that it was understandable that having lost both parents, I wouldn't wish to sustain further loss. Still, in time he came around and agreed that I'd made the right choice."

"And your siblings? What happened to them?"

"At the time my brothers were already eighteen and seventeen, so they were off and on their own within a year. Jerrod headed west to follow our father's dream of living in California. Harold married the daughter of a United States senator and they live in Washington."

"And your little sister?"

"Beth was just fourteen but with all the work involved in keeping this place going she grew up fast. When she was eighteen, she fell in love with a British photographer who had come to the island that summer. She ran off to London with him, sending word they had been married by the ship's captain on their voyage across the Atlantic."

"How romantic. Is she happy?"

Nola laughed. "Well, she's certainly busy. Her husband is the court photographer and they live in the country where Beth is busy raising sheep and three children."

"So why did you stay?"

Because this is home — for all of us — and someone has to be the keeper of that haven of solace and comfort.

"They have their lives and homes. This is mine."

"And when was the last time you visited any of them? When was the last time you left this island, Nola, for anything but business?"

"Now, Ellie," she began, but the actress held up her palms.

"Don't you 'Now, Ellie' me, Nola Burns. You've talked of the past and the dreams you had as a girl — dreams that never included running this tearoom for the rest of your life. Let's see, your excuses probably run along the lines of 'It's the busy season,' " she mocked in a falsetto tone. "Or 'Maybe next year.' Well, take it from me, my friend, those next years go by fast and

154

before you know it they've passed you by and you're left with only memories."

Ellie's eyes filled with tears and Nola rushed to her side. "Oh, Ellie, I didn't mean to upset you."

"Oh, don't mind me. These days I seem compelled to stick my nose into other people's lives. It's just that sometimes I get so caught up in thinking about all that Phil and I . . ." She leaned forward and clasped Nola's hand. "I like you, Nola, and you deserve so much more than . . ." She started to cry in earnest now.

Nola gave Ellie a moment to compose herself. "I take it then that you would be against the idea of expanding the services of the tearoom to offering the occasional evening recital or poetry reading?"

Ellie wiped her eyes and took a deep breath. Nola had become used to the actress's sudden shifts in mood. Suddenly she was all business. "Actually, it's a very good idea, but as you've already realized, it can't be an evening thing."

"What if we did something on Saturday afternoons at four?"

Ellie's eyes went wide with surprise and she let out a low and most unfeminine whistle that brought Lancelot's ears to attention. "You've already decided to do this, haven't you? What about Mrs. Gillenwater and her friends?"

"Well, I was thinking that they could hardly object if we took an offering instead of charging — and gave the money to charity," Nola said, thinking aloud.

"And the point of that would be what? I thought this was a way to raise more money from the business."

"The idea is to promote the business," Nola ventured. "If we could raise funds for charity, think of the goodwill that would create."

Ellie looked doubtful but at least Nola could see she was considering the idea. "It might work," she said. "You could try it once and if it didn't work then there's nothing lost. On the other hand, if you announce a whole program of such things and then the first one falls flat . . ."

"Oh, Ellie, what a good idea," Nola said as she hugged her friend. "I hadn't thought that it could be a one-time thing to see how it goes. And it wouldn't take much to put it together. If we served just tea and cakes no one would order from a menu and I could handle the setup and cleanup myself."

"And I know the others would be delighted for the opportunity to perform — even the countess," Ellie replied. "And what do you think our friend Starbuck will say about all of this?"

Nola bristled. "It really is none of his affair," she said, but then remembered that the actors worked for Starbuck. "You don't think — that is, he wouldn't . . ."

Ellie shrugged. "He might. On the other hand, he mentioned tonight that he has business in New York for the next two weeks. If we put everything in motion while he is away . . ." She smiled and shrugged again. "What can he say?"

Nola did not like subterfuge. On the other hand, surely he couldn't object to her staging an event for charity. "After all," she reasoned, "it could also be as good for his season at the cabaret as it is for the tearoom."

But deep down she doubted that Starbuck would see things that way.

CHAPTER EIGHT

Harry was beat. His meetings in New York had not gone well.

"You're spreading yourself too thin," Alistair Gillenwater warned him on the trip back. "This business of writing an operetta — well, frankly, Harrison, that's all well and good. A man should have a hobby, but in your case, you've —"

"I write plays professionally," Harry interjected.

"Well, label it what you will. The fact of the matter is that it's your head for business that has brought you the successful lifestyle you enjoy. Now if you're intent on giving that up and becoming one of those struggling starving artist types, so be it, but take my advice, son, and stick with what you do best."

It had always mystified Harry that protocol seemed to dictate that a person was allowed only one area of success — if that.

The idea that a man might pursue a variety of disparate interests seemed to intimidate those who held the purse strings. After all, no one had ever been able to explain why God would give a person multiple and diverse talents and then not be troubled when the person chose one of those God-given talents and discarded the rest.

He slumped against the seat of the railway car, hardly noticing as the train chugged past Tom Nevers Pond on its way to 'Sconset. He couldn't deny that Alistair had a point. At first Harry had enjoyed modest success on the New York theater scene with a series of revues he had written and staged. But when he had turned his attention to more serious topics — real plays with plots and memorable characters and high drama — his efforts had been met with skepticism. And rejection always made him all the more determined to succeed. And succeed he did. He'd written and staged not one but two plays on Broadway last season. Both had played to packed houses and received rave reviews from the critics.

But he was well aware that others were more interested in his talent for taking a business idea and bringing that to fruition. He had a kind of sixth sense when it came to timing a venture and predicting what people might want at any given moment. It was that insight supported by his unique ability to deliver a project or product on time and under budget that had gained him a reputation for being someone investors could rely on to provide a significant return on their dollar. The one thing that had never resonated with his partners and investors was his theory that theater could be used to teach, to build awareness and understanding, and to change the world for the better.

"But, Harry, why would we want to change the world?" an investor had once asked. "It works just fine the way it is."

"For you," Harry had muttered as the man walked away still laughing at the ridiculous notion that a play could change hearts and minds, or that he would ever want such a thing.

Harry closed his eyes and let the gentle rocking of the railway car lull him into a state of half sleep. As always, when the world of business became too stressful to bear, he escaped into the world of his imagination, storytelling on the stage. He thought about his current work — the play set to music. The very fact that he thought about almost nothing but this play told him that it was something different from anything else he'd penned. *Simple Faith* had all the earmarks of a major theatrical experience — a life-changing, heartrending experience. It could be a major artistic and financial hit. Harry was sure of it. In a single evening hundreds of people who may not have darkened a church's door in ages would receive God's message.

Alistair nudged him as the two cars of the train pulled up to the station at the base of the bluff and passengers began gathering their belongings. As they stepped off the platform and into the sunlight, Harry tightened his grip on his small carpetbag and headed for the stairway to the top of the bluff. Alistair fell into step next to him, swinging his umbrella and continuing his litany of details that needed Harry's immediate attention if they were to open the cabaret on schedule.

Alistair Gillenwater had no need of luggage. He owned a fine townhouse on the Upper East Side of Manhattan in addition to the large Federal-style mansion he occupied for most of the year on the outskirts of 'Sconset. Both residences were fully staffed and fully stocked with anything Alistair, his wife Rose, or their children might need. By the time the two men reached the top of the stairway, Alistair was breathing hard.

"You need to get more exercise. I could lend you my bicycle," Harry joked as they reached the footbridge that led into town and Alistair paused to catch his breath.

"Keep in mind that I am a good twenty years your senior, young man. Wait until you're my age and see how well you do with climbing stairs and such."

"Point taken," Harry said, his good spirits restored as they always were the minute he set foot back on the island. It was as if Nantucket were his own personal oasis from the problems and trifles of the rest of the world.

"Now, concerning the cabaret opening," Alistair continued.

"Oh, Alistair, the cabaret will open on schedule and under budget, I assure you."

"It's not just the cabaret, Harry," Alistair reminded him. "Our investors are expecting a package — the cabaret, the golf course and the exclusive inn with the most modern amenities any city dweller could want. It was your idea. They bought it and now it's up to you to deliver."

"Even if Nola sold out tomorrow, I've already explained to the investors that the inn will come next year. First the cabaret and then the inn."

"But you have to make a start, Harry. As

far as I can tell you've made little progress buying Nola's place."

Harry sighed. "Stop worrying, Alistair. Tearooms are quickly becoming a relic of the past. The younger generation of families are going to be looking for something more active, more entertaining. Nola Burns is already struggling to find help. Using my actors to staff the place even temporarily was a mistake of major proportions that robbed her of a fair amount of steady business from the locals. Once her business starts to seriously fall off, it's only a matter of time."

"I don't know, Harry. That place has been Nola's entire life. I don't see her giving up so easily."

"If she has no help and no customers, the decision will effectively be taken out of her hands, Alistair. Now, it's a beautiful afternoon. Can't we just take a moment here to appreciate this glorious day? Look at that sky, that shore. Smell the roses. Look how they've blossomed while we've been away. Now I ask you, what could possibly go wrong on a day as perfect as this?"

As he and Alistair approached the tearoom, Starbuck stopped. Several townspeople were standing outside the gate and eyeing the entrance.

"The tearoom usually closes at six and it's nearly that now," Harry muttered as he quickened his step. He couldn't help wondering if something unfortunate had happened. But when he reached the gate he saw that the few people entering the tearoom were quite lighthearted, even excited. And on the post was a hand-lettered sign announcing an evening of poetry and music "with a freewill offering for charity."

"Charity aside," one local woman huffed, "this is simply not the way we do things around here."

Her companion agreed. "It's one thing to purchase a ticket for a performance in a legitimate theater but this stretches the limits of propriety if you ask me. Nola operates a respectable tearoom — or she did before those people moved in."

The two women hurried to cross to the other side of the street as if simply being seen in the proximity of Nola's place might taint their reputations.

"What now?" Alistair asked as he pressed forward to read the sign.

"It would appear that Miss Nola has come up with yet another new idea for staying put," Harry said and frowned when he realized that in addition to the annoyance he was feeling, there was also a certain measure of admiration for the lady's ingenuity.

Nola could not have been more stunned to see Alistair Gillenwater sitting in the front row just as the recital was about to begin. Alistair rarely defied his wife and Rose's disapproval of the performance had been made crystal clear. Nola was so caught up in witnessing this unusual occurrence that she failed to notice Harry Starbuck until she was on her way to open a window and nearly tripped over him. He was casually leaning against the wall, one ankle crossed over the other, his arms folded, his eyebrows raised as if he was waiting for an answer to some unspoken question.

"You're back," she said. "I'll ask Billy to bring a chair."

Starbuck gazed around the more than half-empty rooms. "No need. It appears that I'll have my pick. You seem to have overestimated your audience."

"Oh, you know how busy people are on Saturdays. I'm quite sure the seats will fill quickly. People have been talking about the recital for days." She was chattering on like some nervous schoolgirl who wanted desperately to impress him. For his part he made no effort to put her at ease. He just kept standing there, staring at her, his brows knitted into a frown.

"But if you prefer to stand, that's fine," she added. "Oh my, it's gotten so warm in here. Perhaps we should leave the front door open. That way as latecomers arrive . . ."

"Exactly what are you doing, Nola?" His tone was casual, even friendly, but his eyes bored into hers.

She released a nervous laugh. "As you can see, I am providing for the comfort of my guests, so if you'll excuse me —"

At that same moment Jasper took his place at the front of the room and tapped on a glass with a spoon to gain the audience's attention. His voice seemed almost too powerful for the room, especially given the sparse crowd he was addressing.

"Ladies and gentlemen, welcome to an hour of the classics for the benefit of the Nantucket Fund for Orphans and Widows. This afternoon you have the rare privilege of enjoying an hour of poetry and music as presented by professional actors from the New York stage. To open our program, it is my pleasure to present Mrs. Eleanore Chambliss at the piano."

A hush fell over the gathering as Ellie started to play. Nola saw that Olga was quietly closing the front door and motioned for her to leave it ajar. She was about to slip past Starbuck and into the foyer when she felt his hand close gently but firmly around her upper arm.

"Your office," he murmured as he steered her across the foyer and into the parlor. He smiled and nodded at acquaintances along the way, but once inside the parlor, he dropped his hold on her and closed the doors.

"You seem upset," Nola said, crossing the room to stand behind her desk.

Starbuck smiled but the humor did not reach his eyes. "I think you owe me an explanation," he said as he collapsed his lanky frame into one of the matching chairs that faced the fireplace. He threw one long leg over the arm, leaning sideways into the chair, then stared up at her and waited.

"I cannot imagine what you are talking about," she replied.

"I am talking about the fact that you are using my actors without consulting me. Are they to be paid, Nola?"

"Not in the traditional sense," she faltered. "The event is free and open to the public. I told you that in my note."

"Your note?"

"The one I left in your office."

"I see. I haven't yet been to my office, so why don't you fill me in on the contents of your message?"

Nola sighed. "I wanted you to know that I had taken an idea the others suggested and adapted it."

"And that idea would be?"

Nola nodded toward the closed doors. "Offering a small event such as a recital or reading to raise money for charity."

"Using my actors to perform," Harry repeated. It was not a question.

"They are human beings, Harry, not your personal property," Nola huffed.

"Nevertheless, I have hired them to perform at the opening of the cabaret and for several weeks following. I have promised investors a return on the money they have put up to finance the building of that cabaret. Did it ever occur to you that offering their talents for free might take a bit of the glow off my plans?"

Nola opened her mouth to protest but he wasn't finished. He swung his legs to the floor and stood. He paced up and down from the fireplace to her desk and back again as he ticked off his grievances in the form of questions. "Did it ever occur to you that I can't afford to have my performers losing valuable time while they prepare for your afternoon gatherings? And let me add that if you think offering people a free concert now and then is going to save this quaint business of yours from extinction, think again."

Nola waited a moment to be sure he had run out of accusations. "Are you quite finished?" she said, moving toward the door.

"I'm still waiting for an explanation."

"I do not owe you an explanation. This is an event for charity and it will surely be publicity for the opening of the cabaret. The way I see things, I am indirectly doing you a favor."

"You don't know the first thing about such matters," he snapped. "They must be carefully timed, carefully planned. You don't just —"

"And you do not own the exclusive rights to creative thinking. I am quite capable of putting such events together. Perhaps they will not have your flair for the dramatic, but in spite of today's small turnout, they do have a certain appeal and word will spread. The very fact that I did this on my own rather than coming to you for permission is the real problem here."

"Not at all. The real problem here is that you had every opportunity to tell me of your plans and did not."

"I left you a note," she reminded him, but the wave of guilt she'd felt when she had first tested the idea with Ellie could not be denied.

Starbuck laughed. "Yes, that you did, knowing full well I would not see it until it was too late to do anything to stop you. There are more modern means of communication, Nola. Telegrams, even a public telephone at the post office, which if memory serves you visit every day. You can tell yourself whatever lets you sleep at night, but the fact is that you deliberately put this little event together while I was conveniently out of town."

Nola rolled back the parlor door. "Think what you like, Harry. Now if you'll excuse me, I must ask that either you find a chair and enjoy the recital or leave my establishment. I have guests."

"You've crossed a line here, Nola. Fortunately, judging by the sparse attendance, the damage is minimal. I trust you will not be repeating this fiasco."

The final note of Olga's aria trailed off just as Starbuck left, pulling the door shut behind him.

The fact that Nola might have settled on an idea that could work was the real problem. If the woman was capable of pulling off something like this, then getting her to sell

170

the tearoom to him was going to prove far more difficult than he'd imagined. He hadn't missed the way the small but enthralled audience had burst into applause just after he'd left the premises. The sound had followed him practically all the way back to his office.

In spite of what he had said to Nola, he had no doubt that word of the genteel afternoon gathering in the setting of the tearoom would spread. Oh, the townspeople would keep their distance for the most part, but the seasonal visitors were always looking for some new entertainment or activity. If he didn't nip this thing in the bud, they would come in droves. Once the weather truly warmed, Nola might consider moving the performances outside to her lovely gardens. He envisioned guests seated at small café tables sipping iced tea and lemonade as they enjoyed the entertainment with the vista of the endless ocean and sky as backdrop.

Oh, Miss Nola, just stop fighting the inevitable.

She was quite spectacular in an irritating sort of way. She certainly was not like any other woman he had ever known. More often than not, the women he'd known had been focused on winning his favor and at-

171

tention. Nola Burns seemed to take some
perverse pleasure in showing him repeatedly how little she thought of him or his
opinion of her.

"Harry!"

He glanced up and saw Rose and Violet
Gillenwater. They were riding in an open
air carriage, parasols unfurled to block the
sun.

"We were just on our way to meet Daddy
at the train," Violet called.

"Please don't shout, dear," Harry heard
Rose mutter as he approached the carriage.

"Ladies," he said as he removed his hat
and nodded to the Gillenwaters' driver.

"You're already back, then," Rose huffed.
"And where is my husband?"

Harry glanced toward the tearoom. Rose
would never let her husband hear the last of
it if she knew he had attended Nola's recital.
"He had some business he needed to attend
and then I believe he was going straight
home."

Music from the tearoom caught Violet's
attention as those few who had attended
the recital filed out. "There he is," she cried.
"Daddy!" She half stood and waved.

"Really, Violet, your behavior is most
unbecoming." Rose might be chastising her
daughter but her eyes were fixed on her

172

husband, who was standing on the porch laughing at something Olga Romanoff had said. "Alistair!" Rose shouted, startling the horse so that the carriage jumped forward.

Harry put out a hand to steady Violet, but he was a second late and she fell against him. "Perhaps, Miss Violet, you would do me the honor of accompanying me for a walk," he said as he helped her back into her carriage seat. "Your parents may need some time."

"Mama?"

"Yes, go, go." Rose waved a dismissive hand, her eyes still fixed on her husband as he took his time making his way across the street to the carriage.

Harry offered Violet his hand to help her down and then turned back to Rose. "It was business, Mrs. Gillenwater," he assured her. "Purely business."

"Please have my daughter home in an hour, Mr. Starbuck."

Harry knew when he had been dismissed. He replaced his hat and offered Violet his arm as they set off toward the footbridge. He also made a point of giving Violet his full attention and laughing a little too loud at something she said. He had seen Nola standing on the porch watching them as they passed.

■ ■ ■ ■

Nola was well aware that Harry Starbuck had once been Violet Gillenwater's frequent escort. She also knew that Rose had had deeply mixed feelings about the relationship. In fact when Violet had suddenly gone off to Europe, Rose had confided to Nola that it was to mend her broken heart.

Apparently there was no permanent damage, Nola thought as she watched the handsome couple pass her place, so wrapped up in each other they didn't even look her way. *Well, why should he — they — look this way,* she reprimanded herself. *Harry is angry with you and Violet has probably been fully informed by her mother that you are associating with undesirables and are to be avoided at all costs.*

She returned to the tearoom where Ellie and the others were counting the money.

"Nearly twenty-five dollars," Billy announced.

"Small crowd, but big pockets," Jasper added.

"That man in the front row gave a whole five dollars," Deedee said.

"Mr. Gillenwater is a most engaging man," Olga murmured. "Quite refined."

"He is also Starbuck's business partner and is looking to buy this place and put Nola out of business," Ellie reminded the countess.

"How come Mr. Starbuck didn't stay for the recital?" Mimi asked.

"He had — other business," Nola replied, recalling the way Violet had placed her hand in the crook of his elbow and giggled as they passed. She shook off the image and smiled. "It was a wonderful event and I thank you all so very much. Now you've done quite enough. Please go enjoy your evening."

They all protested that they would help set things in order so the tearoom would be ready for business on Monday, but Nola insisted on doing it herself. The truth was she needed the time alone. She had to admit that Harry was within his rights to be upset. She had ignored her own conscience and failed to consider the fact that featuring his actors in her recital might take away from anticipation to see them perform at the opening of the cabaret.

In her zeal to show him that she could control her own destiny, in spite of his intent to put her out of business, she had indeed crossed a line. She owed the man an apology. Tomorrow when he came for rehearsal, she would ask for a moment of his time.

Feeling at loose ends after he'd escorted Violet home, Harry decided to call on his cousin Rachel. He had barely cleared the threshold before he began spilling out his frustrations with the antics of one Nola Burns.

"Harrison, this simply is not like you." Rachel set a cup of tea in front of him and took the chair across from him near the fireplace. "You are beginning to sound like a small boy who has failed to have his way. I would remind you that what Nola does in *her own home* is none of your business."

"Well, it is my business when she involves performers under contract to me. She clearly has every intention of fighting me with every weapon at her disposal."

"And what's wrong with that? Wouldn't you do the same if one of your little ventures were threatened?"

"The woman is waging a losing battle and I'm only offering her a way out." Harry blew on his tea to cool it then set the cup aside untouched. He was still feeling the effects of his frustration. First there were his New York investors demanding action on both the opening of the cabaret as well as the linking of that venture to the luxury inn. Then there had been the unwelcome surprise of Nola's "recital." But at the foundation of everything else was his play. "Oh, what's the point?" he said irritably.

Rachel smiled. "The point, as I said originally, is that this is not like you. Not at all. This entire business of turning lovely little 'Sconset into a personal playground for your rich friends seems to have turned your head — and heart."

"I have to make a living," Harry grumbled.

Rachel laughed long and loud. "Don't play the pauper with me, my dear cousin. Now how's the play coming along? I hear you've decided to make a perfectly good drama into an operetta? I was unaware that composing was part of your talents, Harry."

"It's not. I'm trying to do it using old hymns and classical pieces."

"And how is that working out?"

"Not well. Some of the lyrics really need original tunes. I can hear the words and even some of the music in my head, but I need to get it out of my head and down onto paper, and I don't know how to do that."

"So hire someone. There must be dozens of lyricists and composers wandering the streets of New York who would be delighted to take a holiday on our lovely island."

"As you've pointed out, I have other matters that demand my time, including the gala coming up in just eight short weeks."

"You always were trying to do too much at the same time."

"I don't understand what you mean. I can't very well help it if God gave me a variety of interests."

"No, and it would be a sin for you not to make use of those gifts. What I am saying, dear cousin, is that perhaps the time has come when you must choose. Always before you've been talented enough to pull it off, but this time, it sounds as if . . ."

"You think I should give up the play?"

"That's not at all what I said," Rachel argued. She stood. "Here's my advice — you did come for advice, didn't you?"

"I always do."

"Then as I see it you need to get on that bicycle of yours and, on the ride home to 'Sconset, set aside your worldly worries for a time. You've always found answers in your faith, Harry. Could it be that you are so caught up in everything you've promised others that you've lost sight of what you want and need for yourself? Have you failed to give yourself the quiet and solitude you need in order to hear God's answers?"

"I pray."

"A prayer goes both ways, Harry. For once in your life stop trying to control everything around you. Set some priorities. Try listening instead of talking and perhaps you will find the answers you need."

CHAPTER NINE

It might have been downright cowardly not to go directly to the tearoom and tell Nola and the others what he'd decided, but when Harry had passed the Lang house on his way back from Rachel's, he'd decided to stop by. He wanted to make sure that Jonah understood the urgency to have those cottages ready for habitation by midweek at the latest. When Judy had asked why the sudden hurry, Harry had told her that he was going to need the actors for rehearsals all day every day and they should have their own quiet place to go back to between sessions.

"But what about the tearoom?"

"Miss Nola has had ample time to find help. I've been as patient as I can, but I can't ask my performers to continue to pull double duty. I'll stop by the tearoom tomorrow and let Miss Nola know that she has three days to find replacements."

Judy Lang was already reaching for her shawl as he left, and he knew that she wouldn't wait until morning to make sure Nola heard the news.

It was fine with him, he decided as he pedaled back to his own cottage. It would save him a trip and was the first step in severing all ties with Nola.

His cousin had counseled him to pray and listen. Well, he had prayed on the ride back to 'Sconset from her house. And he had listened and what he had heard, to the accompaniment of the turning tires, had been a clear message. The only way he was ever going to get on with everything he had to accomplish before the opening of the cabaret was to get Nola Burns out of his life. It had been premature to approach her about buying her property in the first place. He didn't plan to start on the inn until spring anyway. There would be plenty of time for that once the cabaret was up and running.

No, this was the best solution — the only solution. Move his actors into the cottages where they belonged. Move the rehearsals to the hotel. Place all his energy on finishing the cabaret and putting the operetta into shape and he'd have no time at all to dwell on any business he might have with Nola Burns.

■ ■ ■ ■

Nola had been sitting in her parlor reading from a book of meditations when Judy Lang let herself in the front door. Surprised to see the older woman at such an hour, Nola met her in the foyer. "Is everything all right, Judy? Did you forget something?"

"Harry Starbuck came by our place just now all charged up to have Jonah get those cottages finished. That man is going to put you out of business if it's the last thing he does."

Nola was trying to make some sense of Judy's ramblings before she could attract the attention of the others. But on the floors above, bedroom doors opened and soon the Kowalski twins as well as Jasper and Billy were leaning over the banister that wound its way from the foyer to the third floor looking down on them.

"Come inside, Judy. I'll get you some water," Nola said as she tried without success to lead her into the privacy of her parlor.

"Might as well start packing. You are being evicted," Judy called up to the others. This announcement elicited gasps from the twins and brought the two men down the stairs as if they might be called upon to defend their female counterparts.

"What is all this racket?" Ellie asked as she emerged from her room, her hair covered by a towel.

Nola sighed. "Get the countess so we can all hear the news that Mrs. Lang has brought us." She crossed the foyer to the tearoom and turned up the kerosene under a wall sconce.

"Now, tell us exactly what Mr. Starbuck said, Judy."

"He told Jonah to get what supplies he needed to finish the cottages from the construction site at the cabaret. He wants the cottages ready for occupancy by Wednesday latest. He also mentioned that if Jonah needed him he'd either be at the hotel conducting rehearsals for the opening or at the cabaret making sure it opens on schedule."

"I don't understand," Ellie said softly.

"Furthermore, Nola," Judy continued as if Ellie had not spoken, "he said that I should tell you that he would be needing the entire acting company for rehearsals two times a day — morning and afternoon."

"And how are we supposed to help Miss Nola?" Billy demanded.

"You aren't," Nola replied quietly. "That's

the point that Mr. Starbuck is trying to make."

"But you have no staff and you saw how packed the trains have been already. By the end of this week there won't be an empty hotel room in town and . . ." Ellie seemed close to tears as she laid out what everyone already knew. "Oh, I can't believe this of Harry. He simply is not this cruel."

"It's business," Nola said. "He is protecting his interests. One cannot fault him for that."

"Two rehearsals a day?" Jasper muttered.

"At least we'll have our evenings," Mimi said.

"Yeah, right up until we open. Then what? Two rehearsals a day and performances at night?" Jasper asked.

"That's hardly the point," Ellie said. "Miss Nola is going to be without help. She and Mrs. Lang will have to serve customers on their own, at least until she can find appropriate staff to replace us."

"Please," Nola entreated. "The performances are why you came here. You've been working so hard. Of course, I shall miss listening to you in the evenings," she added wistfully, "but we all knew this day would come sooner or later."

"We could strike," Jasper suggested.

"Yeah," Billy agreed eagerly. "Unions all around the country are organizing and walking off the job and . . ."

"Please, no," Nola cried. She forced herself to soften her tone as the group turned its attention to her. "This is your livelihood," she reminded them. "You do not have the protection of a union. If you strike, Mr. Starbuck will simply find other performers to hire."

"But, Miss Nola," Deedee cried, "what will become of you?"

"Come now, Mrs. Lang and I have weathered storms far more disastrous than this. You have a duty to these people — and to the contract you made with Mr. Starbuck." She could see that she had made her point. "Now then, shall we all retire for the evening? Tomorrow things are bound to look much brighter and who knows, perhaps Mr. Starbuck will reconsider."

We have an agreement, she thought as she walked Judy out to the porch and caught sight of a lamp burning in Starbuck's office window.

But Harry did not reconsider and John Humboldt told Nola that in light of her decision to stage the recital without his approval, she had effectively made the agree-

185

ment null and void.

By midweek the actors had moved from the rooms at Nola's to the cottages down the lane. As promised, they began rehearsing at the hotel morning and afternoon, but in spite of Starbuck's obvious determination to keep them so busy they would have no time for Nola or her tearoom, they improvised.

Under Ellie's direction the troupe came to the tearoom every evening as soon as rehearsals ended and stayed for a couple of hours, cleaning, washing dishes and preparing for the next day's business. Nola protested that they needed their rest and time to learn the ever-changing lines and lyrics of Harry's operetta since in lieu of hiring a composer he had evidently decided to stick with his original plan to set the entire thing to various classical pieces.

"It's a disaster," Ellie told Nola one evening. "I won't say that in front of the others, but frankly Harry is out of his element with this thing. It's a good thing he has a head for business."

"But he's such a gifted playwright," she reminded Ellie, thinking of the original script she had read in his office weeks earlier. A script that had filled her with wonder when she'd first read it.

"He is that, as well," Ellie agreed. "I just wish someone could convince him that he should have left well enough alone. He's stretching his limits in thinking he can take his words and set them to music."

In spite of the sympathy she felt for the actors — and for Harry — when it came to the operetta, Nola had her own problems. Foremost was the matter of staffing for the tearoom now that he had made it impossible for the actors to do more than help in the evenings after closing. She'd made little progress in finding new employees. The truth was that Ellie and the others had worked out so well that simply finding competent help was no longer an option. Everything about them from Olga's regal greeting of patrons at the door to the twins' sunny personalities as they fawned over each customer had attracted the summer visitors — if not the locals. In fact, the more enthralled her summer visitors were with the actors, the more Nola's fellow townspeople became convinced that she was making a mistake and would regret befriending people of the theater — including Harry Starbuck — in the long run.

Well, they can stop worrying, Nola thought as she sat down to open a stack of mail that had accumulated over the last two days while she tried to come up with a plan for finding new help.

The third envelope from the bottom was another blue envelope. No name or address on the outside but it was sealed just as the first one had been. Nola opened the flap and pulled out the single sheet. Again the message was composed of letters and words cut from newspapers and magazines.

Miss Nola, Miss Nola, why won't you
   heed
The fact that we're doing you a good
   deed?
Those people will be your downfall
If you don't see that, you have some gall.
                                      A friend

The rhyme was so awkward as to be almost comical, but this was hardly a joke. Someone had gone to a great deal of trouble in composing the message, constructing it from cut-out words and finding away to insert it with her regular mail.

And why would Harry spend time making up these silly warning notes when all he had to do was move the actors out and leave her with no help at all? Someone else was behind these warnings. But who?

■ ■ ■ ■

After the actors moved out, Nola lay awake after another sleepless night. The house was too quiet these days, especially in the evenings. She missed the laughter and conversation of the rehearsals. She missed the sounds of the actors settling in for the night. She missed her late-night chats with Ellie. Without them, the house felt empty. She thought of something Harry's cousin Rachel had once said when someone asked how she could stand being all alone in that house on New Street all the time. "Oh, we have each other, my house and I."

Rachel had a reputation for being a modern woman — not always a statement of respect among her neighbors, but Nola had long admired Rachel's penchant for bold self-expression. Perhaps when she was in her forties — as Rachel was — and people no longer gave a thought to the idea that she might one day find some poor widower to complete her, she would give free rein to the bold ideas and wild imaginings that sometimes assailed her.

Surely there was some compromise she could offer Harry. It was completely understandable that Starbuck had been taken by

surprise when he discovered she'd scheduled the recital. *But we had an agreement,
Harrison Starbuck.*

From her wardrobe she reached for one
of half a dozen starched, high-collared
blouses and her gray serge skirt, then put
back the skirt and took out turquoise
lightweight wool instead. She selected a
length of matching velvet ribbon from the
collection on her dresser and fashioned a tie
at the collar of her blouse. That should get
his attention, she thought and was immediately stunned that she was choosing
her attire to impress Harry Starbuck.

"Well, this is business," she reminded her
reflection in the mirror as she twisted her
hair into its usual serviceable chignon and
stabbed it with the necessary pins to hold it
for the day. She put on her black leather
shoes and then shrugged into a fitted black
linen bolero jacket. Sparing herself one last
turn before the mirror, she chose a small
brimless black turban-style hat from her collection and pinned it into place. "Now, off
with you before you lose your nerve," she
ordered as she headed down the back hall
and into the kitchen.

Jonah Lang was helping himself to a
second cup of coffee before heading out to
work for the day. He nodded in Nola's

direction.

"You going over to the mainland?" Judy asked.

"No, why would you think that?"

Judy gave her the once-over and raised one eyebrow.

Nola blushed. "I have a business appointment," she replied. "I won't be long," she promised and hurried out the kitchen door.

In the yard she took a moment to gather her thoughts and through the open window heard Jonah ask, "Do you think she's going to try and get Harry to change his mind?"

"Yeah, I'd say she's off to plead her case."

Plead her case? Most certainly not, Nola thought as she squared her shoulders and set off down the street. *Nola Burns does not plead with anyone — certainly not a man who thinks he can shape the world to his own pleasure and needs.*

"Morning, Miss Nola," Ian sang out as he paused in the washing of his store window. "The mail up yet?"

"Good morning, Ian. Actually I was on my way to see Mr. Starbuck. Do you know if he's in his office?"

"Come and gone," Ian replied, studying her with fresh interest. "I saw him head off down toward the east end with Horace

Gibbs not twenty minutes ago." Ian pointed in the direction of the construction site for the cabaret. "Horace had a bunch of rolled-up papers under one arm. I expect they might be down there awhile. I could tell him you were looking for him when he gets back."

"Thank you, Ian, but that won't be necessary. I'll just go and see him at the . . . down there."

"That urgent, huh?" Ian asked, his eyes afire with curiosity.

Nola forced a laugh. "Not at all. As you said, it's a lovely morning and this may well be my last opportunity for a walk on such a day. We're getting to be quite busy at the tearoom."

"Aye," Ian replied. "I sure hope that's the way it stays for the remainder of the summer. I've got a store full of goods I need to move."

"Which reminds me," Nola said with a smile. "I could use another dozen of those fine table napkins you ordered for me last season."

"Got my table linen order in last week. I'll send over a baker's dozen as soon as it's unpacked."

"Thank you, Ian," Nola said. "Put it on my account and give my regards to Mrs.

McAllister."

Ian's wife had joined the ranks of those who thought Nola had made a grave error in associating with the actors. But faced with disapproval from practically every quarter in the small village, Nola had decided that her best defense was no defense at all. She simply went about her business as she always had and treated everyone the same as she had before the actors arrived. She would not make excuses for her decisions no matter who was concocting these silly notes of warning.

Without hesitation, lest she lose her nerve, she strode the rest of the way through town, nodding to those she passed along the way but not stopping to visit. As she neared the end of Broadway she kept her focus on the low-pitched shingled roof capped by two louvered square cupolas that seemingly overnight had become the town's newest landmark. Nola had avoided the place even as others in 'Sconset had watched it so closely it seemed as if some of them had witnessed every nail being driven.

Even from several doors away, she could hear the sounds of hammering and sawing coming from inside. And as she came closer she could not help but admit that this was a handsome building. Shutters framed the large windows that ran along the front and sides of the cedar-shingled exterior. In addition there was a welcoming porch, not unlike her own, stretching across the entire front of the building and wrapping around to one side where it ended in an enclosed pavilion.

She paused for a moment to take it all in. She could understand why Harry wanted to buy her out. Her home and tearoom would be the perfect retreat for those special visitors who wanted to be in the thick of things and at the same time a bit removed from the general activity in the village. The cabaret certainly was a far cry from the shadowy shuttered place she had envisioned. It was light and airy and inviting.

Nevertheless, she thought as she stepped inside, there were other options. In Nola's opinion Harry had become so used to getting whatever he set out to acquire that the very idea someone might refuse to cooperate was unthinkable.

"Well, well, well," Harry murmured, tipping his chair back as he watched Nola Burns enter the cabaret. She stood just inside the door for a moment, no doubt allowing her eyes to adjust from the bright sunshine of the day to the dimmer sawdust-filled interior. She was wearing an ankle-length skirt the color of the sea on a July day and he couldn't help wondering if she'd worn the uncharacteristic color in order to impress him.

She approached Horace, asked a question and Harry saw Horace point in his direction. He watched her cross the large hall, dodging workmen and carpenters along the way. He waited until she was standing across the table that served as his desk, then slowly got to his feet. "Miss Nola."

"Hello," she mouthed, her soft voice drowned out by the voices of the workers calling out instructions and the sounds that came with finishing off the interior of a large room still in need of lighting, flooring and a stage.

Harry indicated the open rear entrance to the building. "Out here," he shouted and waited for her to precede him onto the back landing. There he shut the door against the chaos inside and turned to her. "What do you think?" he asked, indicating with a sweep of one hand the building and surrounding grounds. "Tennis courts," he explained, following her gaze to the side of the building where the ground had been chalked off in a grid. "Croquet over there."

"Very impressive," she replied, working

the fingers of her cotton gloves more tightly into place. "Are you — that is, will you be ready to open on schedule?"

Harry was thrown by her question. Nola was usually one to come directly to the point. This polite chitchat was unlike her. He squinted at her. "We'll be ready. Now, how can I help you, Nola?"

"I won't keep you," she replied, suddenly all business. "I can see that you have a great deal to accomplish in a very short period of time, and with rehearsals and all, you're quite busy. I have come to apologize."

"I see."

"You were perfectly within your rights to be upset that I had staged the recital using talent you had hired. That will not happen again."

"Apology accepted. Was there anything else?"

"Yes, I have also come to suggest a compromise," she announced without missing a beat.

Harry's squint evolved into a frown. "A compromise?"

"Yes. I can certainly appreciate that your acting troupe needs to have ample rehearsal time, especially now that you've reconstructed the piece to be played as an operetta. And I perfectly understand your desire to have them go over the material not once but twice a day, especially since — from what I've heard of the rehearsals to date — the play does seem to change significantly from day to day and they are constantly being challenged to learn new lyrics and melodies."

Harry eyed her more closely. Was she making fun of him? Surely Ellie had confided to her that rehearsals were a disaster. "Go on."

"And furthermore I would remind you that we had an agreement."

"One you violated," he pointed out.

"I don't recall anything being said about whether or not I could offer entertainment in my establishment. But that's hardly the point. The point is that, while I am sure this was not your intent, your decision to have the group rehearse morning and afternoon leaves me in a bit of a bind."

Well aware that in business sometimes silence spoke more eloquently than words, Harry made no response. His action had the intended result of flustering Nola and he couldn't help noticing that the rosy hue that pinked her cheeks was most becoming. It occurred to him that it had been several days since he'd seen Nola and he had to admit that he'd missed her.

"You see," she hurried to add, "it occurred

to me that if the troupe rehearsed morning and evening, they would still be able to staff the tearoom in the afternoons until I can find suitable replacements."

"And just what progress have you made on that front?" Harry asked. "It seems to me that you haven't yet even begun the search." His gentle accusation needed no response. He was well aware that the best workers had long ago been snapped up by other businesses, not only on Nantucket but in resort communities up and down the eastern shore.

"I . . . That is . . ."

"You see, Nola, staffing your little tearoom is hardly my concern. In fact, we are both well aware that it would make life much easier for me were your business to suffer. Now, if there's nothing more?"

Her eyes widened. "Obviously it was pointless to come here and attempt to conduct a reasonable discussion of the matter. How can you pretend to be a man of faith and wish suffering on others?" She turned to go then realized the steps down from the landing were not yet in place. Trapped, she turned back to face him, her mouth working in frustration, her eyes now dewy with the tears of her anger.

"Nola," he said, taking a step toward her.

"I did not say I wanted to make you suffer. That's the last thing I want. I said that *if* your business fell on hard times — of its own accord — that would be to my advantage. It's a simple truth."

"Well, here is a simple truth for you, Mr. Starbuck. My business will not fail. It did not fail when my mother became ill. It did not fail in the years when it was the sole source of income for my siblings and myself, and I assure you that it will not fail now." Her eyes flamed with the strength of her determination.

"Don't you ever get tired?" he asked.

She blinked. "I don't have that luxury."

"But you could, Nola. You don't have to work this hard, fight this hard."

"It's my home," she whispered and looked down. "It's all I have."

"No, it's not," Harry replied. "You have friends and a family you never have time to visit and a gift for making beautiful music."

"I have said what I came to say," she said and her voice quavered as tears welled in her eyes.

Harry had to knot his hands into fists to keep from wrapping his arms around her. The idea surprised him so much that he turned away and she seized that moment to pull the door open, pinning him against the landing railing while she hurried across the chaotic construction site toward daylight.

He was recovering his senses and trying to decide whether or not to go after her or wait until she'd calmed down when he saw a worker carrying one of the long wide planks intended for the stage floor on a collision course with Nola.

"Watch out!" he heard Horace shout just as the worker swung around, catching Nola full in the back of the head with the board.

She crumpled to the floor and lay there without moving. Workers from all sides of the room rushed to her aid. For an instant Harry's heart seemed to stop beating. Only his brain hammered out a single rhythm. *Nola. Nola. Nola.*

"Get a doctor," Harry ordered and two of the men ran for the front entrance as he knelt next to her. "Nola?"

Nothing. Not a sound or a flinch. Her face was pale and relaxed as if she were simply taking a nap. Harry felt the kind of panic that comes with losing something precious, something you didn't even know you valued. "Nola?" he shouted and touched her shoulder although he wanted to gather her in his arms.

"She's breathing, boss," Horace observed. "Maybe let her alone till the doc gets here.

She's gonna have one whopper of a headache, I'll wager."

Harry eased himself to a seated position
on the dusty floor and took Nola's hand in
his. He pulled off her glove and stroked her
fingers as he closed his eyes and sent a silent
prayer up to Heaven that she would be all
right. *Whatever Your plan, please, just let her
be all right.*

To his relief, he felt her fingers close
around his.

CHAPTER TEN

Nola had trouble getting her eyes to open and she certainly could not understand why she was flat on her back surrounded by men talking in low murmurs. Someone was holding her hand while someone else gently lifted her head and pressed a wad of fabric underneath to form a pillow. Everything smelled of unfinished wood and paint.

"Where's that doctor?" she heard a familiar voice growl.

Starbuck.

She tried to call his name and managed only a low groan. Behind her closed eyes her head throbbed.

"She's coming around," someone said.

Then from some distance away she heard a stranger's voice announce, "Here's the doc. Get back to work, all of you."

"Nola?"

She managed to open one eye and the first thing she saw was Harrison Starbuck's handsome face swimming just above hers. He gave her a shaky smile but his eyes were dark with worry. "Lie still," he ordered and Nola sighed. He did have such an annoying habit of commanding others. Usually he did it with charm and even levity, but the way he was looking at her defied her to challenge him.

Reason enough, she decided, and struggled to sit up.

"Nola!" This time his voice was a shout and she grimaced as the sound ricocheted around the fierce pain in her head.

"There, there, Miss Burns," a gentle female voice entreated. "Lie still so I can have a look." Dr. Lois Wainwright and her sister ran the spa and homeopathic health facility just down the street from the tearoom. Nola had never had occasion to need their services until now, but she had heard high praise for their holistic approach to medicine and healing.

Comforted by the fact that she was in good hands, Nola collapsed back. She expected to find herself once again resting on the hard floor with its makeshift pillow that smelled of turpentine. Instead she was lying against the firm pillow of Harry's chest. His breathing came in shallow but regular beats. When she turned her head so the doctor could examine the site of her injury, she found her cheek pressed against his shirt. The warmth emanating from beneath the soft fabric accompanied by the rhythmic beating of his heart soothed her.

"She's going to recover, isn't she? I mean, fully recover?" Starbuck asked.

"Let's get her back to her house so I can conduct a more thorough examination," Dr. Wainwright instructed. "I'd like her to lie flat for the time being. Could we borrow one of the wagons outside to transport her?"

Arrangements were hastily made, the men obviously relieved to have something concrete to offer. They brought another of the wide planks intended for the stage floor and gently moved Nola onto it, then carried her to the door and outside. The driver of one of the work wagons was waiting and the sudden brightness of the sunlight made Nola cry out and throw her arm across her eyes. Immediately the light dimmed as if the sun had suddenly gone behind a cloud. She squinted up and saw Harry holding his straw hat over her face like an umbrella. "Let's go," he barked, and the driver snapped the reins.

The ride was no more than a few blocks, but 'Sconset was a tight-knit community and even before the wagon stopped at the tearoom, a crowd had gathered.

"Nola, child," she heard Judy Lang cry out. Then Nola heard Judy direct her distress at Harry. "What have you done?"

"I . . . It was an accident," he sputtered. Nola smiled because he sounded so much like her brothers when they'd all been teenagers and defended themselves against their mother's outrage.

"I apparently walked into a board," Nola explained weakly, surprised to realize that she had more recollection of the incident than she had first thought. She frowned as the memory of her argument with Harry came back to her. "We'll have to shut down the tearoom for a few days," she told Judy. "You can't do it all alone and Mr. Starbuck needs —"

"What *Mr. Starbuck* needs," Judy huffed, "is to hold his horses. The world is not going to come to an end if he has to give up the reins for a few days." Once again, she turned her ire on Harry. "These young people kicked out of Nola's perfectly good rooms and moved into those musty old fishing shacks. What do you care where they sleep and more to the point, if they want to wait tables and such *on their own time,* I'd like to know how that is any of your business."

This tirade accompanied the transport of Nola from the dray, up the front walk and into her bedroom. Because Harry and the driver were carrying Nola on the makeshift gurney, he could hardly escape Judy's rant. Since he was at her feet, Nola could see him and observe the fact that more than once he had opened his mouth to protest Judy's accusations and then shut it again until now it formed a thin hard line across the lower half of his face.

Under the guidance of Dr. Wainwright, Harry and the driver transferred her onto the bed and the driver took the board and left the room.

"You come waltzing back into town thinking because you've made yourself a pile of money, people will forget all the mischief you used to get into when you were a kid," Judy continued as she bustled about, removing Nola's shoes, gloves and hat and setting them aside. "Seems to me you haven't changed one bit. Still stirring up trouble and now see what it's come to?"

"Perhaps, Mr. Starbuck," the doctor said quietly, "it would be best if you waited in the outer room while I examine Miss Burns."

Judy took this as her signal to escort Harry to the door and shut it firmly behind him.

"You mustn't blame Harry," Nola said softly when Judy returned to the side of the bed and followed the doctor's lead in helping Nola sit up enough so that they could remove her jacket and loosen the rest of her clothing.

"You let me handle that young man and the rest of it," Judy said, her voice soft and soothing now. "You just concentrate on following the doctor's orders and getting your rest."

It was a mark of how terrible Nola was feeling that this seemed like a good idea. She could barely focus on keeping her eyes open much less on how Judy was going to manage the tearoom for the foreseeable future. She heard the doctor say that there was no sign of concussion, but fell back asleep before she could make heads or tails of the instructions about diet, medication and symptoms to watch for that the doctor was dictating to Judy.

When she woke, the doctor was gone. She was now dressed in her nightgown, her hair pulled into a loose braid. She vaguely recalled trying to cooperate as Ellie helped Judy change her into her nightclothes, but she'd been more like a rag doll than any real help. Outside it was still daylight but whether the same day or the next, Nola could not say. Beyond the closed door of her bedroom, she heard voices.

"I'll be glad to say you called," Ellie was telling someone.

"Young woman, do you have any idea who I am?" The unmistakable boom of Rose Gillenwater's normal speaking voice penetrated the solid wood door. "Miss Nola's mother was one of my dearest friends and since her passing — may God rest her soul — I have taken my responsibility to her children to heart. Now I have no idea why someone did not send for me the moment this happened yesterday morning, but I am here now and I will see her."

So it was now Tuesday, Nola thought, realizing that she had lost an entire night and day. The tearoom, she thought. Judy can't manage that and also care for me. Nola decided that she would get rid of Rose as quickly as possible and then see about getting some help for Judy.

"Ellie," she called, her voice coming out in a croak. She cleared her throat and tried again. "Ellie, it's all right."

"There, you see," Rose said dismissively as she opened the door and swept into the room. "Child, what were you thinking?" she demanded the moment she set eyes on Nola. "One simply does not —"

"Hello, Mrs. Gillenwater. How nice of you to come by. Have you and Mrs. Chambliss been formally introduced?" Nola indicated Ellie, who stood just inside the door, a worried frown marring her otherwise perfect features.

"Yes, yes." Rose leaned closer and whispered, "I will see to organizing proper care for you the moment I leave here, Nola. In the meantime . . ."

"Oh, Rose, Ellie is not hired help — well, she is . . . was. But she's quite famous in the New York theater. Aren't we fortunate that she has decided to come here to 'Sconset and give us all the opportunity to enjoy her talents?"

Rose sniffed. "I'm sure she's quite the star in certain circles," she said with a token smile thrown in Ellie's direction, "but hardly the person who should be attending you in your hour of need, dear Nola. I can't imagine what Dr. Wainwright was thinking. I've asked Mr. Gillenwater to consult with our personal physician in the city — perhaps we should bring an authentic medical professional here to examine you."

"I have been examined, Rose, and as you can see, I am improving hourly." She pushed herself higher onto the pillows and immediately Ellie was there to adjust them to her comfort. "What I really need is for you and the other ladies of the church to use your considerable resources to help me find staffing for the tearoom as soon as possible. We may have had to close for a day or so, but . . ."

Rose's eyebrows shot up. "The tearoom is open, Nola," she said and frowned at Ellie. "I simply assumed that . . ."

Nola shot Ellie a glance.

"Harry told us to help out," Ellie explained.

"Harry did that?" Nola asked. *For me?*

"The man's clearly feeling guilty for having been the cause of your injuries, Nola," Rose announced, taking the glow off Nola's pleasure by stating the obvious truth.

"Thank him for me," Nola said to Ellie. "And tell him I'll see to other arrangements as soon as possible."

"Thank him yourself," Ellie replied with a smile. "He comes by here practically every hour to be sure you're all right." She nodded toward a large vase filled with a display of spring flowers on her dresser. "He brought those on his last visit."

"Guilt, guilt, guilt," Rose murmured. "I shall tell Mr. Starbuck that his concern is unwarranted, Nola, and unseemly. You're a single woman, after all."

"And he's a single man," Ellie blurted, clearly not seeing the problem.

"Precisely," Rose announced as if she had finally gotten through to Ellie. "I do not know — or care to know — how things are managed in your world, Mrs. Chambliss. In our social circle, there is a certain code of behavior that women like Nola must adhere to or risk losing not only their standing in the business community but the respect of the populace in general. This dear woman has already placed her spotless reputation in jeopardy for you people." She bent and gave Nola a dry kiss on the forehead. "Do watch yourself, Nola. In your weakened state I would hate to see you mistake that rake's attention for true concern." Without so much as a glance at Ellie, Rose exited the room as if outside the door lay souls to be saved.

Nola glanced up apologetically at Ellie and was surprised when the actress burst into laughter. "She's like a character out of a badly scripted play," she managed between peals of laughter. Nola couldn't help but join in, but before either woman could recover from their fresh onset of mirth, Harry Starbuck stepped into the doorway.

"Feeling better?" He remained standing near the doorway while Ellie sat down in the rocker across the room and picked up some mending.

"Yes, thank you." Nola pulled the covers higher. It was one thing to think of Harry in her bedroom when she was fully dressed, unconscious with a possible concussion and surrounded by others. It was quite something else to have him there with just Ellie as chaperone. She could just imagine what Rose Gillenwater would say.

Rose! Harry had to have been standing outside the door when the older woman left. Rose would have seen him. And he in turn would have overheard the matriarch's insults to Ellie.

"Has the doctor been by this afternoon?" he asked, glancing around the room, looking anywhere but directly at her.

Casual conversation? No, look at him. He seems upset.

"She was here," Ellie said. "Nola is to try getting up for a little while beginning tomorrow. If that goes well, within a few days she should be good as new."

Harry didn't really seem to be paying attention. He was scowling, not at Ellie or her, but at the floor. Nola rushed to fill the silence. "Ellie tells me that you've given the troupe permission to help Judy until I can get back to work. I assure you that they'll

212

be free of me and this place within a few days."

"There's no reason we can't rehearse in the morning and evening. Since I often have other business that needs attention, it's a good plan, Nola." Harry looked directly at her for the first time and studied her for so long that Nola could not bear his examination and turned her attention to the window.

"It appears to be a lovely day," she said, all too aware that Harry had fully entered the room and was now sitting on the stool in front of her dressing table.

"Do you agree with the Gillenwater woman, Nola? Has your association with us truly damaged your reputation with the townspeople?"

Ellie glanced up for the first time but immediately returned to her sewing.

"Oh, Harry, no," Nola assured him. "There are always going to be those who are overly protective, but they'll come around in time."

"But if I hadn't provoked you, you never would have been at the cabaret and none of this would have happened."

"It was an accident. In fact I probably was at least partially to blame, not looking where I was going and . . ."

"Why do you do that?"

"Do what?"

"Take responsibility even when you are the victim?"

"I am hardly a victim, Harry. It was an accident. Please don't concern yourself with . . ."

Harry grinned down at her. "Ah, yes, you've been warned not to take my concern seriously, I believe."

So he had also heard that part. "Mrs. Gillenwater can be . . ." Nola searched for a suitable word while Harry leaped in with several suggestions.

"Overbearing? Autocratic? Domineering?"

Nola permitted a smile and she heard Ellie chuckle. "I was going to say 'difficult.' She can certainly make her opinions known but it is always done in the interest of maintaining decorum. She's a pillar of the community and the church," Nola reminded them both sternly. "And aside from all that she has been very good to my family and to me."

"And she allows no room for alternative opinions or ideas," Harry said. "Take faith, for example."

"Surely you cannot question her devotion to the church," Nola exclaimed.

Harry shrugged. "The way I see it the lessons in the Bible are all about love — loving your neighbor, loving people who are different, loving those less fortunate, less educated. Rose Gillenwater is certainly a pious woman, but she doesn't strike me as a loving woman."

And how do I strike you?

Nola suppressed that thought and instead said, "The Bible also suggests we not judge one another."

Harry leaned forward, his eyes alight with interest. "That's exactly what I was thinking about when I wrote the play. God's love is universal — it's the very reason those who fall away always have the choice to return to God — but that all comes with responsibility."

"You have this habit of changing subjects in the middle of a conversation, Harry. It can be most unsettling."

"I am not changing the subject at all. Take you, for example. If I had known you then I might have been modeling the lead character on you. You take responsibility very seriously — some would say too seriously. You raise your siblings, you manage this business and Oliver says he can't recall your ever missing a Sunday playing for services."

"Honestly, Harry, you make me sound as regimented as some spinster schoolmarm." Nola's head was beginning to throb and she was having trouble concentrating. She reached for the glass of water on her nightstand.

Simultaneously Ellie and Harry rushed forward to get the water for her, but Harry was closer. When he handed her the glass there was no choice but to brush his fingers with her own.

"I don't think anything of the sort," he said as he steadied the glass in her hand and then immediately stepped away, turning his back to give Ellie time to take the glass from her and then assist in rearranging the covers. "Look, I'm well aware that there are many people in this community who are less than thrilled to have the actors here. Some don't even want me here, but this is my home, too, Nola, and I believe that what I am trying to do will not only enrich my life. It will enrich the lives of everyone who lives here."

Nola opened her mouth to protest, then closed it. She would not insult him with platitudes. "People don't always care that much about money, Harry."

"I'm not talking about money. I'm talking about progress, about change. It's inevitable but it can be shaped to the best advantage of those it affects."

"And yet people often struggle when

things start to change too quickly," she said.

"This isn't just about changing old ways into new or bringing in more modern ideas," he said. "It's important that you understand that for me the theater is more than just a hobby or diversion, Nola."

"Why?"

"Because live theater has the power to teach, to inspire, to provoke thought and action. It can change the way people decide to live their lives."

"I suspect Nola is asking you why is it important that she specifically understand?" Ellie said, and it was clear from the curious expression in her eyes that she was also interested in that answer.

He glanced toward Ellie and then back at Nola. "I'm not sure," he muttered and Nola caught Ellie's hint of a smile as she stood and put her mending aside.

"Well, the important thing for Nola at the moment is rest. Come along, Harry," she ordered as she escorted him to the door.

"Of course," Harry said, retrieving his hat from Nola's dresser. "I'll stop back tomorrow, if that's all right."

"I'd like that," Nola replied and meant it.

Back in his office, Harry forced his attention to the pile of invoices and pending orders for supplies that were stacked in neat piles on his desk. Deliberately he set aside the most recent version of the script. He checked the charges from one vendor, then compared bids from three others, all the while forcing himself to concentrate against the memory of Nola's wistful voice.

I'd like that.

"Hey, you there!"

Ian McAllister's gruff voice interrupted Harry's reverie. Harry stepped out onto his landing in time to see Ian chasing a gang of three older boys down the lane.

"Ian? Everything all right?"

Ian was breathing heavily as he gave up the chase. "Too much time on their hands," he called up to Harry. "Used to be they'd just turn the rain barrel over or some such mischief at night. Now they've gotten brazen enough to pull that stuff in broad daylight."

Harry went down to help Ian turn the barrel upright again and noticed a cracked pane in the rear window of Ian's store. "They did this, as well?"

"Not sure. I found that a couple of days ago when I was opening up. Just haven't had the time to get it fixed."

"I'll ask Jonah to stop by and replace the glass," Harry offered. "Did you report the

218

damage?"

Ian shrugged. "Yeah. I spoke to Officer Daniels and he said he'd step up night patrols, but I intend to make sure everything's locked up tight and I'd suggest you do the same, Harry."

As he returned to his office, Harry couldn't help thinking that he was glad Nola was in the habit of locking up no matter what time of day it was.

CHAPTER ELEVEN

There was one advantage to being forced to stay in bed. Nola had little to do but enjoy the view from her open window and think. The late June breeze stirred the lace curtains carrying the scent of roses and lavender her way. On the other hand, the open window also gave her access to the conversation of others who passed by on their way to the beach or to shop in town.

"We should go here for lunch one day," a young female voice commented and Nola felt the usual glow of pride in her establishment.

"That place is for old people. My *grandmother* goes there," the companion replied.

"Yeah," a third voice chimed in. "We need a place where we can go with those Gillenwater boys we met on the beach yesterday."

"My mother said I was to stay clear of those boys," the first girl said.

"Parents always warn you to stay away

from the interesting ones," the first girl sighed. "If there were only something to do — an ice cream parlor where we could go without having to make excuses," she moaned as they moved on down the street and their voices faded into distant laughter.

Restless with the boredom of her confinement, Nola's thoughts turned as always to business. The girls had a point. Although most of her patrons were summer visitors, she couldn't help admitting that unless they came in with their parents or grandparents, she had seen almost no young people this season. Those who had come for lunch or tea had clearly been there under duress as their elders insisted on sharing the memories of their own youth.

Nola knew that word of mouth was everything for a business dependent on tourists. If the younger generation's memory of Miss Nola's was that they were forced to go there with their parents, then what did that bode for the future of her tearoom?

The girl had mentioned ice cream.

Somewhere in the attic was an old ice cream churn. Nola's father had been famous for the strawberry ice cream he made each year for the church's annual clambake. What if she could offer a monthly ice cream social? Perhaps on a Friday evening. In the garden. With paper lanterns strung among the trees. After a performance at the cabaret when the young people were on their way home. She closed her eyes and envisioned the scene — girls and boys in pastel clothing chatting together, sharing an ice cream soda, even falling in love.

Nola smiled. A boy and girl who met and fell in love in her garden would surely become customers for life, would surely tell others about the magical place where they had spent so many lovely summer evenings. She imagined a girl with hair braided to her waist sitting across from a tall broad-shouldered young man. They were sharing an ice cream soda and he was laughing at something she said. His face was in shadow but she knew that laugh.

Starbuck.

Nola's eyes flew open. This daydreaming was a pure waste of time. Of course, he would come to mind. He'd been in and out of the place on a regular basis ever since her accident. She sat up and swung her legs over the side of the bed, reaching for her robe at the same time.

"Judy?" she called as she stood and tied the robe tight around her. "Judy?" she called again above the clang of dishes being washed in the kitchen.

"Oh, bother," she muttered and walked barefoot into the front foyer and through the closed and deserted tearoom into the kitchen.

"What are you doing out of bed?" Judy demanded. "And no shoes? You'll catch your death on top of everything else."

"Do you remember Papa's ice cream churn?" Nola asked, ignoring Judy's protests.

"I remember he had one," Judy replied, momentarily taken aback by the turn in conversation.

"I wonder if it's somewhere in the attic," Nola mused as she moved toward the back stairway.

"Stop right there, Nola Burns," Judy demanded. "If you are so intent on finding this ice cream churn I will send Jasper or Billy to look for it tomorrow after they get through with their play practice. Now you just get yourself back to bed while I finish closing up here. I made you some nice chicken soup for your supper and . . ."

"I have a new idea," Nola said as she started gathering a bowl and spoon as well as a plate and knife and setting a place at the kitchen table. She glanced over at Judy, who was observing all of this with her hands planted disapprovingly on her hips. "I'm fine," she assured her.

Judy rolled her eyes and relieved Nola of the bowl as she slid the cover off the simmering soup. "Sit," she ordered.

While Judy served up soup and cheese and a slice of her crusty wheat bread, Nola told her about the overheard conversation and her idea to expand the tearoom services to include an ice cream parlor. The more doubtful Judy looked, the more entrenched in the idea Nola became. She was well used to people telling her she couldn't do something. It had the effect of only making her more determined to prove herself.

"Nola?" Judy placed the back of her hand to Nola's forehead. "You all right?"

"Of course." Nola shook herself free of her revelry and expanded on her idea for adding an ice cream parlor to the tearoom.

"What is this really about, child?" Judy asked.

Surprised at Judy's weary tone, Nola gave the older woman her full attention. "I don't know what you mean," she said.

"I mean, look around you. It's you and me, my girl. Cooking, cleaning, serving — and you want to start an ice cream parlor on top of that?"

"Ellie and the others are still helping."

"And look at them. They run to rehearsal

224

then come here then back to rehearsal. When do they sleep? They can't keep that up, Nola."

"I know," Nola admitted. "But . . ."

"If you ask me — and I know you didn't — you need to stop trying to put one over on Harry Starbuck and maybe think about what he offered you that first day he stepped onto the porch here."

"And what is that?"

"A way off this island. I'll admit I never would have thought he'd be the one to bring you that. That boy was always going against the grain, always testing the waters and stirring things up."

"Harry has nothing to do with this."

"Harry has everything to do with it." Judy reached across the wooden table, warped by decades of rolling out dough and kneading bread, and patted Nola's hand. "You don't have to keep fighting, Nola. You did what you promised your mother you would do. You kept the family together. You made sure they were all educated and set out on paths of their own choosing. You paid the bills and kept this house in the family."

"And now," Nola protested, "I am simply suggesting a way we can sustain the good life we've built. After all, one must keep up with the times and for young people in this

225

day and age a tearoom is simply not fashion-able."

"Don't you want something more? You are twenty-seven years old, Nola. Isn't it time you went out into the world and found out if Nantucket is truly where you want to spend your whole life before you just give yourself over to it?"

Nola leaned back and folded her arms stubbornly across her chest. "This island is my home," she grumbled. "Besides, if this life is good enough for Rachel Williams, surely —"

"Rachel Williams knew exactly what she was choosing. You don't," Judy replied bluntly. "Oddly enough it's her cousin who's giving you the possibility to see for yourself if indeed you're like Rachel."

"Harry is interested in one thing — get-ting his hands on this property so he can . . ." She swallowed. "So he can turn it into some monstrous opulent palace for his rich friends and make even more money than he already has."

Judy got up and began clearing the table. "You don't believe that — and neither do I. Seems to me that you're being as childish about this as Harry is. The two of you are like kids in the schoolyard, each determined to show up the other. Well, this isn't a game,

Nola. This is life — your life. I don't think God intends for you to keep wasting that precious gift by trying to beat Harry at his own game. Now eat your supper and get yourself back to bed and I'll have Jasper or Billy check on that ice cream churn tomorrow."

Chastened by Judy's outburst, Nola ate her supper and watched the woman who had been like a mother to her move around the kitchen. She couldn't help noticing how from time to time the older woman grimaced as she reached to replace a dish on a high shelf or hoisted a heavy water-filled pan onto the sink counter to soak. It was true, then. In her zeal to avoid change, Nola had failed to consider the effect her stubbornness might have on Judy. What would she do when Judy could no longer bake and cook? When Nola herself could no longer keep up with the large house? Why had it never occurred to her that Judy and Jonah might be ready to take some time to themselves without having to work?

She wasn't even aware of the tears that were staining the satin lapels of her robe until Judy paused on her way out to the sideboard in the tearoom, her hands filled with clean cups.

"Oh, honey," Judy said softly as she set

down the cups and pulled Nola to a standing position and embraced her. "If you want to make ice cream, then order the berries and I'll search the files for your father's recipe."

"This is all I know, Judy," Nola blubbered against the older woman's soft shoulder. "Losing this place would be like losing a part of myself."

Judy rubbed her back and held her close. "You can't lose what you never had time to look for, darling girl. That's all I'm saying."

On the Sunday before the church's annual clambake, Nola was back in church, but she left so quickly Harry didn't have a chance to talk to her.

"One can only hope that the blow she suffered has brought her to her senses," Harry heard one choir member whisper as she watched Nola say her goodbye to the minister and hurry off.

"Well, I do think it was nice of Mr. Starbuck to allow his actors to help out while she was convalescing," the woman's husband replied.

"Still, the sooner she cuts those ties, the better. After all, she has to live here long after those people pack up and leave."

The woman had a point. Harry could not

deny the improvement in attitude he'd seen toward Nola once he decided to move the actors to the cottages and hold rehearsals at the hotel. And maybe this woman was right. Now that Nola was up and around again, maybe it was time to cut those ties. Since he was still in the habit of dropping by the tearoom daily to check on her progress, he decided that he would have to stop that, as well. He would call on Nola later in the afternoon just to be sure she was truly recovered and if so, then he would end it.

While he was at it, he could return a sheet of music that had fallen from her loose-leaf binder at services. He'd seen the page drift to the floor and realized that in her haste to leave, Nola had failed to notice the loss. Of course, he could have given it to someone else to take to her. He could have let it lie. But instead he retrieved the music, folded it neatly and placed it in his pocket.

At his cottage, he prepared himself a cold lunch of leftovers from his supper the night before at the hotel and carried the plate out to the side yard. Sitting at the rustic table he'd inherited from the former owner, he ate without really appreciating the food or his surroundings. He pulled out the paper and pressed out the folds with his palm. As he chewed on his lunch, he mentally played out the notes, beating out the time with his hand.

A fugue, vaguely familiar and yet different. He hummed aloud, following the rhythm on the page. And then he smiled. Nola Burns was trying her hand at composing. He was certain of it and if these few lines were any indication, she was quite good at it. And then in light pencil at the top right corner of the page he saw two words that had been erased. *Simple Faith.*

"Well, well, well," he murmured as he left the remains of his lunch for the birds and headed back down the lane toward town. "So, you've had some thoughts about my operetta after all, Nola Burns."

The tearoom was closed and yet the place seemed alive with distant chatter — even laughter — accompanied by a percussion that sounded like someone grinding rocks. Harry followed the sounds around to the side porch and saw Nola sitting in a wicker chair under an arbor of roses, her face alight with laughter. In front of her, Jasper sat on the ground arduously turning the handle of an old-fashioned ice cream churn while Billy fed the thing chunks of ice. At a side table Ellie and the Kowalski sisters were surrounded by full bowls of capped strawberries. Olga observed the activity with her usual expression of disdain.

Billy spotted Harry first. "Come on, boss, give it a turn," he called. "Our arms are about to give out."

Harry liked Billy Andrews. He was a talented actor without the usual insecurities that caused other performers to fall back on haughtiness as protection against the outside world. His love for the theater matched Harry's own and the truth was that Harry was keeping Billy in mind for the role of leading man if his operetta ever made it to Broadway.

Harry strolled the rest of the way down the side porch, removing his jacket and tossing it onto one of the rocking chairs. He rolled back his sleeves as he approached the churn. He could feel Nola watching him closely but he did not meet her gaze. "Looks like hard work to me," he commented.

"Yeah," Billy replied, "but the pay is great. Fresh strawberry ice cream on top of Mrs. Lang's lemon pound cake capped off by whipped cream."

"Your turn, sir," Jasper said, relinquishing his place at the churn.

Harry pushed back his hat and scratched his forehead as he studied the situation. "Seems to me, boys, that if we moved this thing onto that table there out of the sun, the ice wouldn't melt so fast and we'd be in the shade as well."

Billy gave his head a smack. "Now why didn't we think of that?" With Jasper's help, he heaved the churn onto the table next to Nola. "Guess that's why you're the one in charge, right, boss?" he teased.

"Guess so," Harry replied and he finally looked directly at Nola.

"Anyone for lemonade?" Ellie called.

Billy's hand shot up as he and Jasper headed for the kitchen door.

"Excellent," Ellie said with a grin. "Come inside and squeeze the lemons for me."

Once the others had gone inside, Harry concentrated on churning the ice cream and silently thanked Ellie for giving him this moment alone with Nola.

"I should go help," Nola said.

But when she made a move to rise, she faltered. Immediately Harry reached for her, steadied her and eased her back onto the chair. "I'm pretty sure that even a bunch of actors can handle making a pitcher of lemonade," he said. "Looks like you're not yet fully recovered."

"Just a bit dizzy. My father would have said I don't quite have my land legs yet." She leaned back in the chair.

"Must have been hard on your mother

with your father being off to sea so much,"
Harry commented as he returned to his
churning but kept one eye on Nola.

"My mother had a difficult life."

"And you?"

He saw her eyes widen at the unexpected
question.

"My life has been just fine," she replied,
but she sounded less confident than she had
in the past.

"Don't you ever have dreams for a different future, Nola?"

She folded her arms around herself as if
the balmy temperature had suddenly
dropped by several degrees. "My dream is
to stay here. You're the one who went dash-
ing off to find adventure. Did you find what
you wanted?"

Harry shrugged and continued churning.
"Maybe."

"There's no denying that you've certainly
made your mark. To be such a success in
business and also —"

"My business success is nothing more
than a means to an end."

"To what end?"

"To earn enough money so that I can
comfortably devote the rest of my life to
writing for the stage — to creating plays
devoted to teaching God's lessons while

233

entertaining the audience." He stopped churning and untied the bandanna from around his neck, then used it to wipe his brow. Stuffing the bandanna into one pocket, he pulled out the sheet of music from the other. "You dropped this at church this morning."

He watched as she unfolded the single sheet, saw her cheeks color slightly and heard the barest intake of her breath as she realized what he'd found. "Thank you," she murmured and quickly refolded the page and tucked it into the pocket of her skirt.

"I'd like to give that melody a try in rehearsal, Nola. If you don't mind."

"No, it's not nearly ready — not nearly good enough."

"It's a work in progress," Harry replied, then grinned. "Like my operetta. Give it some thought, Nola." He returned to the churning. "Almost ready," he said, removing the top to test the ice cream. "You made enough for an army here. No wonder it took so much churning."

"Nola's going to offer ice cream here in the tearoom garden," Ellie explained as she arrived with a pitcher of lemonade and set it on the table with the berries and whipped cream. "That's the test batch. Mimi," she called back toward the kitchen, "ice cream is ready for tasting. Bring out the cake."

Harry looked down at Nola who met his gaze with defiance. "It will be good for business," she informed him. "We need to attract a younger clientele."

"I didn't say a word," he pointed out, then offered her his arm to escort her to the table where the others were already cutting hunks of lemon pound cake and placing them in bowls.

"Jasper and I are going to the beach," Billy announced once they'd each prepared a sundae and taken a seat around the long table. "Do you girls want to come?"

Harry saw that this was directed at the Kowalski twins who eagerly accepted.

"Ellie?" Billy asked when he realized she hadn't been included.

Ellie laughed. "That's for you young people," she replied. "I'm going to take the rest of this afternoon for a nice walk and then some reading."

"Countess?"

Olga lifted one eyebrow. "I walk in the evenings . . . alone."

"Right," Billy murmured. "I forgot."

"Nola? How about you?" Jasper asked.

"Sounds like an excellent idea," Harry said before Nola could answer. "Salt air and sunshine will do you good. You four go along. Miss Nola and I will see you down there once we get everything squared away here," he announced.

Instead of looking at Nola for agreement, he polished off the rest of his sundae and began gathering empty dishes onto a tray. "You're not planning on being open during the clambake? Everyone will be down at the beach, not here in town."

"Not everyone. But no, the tearoom will not be open. How could I deny these wonderful souls the pleasure of an old-fashioned clambake?" She smiled at Billy as he scraped the bottom of his bowl and added it to Harry's stack.

"Nola's going to give away free samples of her ice cream at the clambake," he said. "It's her way of advertising the opening of her ice cream parlor."

"Really?" Harry couldn't help but be impressed. The woman had a head for business. He'd give her that.

"Well, not an ice cream parlor per se. I mean the plan is to use the garden here for the occasional ice cream social. Something for the younger set to enjoy."

Harry glanced around at the space. "You'll need more tables," he said more to himself than to her. "I have some small café tables with matching chairs that I ordered for the cabaret, but they aren't right for that space. They'd work here, though."

"I appreciate the offer but I can't afford to buy new furnishings until I see if the idea is a success," Nola said.

Harry shrugged. "I was going to send them back. You'd be saving me the cost of that. We'll work something out," he assured her and headed off to the kitchen.

"Come on, girls," Jasper called. "By the time we get back to the cottages to collect our swimwear and then down to the beach the afternoon will be half-gone already. That okay with you, Mr. Starbuck?"

"Fine. Enjoy yourselves."

Jasper and Billy each took a Kowalski twin by the arm and headed off. Ellie leaned down and kissed Nola's cheek. "Don't overdo," she advised. "Come along, Countess."

"Olga is quite apprehensive around you," Nola said once they'd all left. "You do have that effect on people, Harry." She brushed past him on her way into the kitchen.

"I certainly don't seem to scare you," Harry countered as he followed her and set the dirty dishes in the sink.

"I don't work for you. Olga confided to me recently that she's concerned about her future in the theater. Now that she's getting older, she's aware that roles she might play are limited. And both Jasper and Billy care a great deal about impressing you. It makes them vulnerable. It's quite a powerful thing to hold a person's future in your hand."

"People determine their own futures, Nola. If they do a good job then they'll succeed. Neither I nor my personal opinion of any one of them has a thing to do with it." He had always been known as an easygoing if somewhat unconventional employer. A man who asked no more of others than he expected of himself — and those who worked for him were well aware of that. At the cabaret he had done his fair share of the labor when a worker had fallen ill or been injured. It bothered him that she might think he was some kind of demanding overseer. "Ask anyone who works for me and they will tell you —"

"As I said, I do not work for you." She ran water into the dishpan. "I'll see to these later. If you'll just pack the ice cream in ice, I'll get my parasol so we can take that walk."

"Now who's giving orders," Harry grumbled as he stalked outside.

From her bedroom window Nola watched as Harry meticulously cleaned up the mess left after making the ice cream. His shirtsleeves were still rolled back and she watched in fascination as he lifted the wooden churn as if it were no heavier than the pitcher of lemonade. He settled it on one shoulder and carried it off to the kitchen. A memory stirred.

That night when she had gone to find her brothers after her mother collapsed and Harry had run for the doctor, he had come back. He had stayed until he was certain her mother was going to be all right. And when he had reluctantly taken his leave, Nola recalled now that her mother had said, "Harrison Starbuck is going to make a fine family man one of these days. In spite of his reputation for rebellion, he cares so deeply about other people — especially people in need."

Nola couldn't help wondering what her mother might think of this Harry Starbuck. A minute later he was back in the garden, brushing the caps of the strawberries from the table onto the tray. He glanced around, then tossed them onto the compost heap she kept behind the garden shed.

Licking his fingers, he took a visual tour of the garden as if to be sure he wasn't missing something, then satisfied, he gathered the last of the glasses and utensils onto the tray and carried them into the house. The garden was as pristine as it had been earlier that morning. "I'm just getting my jacket," he called. "I'll meet you out front."

The screen door to the kitchen banged shut behind him as he rounded the side of the house, rolling his sleeves down and fastening the cuffs. She couldn't help noticing the boyish way he chewed on his tongue as he worked the fastening. It made him seem more vulnerable than she'd ever thought him before. Even as a young boy he had always seemed to be perfectly in control. She wondered why he had not yet married and decided that her mother had been wrong about him. The only "family" Harry concerned himself with was the company of actors charged with staging his latest play.

They crossed the footbridge to the stairway in silence, then Harry took her elbow as they started down the stairs. "Thank you," she murmured, trying hard not to dwell too long on the warmth of his fingers through the thin lawn fabric of her sleeve. When they reached the last step, he immediately released her and walked alongside, his hands clasped behind his back. She couldn't help recalling the flirtatious way Violet Gillenwater had snaked her hand through the crook of his elbow when the two of them went walking.

"I'm thinking that four small tables each with four chairs will present an inviting environment without appearing too deserted on those occasions — rare, I'm sure — when you have no customers for your ice cream." It was as if no time at all had passed since he'd first offered the idea of café tables.

"I will make do with what I have, Harry," Nola said. "But I do thank you for the kind offer."

"I have a dozen of the things with four chairs for each, but a dozen in that space would be too much. Six, perhaps — eight at most."

Nola sighed. "Do you ever listen, Harry Starbuck? I mean it's no wonder you were in constant trouble at school." She stopped and faced him, lifting her parasol higher so she was certain he could see her face. "I do not need — or want — your tables and chairs."

Harry grinned. "Come on, Nola. Of course you do. Do you think these young prima donnas from the city are truly interested in 'roughing it'? Roughing it for them means going without the upstairs maid for a week. It means dressing themselves for the day without help. It means . . ."

"I am well aware of the expectations of my clientele, Harry. I am perfectly capable of attending to their needs on my own."

Harry studied her for a long moment, so long that Nola could feel the sun warm her face through the protection of the parasol.

"That's your problem, Nola," he said. "You've never allowed yourself to need anyone." He walked on without her.

Nola stood rooted to the spot where he'd left her. Should she go after him and protest the unfairness of that comment — especially coming from him? Should she return to the tearoom? Should she ignore him and join the others?

Billy was waving at her from the beach. "Nola! Over here!" He indicated two beach chairs that they had placed in the shade of a decaying old shipwreck. "Best seats in the house," he shouted.

Just then Deedee ran up behind him and dumped a child's sand bucket filled with sea water over him. Billy gave a cry of alarm and took off after her. The four young people were soon splashing happily in water up to their waists. Nola couldn't help smiling at their antics.

And what's so wrong with how I live my life? It gives me pleasure — and purpose — to help others the way I've helped these delightful young people. The way I helped my brothers and my sister build lives for themselves when others would have split us apart. The way I've . . .

"I'd like to apologize."

Nola had been so intent on watching the others and reconstructing her defenses that she hadn't noticed Harry retracing his steps. He was next to her now, his expression contrite. "What I said — it was unfair. I barely know you, after all." He grinned and cocked his head to one side. "I wouldn't mind remedying that, though. It occurs to me, Nola Burns, that if we stop fighting each other, we could be a staggering force for good."

"I wasn't aware we were fighting, Harry," she said sweetly. "I thought we were out for an afternoon stroll along the beach."

Harry laughed. "Excellent point, my lady. Shall we?" He offered his arm.

Nola hesitated then accepted his peace offering. Inside she felt a tremor of pleasure as she considered how it must look from the bluff above — the two of them walking across the sand to the beach chairs. She glanced back and saw the unmistakable figure of Oliver Franks watching them. And although she was well aware that Oliver and Minnie Franks had joined the ranks of those who disapproved of her associating so closely with Harry and his troupe of actors, she could not help feeling relief that it was Oliver and not Rose.

CHAPTER TWELVE

On the day of the clambake, the men and boys were the first to arrive on the beach to deliver the stones, logs and potato sacks. Next the girls came to gather the seaweed so vital to the proper preparation — and to have an excuse to flirt with the boys. They wore their best summer dresses in spite of the need to climb over rocks and scour the shoreline for just the right variety. The local girls showed the summer girls how to look for rockweed, favored because it had pockets that allowed the best combination of air and water to create the steam necessary to cook the meal. The girls wore their hair braided and interwoven with colorful ribbons or piled atop their heads like crowns. The boys watched them even as they pretended to focus on the work of delivering the logs and rocks for the large fire pit they would dig later.

"Look at them," Ellie sighed as she helped

Nola set up the stand for serving her ice cream samples. "The potential for romance is so thick you can almost smell it. Ah, to be young again and in love."

Nola had been watching a group of men digging the first of the cooking pits. Harry Starbuck was at the center of that group, wielding the shovel as the other men shouted encouragement and waited their turn at the digging. At Ellie's comment she forced her attention up the beach to where the girls were giggling as they carried mounds of rockweed in buckets of sea water over to where the boys had gathered. "It's a bit like a dance — a kind of ballet," she said wistfully.

"Why, Nola Burns, you are such a romantic," Ellie teased. "So, tell me, when you were that age, was there one boy?"

No!

Yes. The incorrigible Harrison Starbuck.

Nola shrugged and turned her attention back to attaching bunting to the table of the stand.

"There was," Ellie guessed, moving around so that Nola had no choice but to face her. "You're blushing." She popped herself onto the edge of the table and leaned closer. "Tell me everything. Was he quite handsome?"

Nola laughed. "Oh, Ellie, at that age all older boys are attractive," she said.

"Ah, so he was older — unattainable?"

"This is ridiculous. I don't really recall." But she did. Suddenly every detail of the clambake the summer that her brothers and Harrison Starbuck graduated came rushing back. The fact that commencement exercises were scheduled for the following day and that everyone knew of Starbuck's plan to leave the island for New York made that clambake seem more bittersweet than any that had come before — or after. For in spite of the fact that she and Starbuck had barely encountered one another on more than a dozen occasions, she had felt so keenly the agony that she might never see him again.

"Oh, dear Nola, how sad you look. Did the cad break your heart?"

"Of course not," Nola replied and tried to cover her snappish answer with a laugh. "How could he when he barely knew I was alive?"

"And you never had the chance to let him know? Did he marry?"

"He moved away," Nola said. "Ah, here come the others." She had never been so happy to see Judy and the troupe of actors as they pulled up in a box cart loaded with the supplies needed for serving the ice cream.

"You wouldn't happen to have a jug of your famous limeade in that cart, would you, Mrs. Lang?" Harry asked.

Nola wheeled around. He had removed his hat and was mopping sweat from his brow with the ever-present bandanna. She tried focusing her attention on anyone but him. Still, she felt her cheeks burning at the very real presence of the boy who had once haunted her girlhood dreams.

"You'll have to ask Nola," Judy replied. "She's in charge."

"I see." Harry turned his attention to Nola, a twinkle of amusement lighting his eyes. "Should have known," he added. "Here, let me give you a hand with that, Mrs. Lang." He moved to the cart and helped with the unloading, chatting with the others and flirting with Judy in the process.

Is that how you see me? Nola wondered, her high spirits of earlier crushed by the realization. *Am I eternally the bossy one? The one always in charge?* She turned away and looked for something to occupy her, something that would block out his laughter, his deep velvety voice, his very presence.

"Here." Harry thrust a paper cup filled

with limeade under her nose and then gulped down another cupful in practically one swallow. "You're looking quite well today, Nola. No aftereffects from the accident?"

"I'm fine," she said, still unable to tear her eyes away from his.

He plopped his hat on her head and pulled it down so that the brim shaded her face. "Still, that sun's hot today. We wouldn't want to mar that beautiful skin of yours with freckles and such."

"I have a hat," she protested, touching the brim of his.

"This one suits you, I think. Hang on to it for me. I'm going for a swim."

And before Nola could further protest he took off running across the beach, pulling off his shoes and socks and shirt at water's edge and leaving them in a pile as he plunged into the water.

"Was it Harry?" Ellie asked, coming alongside her and watching Harry swim against the current. "That boy from long ago?"

Nola choked on the last of her limeade. "Whatever would make you think that?"

Ellie wrapped her arm around Nola's shoulder. "It doesn't matter, really. If it was, maybe God's given the two of you a second chance and if it wasn't maybe God's decided it's high time you had your first chance at true love."

"I doubt God has time to concern Himself with such trivial matters," Nola said primly as she turned away and began organizing the dishes for the ice cream.

Harry swam as if his very life depended on each stroke. He pounded the water with his power, fought against each current, every wave that threatened to carry him back to shore. Back to her. When he had exhausted himself he rolled to his back and floated just beyond the breakers as he looked up at the cloudless sky.

What is it about this woman? What do You want from me when it comes to her? Leave her alone? What?

It had all started so innocently — a simple business transaction. He'd gone through hundreds of them in his lifetime and admittedly some had run their course more smoothly than others, but this one was different.

Because she's a woman?

"Because she's *this* woman," he corrected himself. With anyone else he would have long ago walked away or turned the entire project over to Alistair to handle, but he'd found it impossible to leave her alone. When he wasn't face-to-face with her, he was thinking about her, reliving some moment they had shared. If he didn't know better he'd think he was falling . . .

In love? Impossible. Nola Burns and me? I know You've got a sense of humor, Lord, but this? I'm all wrong for her — vagabond theater guy meets uptight New England spinster? It's classic melodrama, and forgive me, but bad melodrama at that.

He studied the sky for a sign that he was right. Maybe a sudden gathering of cumulus clouds spelling it out for him. But the sky remained clear, cloudless, calm. Harry closed his eyes and slowly backstroked his way down the beach.

What was it Rachel had advised? Listen?

With a frustrated growl he rolled over and swam back toward shore until he could stand. And as he emerged from the surf, the first place he looked was to where he had left her, but the stand was deserted.

The other men had completed the task of lining two long pits with carefully selected stones the size of grapefruits, then added hardwood logs that would be set on fire. Now he saw the fires to heat the stones had been lit. Nearby the boys and girls had joined forces as they washed and sorted the mounds of clams that had been dug the evening before. Not ten feet away sat a group of mothers and older women, shucking corn and washing yams, all the time keeping a watchful eye on the young people.

"I'm going to change," Harry called to his cohorts, receiving a wave in return as he retrieved his cast-off clothing and walked toward the stairway. He'd left his bicycle on the bridge and as he pulled on his damp shirt scratchy now with sand, he refused the inclination to glance up toward the tearoom or rather the windows he now knew were her private quarters. Instead he raced up the stairs and mounted the bicycle then pedaled past Nola's place as if some demon were chasing him.

Nola was halfway back down the stairs to the beach when she remembered that she'd left Starbuck's hat on the kitchen table after going home to get more spoons for scooping the ice cream. She could picture it lying there, its honey color in sharp contrast to the dark wood of the table. She had stood right in the middle of her kitchen staring at the thing and the way it seemed to dominate the room in exactly the same way that Harry Starbuck dominated any room he entered. How could she have forgotten it?

She considered going back for it, but then she saw Judy trying to haul a heavy block of ice by herself and decided Starbuck — and his hat — could wait until tomorrow. After all, by the time the clambake was ready the sun would be setting and the shadows would lengthen. He wouldn't need his hat at all. She'd send it along with one of the actors when they went to rehearsal the following day.

"Judy, put that down," she called as she hurried toward the stand. "Where are Jasper and Billy?"

"I moved blocks of ice long before those two showed up," Judy fumed, but she set the block of ice down and took a moment to steady her rapid breathing. "You look nice," she said, eyeing Nola from head to toe.

"I look exactly the same as I did before I went to get the spoons." Nola was reluctant to admit, even to herself, that she had taken a moment to repin her hair before heading back down to the beach. She thought about explaining that Harry's hat had caught on several of her hairpins when she removed it. Either she had to put her hair up properly or have it falling down in the midst of serving the ice cream.

"You did your hair up different," Judy

observed. "Looks nice. Better than Star-buck's hat."

Nola couldn't be sure but she thought she heard Judy chuckle as the older woman walked away and scanned the beach for her helpers.

By the time Harry cleaned up and returned to the clambake, the beach was already filled with locals and tourists who had looked forward to the event for weeks. The area was so crowded that it was easy to avoid Nola as he joined the other men to prepare for the closing of the bake. Someone handed him a pitchfork and he worked in tandem with a partner to clear his area of the pit that ran fifteen feet in length, three feet across and two feet deep. Carefully they lifted out the charred and glowing remains of each log to reveal the stones, now white-hot. Trading pitchforks for brooms, the men swept away debris and ash from the stones.

Next the men guided the boys as they gently deposited bushels of clean, damp clams onto the rocks. The sizzle and rise of steam tickled Harry's nose and brought back memories of other clambakes, times when he and his buddies had been the ones responsible for making sure the clam shells did not break or crack as they were deposited onto the rocks.

Home, the sizzling clams seemed to whisper.

Next came a layer of lobsters followed by a layer of corn and then pans of spiced dressing were emptied over the length and width of the large pit. Harry laughed with the others as the girls squealed in dismay over the dying wriggles of the large lobsters. Finally the pile was lined with long baskets layered with tripe and bluefish and potato sacks. The last act in the ritual of preparing the bake was to cover the huge steaming mass with a large canvas soaked in seawater and then cover that with masses of the wet and tangled rockweed until every crevice through which steam might escape was sealed.

"Half an hour till chow time," one of the men bellowed and the crowd cheered, then returned to whatever activity had caught their fancy. There were games and races for the youngsters as well as impromptu sing-alongs for the adults. But most people preferred to simply chat with their neighbors or help prepare the tables for the feast. It was there that he spotted Nola.

She was laughing and he thought it might actually be the first time he had seen her so completely open to the moment. Usually she always seemed to be examining the words of others for some underlying trap. But it was obvious that she and Ellie had developed the kind of trust where each accepted the other without reservation.

He turned away and then back again, his feet seeming to have a mind of their own as he made his way through the crowds of people toward her. She looked beautiful; something about the way she'd arranged her hair in a looser style held the promise that it might easily escape the usual pins and combs and cascade down her back. Harry sauntered in her direction, taking care that he appear simply to have wandered by.

You're acting like some lovestruck teenager.

Struck by that thought, he paused and considered veering off in another direction.

"Harry! Over here," Ellie called. "Come, make yourself useful." She held up a roll of oilcloth that the women were using to cover the long tables.

Harry risked a glance at Nola but she had turned away and was walking back toward the ice cream stand with Judy.

"Sure," he agreed, taking the cloth from Ellie. "Quite a party, isn't it?"

"It's such fun," Ellie agreed. "And terribly romantic, don't you think? I mean, the beach and all. And then the sun will be setting in a little while."

"Why, Mrs. Chambliss, are you flirting with me?"

"Oh, Harry, stop fooling yourself. I can see how you look at Nola. Don't you think it's time you acted on your feelings?"

Harry didn't even pretend not to know what she was saying. "Not meant to be," he said. "We're . . . different. Water and oil. Order and clutter."

"Snowflakes and seashells," Ellie added. "What's your point? Nola is a good woman. She would be as good for you as you would be for her." Her eyes misted over as she clutched his arm with her hand. "Take it from me, Harry. None of us knows how much time we have — perhaps the greatest sin lies in wasting the precious moments God offers. At least ask her to sit with you at the clambake," she advised in a whisper as Nola returned to the table.

But Oliver and Minnie Franks joined the group at just that moment.

"Nola, come sit with us," Oliver invited.

"Yes, please," his wife added. "We've had so little time to catch up lately."

They steered her to the far end of one long table, well away from Ellie and the others.

"Looks like it's time to open the bake,"

Harry said, handing Ellie the roll of cloth. He nodded to Nola as he passed by her on his way to help. "Miss Nola," he murmured, "enjoy your meal."

Nola was all too aware of Starbuck sitting at the far end of the table. His laughter rose above the chatter and the background of the surf rolling onto the sand. And when it wasn't his laughter, it was the laughter of others, especially Violet Gillenwater who had defied her mother and taken her place next to Harry. "Why, Harry Starbuck, you say the most appalling things," Nola heard her say.

It had gotten to the point where Nola was barely aware of Minnie's attempts to include her in the conversation going on at their end of the table.

"Rose," Oliver called out as he stood and relieved Rose of her plate and escorted her to the table. "We have saved a place just for you. And look, Nola is here as well. We were just talking about how Alistair has never missed a clambake in all the time we've . . ."

To everyone's astonishment, Rose's lower lip began to quiver uncontrollably and her hands flailed about as she reached for her glass of lemonade and knocked it over. Her face flushed and blotched, she pushed her way past others and fled.

"What on earth?" Judy Lang said as she mopped up the lemonade.

"I'll go," Nola said.

"Let me come with you," Oliver offered. "Obviously it was something I said."

"No. Stay here," Nola replied, including in that instruction anyone else who might have had thoughts of accompanying her. "She needs privacy."

Rose was sitting on a bench near the road. She was sobbing into an already-sodden lace handkerchief and the choking sounds she was making were not only alarming, they were heartrending. Nola sat down on the bench and offered the woman her own clean, dry handkerchief.

"Rose?"

The older woman shook her head and waved Nola away.

Nola slid closer and put her hand gingerly on Rose's back. "What is it? Has something happened to Alistair?"

As suddenly as the tears had begun, they were gone. Rose wheeled around and stared at Nola, her face filled with fury as her lips worked to find words. "You have the nerve to ask such a thing when it was you who took those people in, gave that woman a position of prominence in your business? Gave her access to my husband?"

Nola tightened her grip on the hysterical woman. "Rose, calm yourself," she said gently. "What woman?"

"The countess," Rose spat out bitterly and then she gave a laugh that was high and cackling and totally devoid of humor. "Countess, indeed. She is a harlot who preys on the good intentions of unsuspecting men and traps them in her lair and —"

"Olga?"

Rose jerked free of Nola and stood. "Yes. Where is she? Have you seen her at all today?"

"She was here earlier, but this sort of thing is not really to her taste."

"No, I suppose not. Her taste runs to enticing a respectable married man like my Alistair into becoming such a fool that he . . ." Her tirade unleashed a fresh wave of tears.

Nola's mind raced. "You're mistaken, Rose. Olga would never —"

"Are you questioning what my boys saw with their own eyes, Nola?" She drew in a long shuddering breath and her voice was high and tight as she added, "When I think that those dear impressionable lads should have witnessed their father — whom they idolize — with that woman in broad daylight."

"I'm quite certain this is all a misunderstanding," Nola said. But she wasn't certain at all. What did she really know of Olga or the others?

"Has my husband ever missed a clambake?" Rose demanded. "Look around. Do you see him here?" She fanned her arm across the gathering on the beach. "No, and why not? He is with that . . . that . . ."

"There has to be some other explanation," Nola murmured.

For the third time Rose dissolved into tears. "It's my fault, of course," she blubbered. "I have such high standards and Alistair has often reminded me that not everyone is as strong as I am when it comes to temptations."

"But the countess was here," Nola said. "Why don't I just go to her cottage? I'm sure there's a perfectly simple explanation to whatever Edgar and Albert might have thought they saw."

"Oh, Nola dear, you've led such a sheltered life. My sons are not fools. They know what they saw."

"And what exactly did they see?"

"They observed their father with that woman walking along the beach. They were oblivious to anyone else, laughing together. Laughing at me," Rose added and her lip quivered.

"You're leaping to conclusions here without . . ."

Rose scowled at Nola. "Sometimes I think I may have done your dear mother a disservice in not making sure that you got out into the world a bit. You are far too trusting, my dear, so naive when it comes to the matter of judging the character of others." She gave one last shuddering sob and stood. "So I seriously doubt that you can explain to me why Alistair had to leave suddenly for Boston this very afternoon."

"He often goes away on business suddenly," Nola reminded Rose.

"He has gone ahead to make all the arrangements for their little rendezvous, don't you see? And soon that woman will follow him. You mark my words."

Nola sat quietly for a moment while Rose continued to pace, muttering to herself and clutching both Nola's handkerchief and her own. There had to be some plausible explanation. Rose was given to jumping to conclusions, especially when she had already formed an opinion.

"I have tried my best to heed Reverend Diggs's counsel and at least tolerate these theater people. For the sake of Alistair's investment if nothing else. After all, I suppose one could think of them as assets in a purely business sense, but . . ."

"That's true." Nola felt a flicker of hope that perhaps Rose was coming to a more rational conclusion about the entire matter.

"But at the same time I have warned Alistair that no good could possibly come of actually socializing with such people." She turned her attention to Nola as if just realizing that she was still there. "I have also warned you, for all the good it's done."

"Mrs. Chambliss and the others have been a great help to me. They have offered not only their time and talent but their friendship."

Rose pulled herself to her full height. "Well, if you consider yourself my friend, Nola Burns, you will do me the favor of disassociating yourself from those people at once. I will make certain you have proper staffing for the tearoom. Dorothy and Lucille and I have discussed it at length. We have found you two young girls of impeccable character. They are from a family here on the island that has fallen on difficult economic times. Not unlike your own situation after your mother died. Surely employing those girls is the charitable thing to do."

"But . . ."

"Let Harry Starbuck provide for those people, Nola. He's the one who brought them here in the first place. He has the means. It's hardly as if you are putting them out into the street."

"You are wrong about them, Rose," Nola said. "They are good people. Mrs. Chambliss, for one, is a woman of strong faith and the others are so giving and —"

Perfectly composed once again, Rose Gillenwater leaned close to Nola's face. "Get them out of your business and life or be prepared to suffer the consequences," she hissed. Then she snapped open her parasol and sailed back across the sand toward a small group of dignitaries. "Ah, Mr. Mayor," she chirped.

"She threatened you?" Judy gasped once Nola had relayed the entire story as they completed setting up for distributing the ice cream samples. "Then maybe we've both been barking up the wrong tree."

"Meaning?"

"The notes. What if —"

"Oh, Judy, don't be ridiculous. Whoever sent those notes has surely realized their prank won't work —"

"You just said that Rose Gillenwater

threatened you," Judy reminded her.

"She didn't threaten me," Nola corrected. "It's just her way. She has certain standards and she expects others to follow them — me especially because she was instrumental in keeping our family together after my mother died. Besides, she was upset. She has this idea that Alistair and the countess have been, well, carrying on."

"Oh, Nola dear," Rose Gillenwater called out from a short distance away. Two plain-faced and clearly nervous young girls were at her side. "May I present Constance and Clara Huff? The young *ladies* I mentioned for employ in your tearoom?"

"I am so pleased to learn of your interest," Nola said graciously. "If you will both come by the tearoom tomorrow afternoon, it will give you the opportunity to observe my current employees and decide if indeed the work suits you."

The Huff girls glanced nervously up at Rose who pressed her lips into a thin line. "I hardly think your current employees set the sort of example these young ladies need."

"I trained them myself," Nola replied, meeting Rose's gaze.

"Very well. Tomorrow, girls."

"On the other hand," Nola added, "perhaps you could get a hint of what's in store for you by helping me to serve the ice cream samples?"

Both girls broke into wide smiles. "Yes, ma'am," they replied and took off toward the ice cream stand where Ellie and the rest of the actors were donning aprons and a line had already formed.

Nola watched them go then turned to face Rose. "Thank you for your concern. They may be an answer to prayer."

With a barely audible harrumpf, Rose turned on her heel and headed in the opposite direction.

CHAPTER THIRTEEN

Unlike the recital, the ice cream samples were a spectacular success, especially with the young people. And the additional help of the Huff girls freed Jasper and Billy to entertain the crowd with an impromptu sing-along as the sun set and everyone gathered around a large campfire. When they had served the last customer, Nola sent the Huff and Kowalski sisters to enjoy the music. She was just licking the last of the melting ice cream from the spoon when she saw Harry coming across the beach toward her.

He was applauding as he might the end of a good performance. "I can see the reviews now," he said. "Tearoom owner warms young at heart with ice cream."

"I didn't see you or Violet stop by for a sample," Nola said. "Perhaps you'd like to take some to Miss Gillenwater. I believe there's just enough for one more dish."

"Why, Nola, you aren't jealous, are you?"

"Certainly not." She thrust a dish of half-melted ice cream at him.

He polished off the scoop in four quick spoonfuls. "Delicious," he murmured as he set the spoon on the counter behind her. "I'd tip my hat to you, but I seem to have misplaced it."

Nola neither moved nor breathed as she took in the nearness of him. The smoke of the clambake fire that clung to his shirt, the faint fragrance of the lime that was his aftershave, the sheer presence of him so near to her. "I'm sorry. I left it behind when I went to change. I'll . . ."

"By the way, Violet went home with her mother. Seems Mrs. Gillenwater was upset about something."

"Yes. She thinks Alistair is preparing to run off with Olga."

"Well, that will certainly be news to Alistair since he's in Boston closing the sale on their townhouse and buying some mansion Rose has had her eye on for years as an anniversary gift."

"Oh, Harry, you should tell Violet."

"It's also to be a surprise for Violet. It's where she and her fiancé are to be married."

"Violet is to be married?"

"Yep. Son of a shipping heir." He touched

268

her hair, then brushed the outline of her jaw with the backs of his knuckles. "You see, Nola, things are rarely as black and white as they may seem."

"Oh, Harry, I just assumed that you and Violet . . ." she whispered. "Would you . . ."

"Kiss you?" he murmured back as he lowered his mouth to hers. "My pleasure," he added a second before his lips — still cool from the ice cream — touched hers.

Down the beach a group of teenagers had set off skyrockets, but Nola was certain that those were no match for the fireworks she was feeling. The gentle pressure of Harry Starbuck's kiss sent sparks up and down her spine.

"You taste like berries," he whispered as he pulled away. "And smell like lily of the valley," he added. "It's a perfect fragrance for you. I noticed it that first day on your porch."

He picked up the picnic basket she'd used to store the used spoons and hooked it over his arm. "May I see you home, Nola?" With his free hand he took hold of her elbow and as they stepped out of the stand, they were swallowed up by the tidal wave of partygoers still exclaiming over the fireworks. Together they walked up the stairway and on to the tearoom while the others went off in other directions calling out their farewells and promises to meet up again the following day.

"Well," Harry said as he set the basket by the back door, "that wasn't exactly the way I had planned to . . ."

"Please don't concern yourself, Harry. It was impetuous but hardly out of character given the circumstances. I mean, after all . . ."

Before she could complete the sentence Harry had set the basket aside and bent to kiss her again. Nola murmured a protest of surprise and he stepped away.

"All outward appearances to the contrary, I am not an impetuous man, Nola. And I most certainly am not given to impulsive moves when it comes to you. I have far more respect for you than that. I intended to kiss you when I saw you alone down there. I thought about little else all during the clambake."

"And this?" she said defiantly as she touched her lips.

To her surprise he chuckled. "Okay, this was pure impulse." He stroked her cheek with his fingers. "Look, Nola, I don't know what's happening here any more than you do, so don't go giving me credit for plotting and planning when it comes to you. All I know is that with everything that's happened, this has become a lot more complicated than my wanting to make you an offer for your property."

Nola took a moment to allow her racing heart to calm itself. "I know. Sometimes I have to wonder about God's true purpose in everything that's happening. I mean, perhaps He meant for us to become friends."

"Exactly. So I was thinking that maybe we could spend some time together — time not dueling with each other."

"A kind of truce?"

He nodded. "I've liked the suggestions you've been making to Ellie about the play. And I can't get that fugue you were working on out of my head. I think it might be perfect for the closing number in Act One."

"I have no professional training, Harry."

"You have something better." He tugged at her ear. "That natural ear for music. So, how about it? Could we start fresh — common ground, so to speak?"

"I did have some thoughts about the opening," she admitted.

He leaned closer. "I'd love to hear those thoughts."

Nola took a step back. "Very well. I could spare an hour tomorrow morning."

"Afraid not," Harry replied. "I've got to meet with the carpenters tomorrow about installing the lighting for the stage. How about tomorrow evening?"

"Four-thirty — just after closing," she bargained.

"And while Mrs. Lang is still around cleaning up," he guessed.

"Precisely." Nola offered him a handshake. And she could not help but be delighted when he took her hand and kissed it with a courtly bow.

"Good night, Miss Nola," he whispered.

"Good night, Starbuck."

Now that Nola had hired the Huff sisters and relieved the actors of any further duty in the tearoom, town locals focused their concern on the fact that Nola was now openly working with Harry on his play. Nola seemed to think nothing of stopping by Harry's office to leave some piece of classical or religious music she'd discovered with a note about its potential use in the operetta. Nola chose to ignore reports from Judy that tongues were wagging all over town whenever Harry dashed into the tearoom in the middle of the afternoon rush to drop off his latest rewrite of the lyrics.

But Nola was thrilled with this opportunity to collaborate on the operetta. At first she was reluctant to question Harry's classical selections, but by week's end she'd become so exasperated with his attempts to make a Viennese waltz work as the background for the play's love song that she had thrown up her hands in frustration. "It's all wrong, Harry."

Harry was taken aback at her outburst. "Well, it needs work, but . . ."

"No. It won't work at all. That's the point. We need something else."

Harry smiled. "We?"

"You . . . It needs something more tender. Something sweet and . . ."

"Then write something that will work."

"I couldn't," she whispered.

Harry placed his hand on hers. "Try. I have to check on something at the cabaret. Work on that melody that I would guess is already playing in your head and we'll start fresh tomorrow."

In spite of her doubts, Nola found the work of composing for his lyrics thrilling. When he liked the melody she came up with for the love ballad, he asked her to see what she could come up with for the closing number. It was as if she'd been preparing for this moment all her life. Melodies she had created in her youth and not thought of

in years now seemed the perfect complement to the words and mood of Harry's
operetta. Hour after hour she sat at the
piano setting down the music that had only
played in her head until now. She was more
certain than ever that her inspiration came
from God and that this was what He had
intended for her life.

And although she had missed the company of the others, and especially her late-
night chats with Ellie, now that music filled
the house, Nola seldom felt surrounded by
emptiness as she had in the past. The truth
was that she barely had enough hours in the
day to manage the tearoom, plan the next
ice cream social and create more original
melodies for Harry to consider. One night
she had gotten so caught up in the project
that she hadn't gotten to bed at all and Judy
had found her the next morning, sound
asleep with her head cradled in her folded
arms while still seated at the piano.

"That man is working you too hard," she
groused.

"Harry has nothing to do with this, Judy."
Nola yawned and stretched. "It's me. Oh,
Judy, what if you were right? What if God is
driving me to do this. It just feels so . . ."

"And what happens once you've finished?
It's bound to be a letdown not to have some

project to work on."

"But I will always have this, Judy. That's the gift of it. For the rest of my life, I will carry with me the memory of this summer — of composing music for a play that could inspire audiences I'll never see. I don't need more than that. I never thought I would have this," Nola said. "And it's all thanks to Harry," she added.

"Humph," Judy grumbled. "Seems to me there was a time not too long ago when you wouldn't have trusted that man any further than from here to there." She held her hands six inches apart. "Now all of a sudden it's Harry this and Harry that. You need to watch yourself, my girl. It's not just the composing that's got you all worked up. It's Harrison Starbuck. He's a heartbreaker, that one. Not intentionally, I'll give you, but a heartbreaker nonetheless."

"Oh, Judy, give me some credit for knowing what's what," Nola said as she grabbed the startled woman and hugged her. "Harry and I respect each other's talents just as we have always grudgingly respected the other's business acumen. The difference is that through our collaboration we have become friends. That's all there is to it and all there ever will be. Now how can that end in tragedy?"

"And what about this place? You don't think he's just suddenly dropped the whole idea of buying you out, do you?"

"No, but . . ."

"You need to see the whole picture, Nola. You and Harry are having some fun now and that's nice. But he's not in this alone. He has people who expect him to come up with this place in the end."

"I know that," Nola said, unable to suppress her irritation with Judy's lecture. The truth was that she had indeed lost sight of that. But now all her doubts about Harry's true motivations came flooding back. What if this entire thing were no more than his latest ploy to distract her while her business continued to suffer?

Judy put down her rolling pin and dusted the flour off her hands as she reached out to enfold Nola in her arms. "Ah, sweet child, you think it doesn't do my heart good to see you so happy? To see you all sunshine and laughter these last several days? All I'm saying is be careful."

"Do you really believe that Harry would hurt me?"

"Not intentionally," Judy agreed. "But you of all people should understand that when it comes to business, sometimes people with the best intentions have to make hard decisions. Just don't forget that. Now go lie down. The Huff girls and I can handle things for one afternoon."

"No, you're right. It's high time I paid attention to my business. After all, in just a few weeks the gala will have come and gone — as will Harry and the others. But we will still have this tearoom to run. I'm going for the mail and then I'm going to contact every inn and hotel on the island until I find you some extra help."

"The Huff girls are doing their best," Judy said.

"The Huff girls are two inexperienced teens trying to do work that was handled by six mature adults. We need more help, Judy."

Not a quarter of an hour later she was back. She entered the kitchen in a rush, allowing the back screen door to slam behind her and startling Judy. She held one envelope and dropped the rest of the mail on the kitchen table, then paced over to the kitchen door.

"You're back awfully quick," Judy ventured.

"Yes." Nola chewed her lower lip as she tapped the envelope against her skirt.

Judy returned to kneading dough.

"The Cabbage Inn in New Bedford is

closing."

That got Judy's attention. "Now? With the season already half-gone?"

Nola nodded. "Alice Rowling was quite ill all spring. Her son tried his hand at keeping the place open, but apparently he's decided to close the doors."

"I'm real sorry to hear about that," Judy replied, watching Nola carefully.

"They have a staff of five hired for the season. We could hire them here. Then the Huff sisters could take on the ice cream socials. They'd rather wait on young people anyway, I'm sure."

"These folks from New Bedford are willing to come here for the remainder of this summer?"

"I don't know," Nola said, pulling out the letter and scanning it quickly. "He doesn't say. Maybe he wants to know there's a place for them before he brings it up. Oh, Judy, this could be an answer to our prayers."

"Well, this would certainly clear up any notion that you've given up on keeping this place up and running."

Nola wheeled around. "Of course, I haven't. Why would anyone think differently?"

Judy shrugged. "There are those who are speculating that with the work you're doing on Harry's play, maybe you're planning to sell and head off to New York yourself."

"Oh, Judy, please tell me you don't believe such nonsense."

Her answer came in the almost imperceptible lift of the older woman's shoulders and her silence other than the occasional slamming of the dough onto the breadboard.

"Judy, nothing has changed," Nola assured her. "At least not about my intention to maintain my home and business right here in 'Sconset."

"So you'll consider hiring these folks from the Cabbage Inn?" Judy glanced up at her.

"I'll send Mr. Rowling a telegram offering his employees jobs as soon as he can spare them."

Judy Lang's smile of pure relief was all the assurance Nola needed that she was making the right decision. She returned to the post office and wrote out the message she wanted to send to the owner of the Cabbage Inn.

"Bad news?" Essie Crusenberry asked as she came from behind her desk.

"The Cabbage Inn is closing. Alice Rowling has been ill for some time. Her son thought he could manage but his heart's not in it."

"Poor soul," Essie murmured. "But you've

been looking for help. It would give you the chance to finally cut free of those theater people once and for all."

"As I have told you before, Essie, *'those theater people'* are good people and they've done a wonderful job helping out at the tearoom. And not once have they complained."

"And why should they? When they got here, you put them up and fed them and let them keep whatever tips might have come their way." Essie shook her head. "Besides, I know you don't like hearing this, Nola, but you've got bigger problems than that. Now even some of the summer folks are beginning to wag their tongues over how much time you and Harry Starbuck are spending together these days. After those rumors about Alistair Gillenwater and that Russian woman —"

"Unfounded rumors," Nola reminded the postmistress.

"All the same, talk is that there are some who think having their young people hanging around your place might expose them to the wrong element."

This wasn't news to Nola. The Gillenwaters had captured local attention for a moment but Alistair had, of course, declared his innocence. He had dismissed what his sons had observed as nothing more than a casual conversation in a public place and had assured Rose that his abrupt trip to Boston had been purely business related. That, along with the diamond brooch he had brought her, seemed to have gained him a reprieve of sorts.

Nola took a moment to form her response to Essie's question with care. "There will always be a few people who misinterpret an innocent friendship or business association, Essie. And frankly, I am so grateful for friends like you who certainly understand that," Nola said as she handed Essie the script for the telegram. "If there's a reply before I come for my mail tomorrow, please ask one of the Gillenwater boys to deliver the message to the tearoom."

Essie followed her out to the street. Her raised eyebrows and smirk of a smile said more than any flood of words ever could. "I thought that Chambliss woman played the piano. Why isn't she the one working on compositions with him?"

"She plays for the rehearsals. She is not a composer." *Oh, why am I forever trying to explain myself to people who have already made up their minds?*

Essie placed a hand on Nola's sleeve. "Look, it's nobody's business, but when

281

you're a female and on your own and trying to earn a living, these things matter. Some people don't like it that you got mixed up with that acting crowd. It's not personal, Nola. Everyone has your best interests at heart."

Three tourists sidled past them, their voices loud with the excitement common to those on holiday. Nola took advantage of the interruption to leave before she said something that she would surely regret.

"Whoa! Where's the fire?" Harry came around the corner just as Nola quickened her step to escape the postmistress. He caught her by the shoulders to keep her from plowing into him. His voice was teasing but his eyes were filled with concern. "Nola?"

"Please excuse me, Harry, I . . ."

Just as she prepared to dart around him, they both turned at the sound of her name being called. Judy Lang was half running, half walking toward them, her breath coming in short harsh gasps. Starbuck hurried to catch up as Nola ran to meet the red-faced woman.

Judy waved a sheet of heavy blue stationery in front of Nola. "There's been another note," she managed.

Before Harry could read over her shoulder

and take in the full message, Nola had read through the contents and shoved the note into her pocket. But he had seen enough.

Miss Nola, you will rue the day
You took up with him who likes to play;
Your mother's memory you disgrace
Repent before more wrath you face.

A friend

"We'll talk about this at home," Nola said as she put her arm around the older woman's waist and started back toward the tearoom.

Harry fell into step beside her. "There's been more than this one note?" he asked.

Judy nodded. "The first was several weeks ago. Essie handed it to Nola with the morning mail. The second came right after Nola's accident and now this."

"Why didn't you tell me, Nola?"

"Please don't concern yourself, Harry," Nola said with a forced lightness. She even gave a little laugh. "You know how young people like to play pranks. It's nothing and the best way to deal with it is to ignore it, right, Judy?"

Judy did not appear to agree. She glanced up at Harry. "What do you think?"

Nola shot Harry a look of pleading over

Judy's head. His mouth tightened slightly but he smiled. "Now, Miz Lang, as I recall when I was a boy here on Nantucket, this was just the sort of thing I might have dreamed up. Getting folks all stirred up over some perceived threat and then sitting back and watching it all play out."

"Yes," Nola added. "That's probably how Mr. Starbuck got his start in the theater. These sorts of things are so feigned," she said. "In fact they are so histrionic that they can't possibly be taken seriously."

Judy glanced from one to the other. "I suppose. Still . . ."

Harry narrowed his eyes. "What was in the other notes?"

Nola shrugged. "More childish pranks. Nothing of importance."

Judy, Nola and Harry had reached the side gate of the tearoom. Harry held the gate for the ladies but made no move to come inside. "You're sure you're all right?" he asked softly once Judy had started up the back porch steps.

Nola gathered strength from his concern. "Perfectly," she assured him. "Now, I'm sure we both have business we need to attend. Good day to you," she called, as much for the benefit of Mrs. McAllister who was coming down the street from the opposite direction and craning to catch whatever might be going on between Nola and Harry.

"I'll see you later this afternoon," Harry called.

Nola hesitated for just an instant before she glanced back over her shoulder and gave him a smile and a wave that she prayed would reassure him and send him on his way.

CHAPTER FOURTEEN

Harry was fairly certain that the motive behind the notes went beyond a simple prank. In the first place it had taken a lot of patience to go to such lengths — making up rhymes, cutting out just the right letters and such. Then there was the expensive stationery. There was something familiar about the color, the thickness of the lined envelope that Judy had waved about. In spite of his reassurance to Mrs. Lang, the one line of the note that he'd seen worried Harry.

 . . . took up with him who likes to play.

The writer of the note was speaking of Harry, warning Nola about her association with him. He was well aware of the gossip currently making the rounds, but gossip had never bothered him before. Of course, Nola was a different matter. She would hate being the topic of gossip. Prepared to retrace his steps and confront Nola so that together they could get to the bottom of this, Harry

286

remembered where he had seen that note-paper before.

In the days when Rose Gillenwater was trying to foster a romance between Violet and Harry, there had been constant invitations to join the family for Sunday dinner or an afternoon carriage ride or to go sailing. *And the invitation always came on heavy blue notepaper.*

When the fourth note arrived just two days after the staff from the Cabbage Inn started work in the tearoom, Judy insisted that Nola contact the authorities. This time the note warned that since Nola had ignored the previous notes, the author would not be responsible for what harm might come her way.

"That will only encourage whoever is behind this," Nola protested. "Can't you see that anyone who would stoop to such measures is probably watching and hoping for some reaction?"

"Oh, child, I don't want to believe there might be some lunatic on the loose here in 'Sconset any more than you do. But this is a serious matter, Nola. This latest message implies that you might actually be in danger. At least stop working with Harry for the time being and let this all calm down."

"All right," Nola replied. "I've done as much as I can anyway and from here until opening night Harry and the others are going to need every moment they can spare to rehearse. Harry himself agrees that there simply can be no more changes until he takes the play to New York."

"Well, finally we might just get things back to normal around here," Judy huffed.

Nola gave Judy a hug. "Please stop worrying, Judy. I have everything under control."

"I'm not going to hold my breath waiting for that," Judy said. "Harry Starbuck seems to have this way of coming around and stirring the pot whether you like it or not."

"He's going to be far too busy for the next few weeks, Judy."

But as if he'd been waiting in the wings to prove her wrong, Harry showed up in her kitchen just an hour later, right in the middle of the noon rush.

"I have to talk to you," he said.

Nola stuffed the latest note into the pocket of her apron. "Harry, I have a full house and a new staff still finding their way. Can't this wait?"

"I think I know who might be sending the notes."

Nola fingered the note. "Is it someone I know?"

"Yes."

"Then please don't tell me."

"Why not? Nola, this person . . ."

". . . is a neighbor and friend who thinks he or she is doing me a favor by warning me to stay away from you and the others. I have to live in the same small town as this person long after all of you go away, Harry. I don't want to know."

"But —"

Judy pushed through the swinging door with a tray laden with dirty dishes. The minute she spotted Harry alone with Nola she paused.

"Mr. Starbuck is just leaving," Nola said. "Aren't you, Harry?"

"For now. But if there are any more notes . . ."

"There won't be if you'll stop hanging around Nola here," Judy told him.

Harry ignored her and focused on Nola. "You will let me know if there is even one more note?"

"There won't be any more notes. Now, unless you intend to tie on an apron and prepare a fresh batch of cucumber sandwiches, please go. We are swamped."

Harry was tempted to take her up on the offer to help out in the kitchen. At least then he'd be able to keep an eye on her. Nola Burns was possibly the most stubborn woman he had ever met. Did she not understand that at just over five feet and not an ounce over one hundred pounds, she was hardly a match for someone who might wish her harm? Not that he thought Rose Gillenwater would actually resort to physical violence, but Rose had a lot of influence over others. It wasn't beyond the realm of possibility that someone might decide to confront Nola directly.

As he entered the cabaret, he spotted Alistair and decided he would have a word with the man about his wife's penchant for sticking her nose into other people's business. But before he could take his partner aside, Billy interrupted.

"It's Ellie, boss. She's taken a tumble."

Without missing a step, Harry followed as Billy led the way backstage.

"We were all just taking a look at things and didn't know that stair railing wasn't secured yet and Ellie, well, she leaned against it and . . ."

Ellie was sitting on an overturned wooden crate surrounded by the entire cast — a cast that now had grown to include several of the resident colony of actors. She was holding her wrist and wincing.

"We sent for the doctor," Jasper said as he stepped aside to let Harry kneel next to Ellie. "Do you think it's broken?"

"It's a sprain. Nothing more," Ellie said. "Please, I'm fine."

"Give her some space and somebody go see what's keeping that doctor," Harry barked. "Just sit tight," he instructed Ellie in a softer tone.

"Whatever the verdict, I'm not going to be able to play for rehearsals, Harry. You'll have to get someone else."

"You let me worry about that."

"Nola could do it," Ellie said.

"Nola's busy. Now hold still. Here comes Dr. Wainwright."

Nola was on her way to the bookstore when she saw the little parade of actors making their way down the street. At the center of the group were Ellie and Dr. Wainwright. Trailing behind were Billy, Jasper and the Kowalski sisters. Starbuck was, as usual, barking out orders and Olga had hurried ahead to hold the door to the clinic open for Ellie.

"What's happened?" Nola asked as she caught up with the Kowalski twins.

"Oh, Nola, it's Ellie. She fell and hurt her wrist."

"It might be broken," Deedee said.

"Or sprained," Mimi corrected. "Either way she can't play for rehearsal and until the musicians Mr. Starbuck hired get here at the end of the week, we have no one."

"Oh, come now. There must be at least one person among the summer resident actors who plays?"

Deedee shook her head. "Well, sure, but no one else knows the music and Harry says we really don't have time for anyone to learn it and . . ."

"But you know it, Nola," Mimi said and grinned at her sister. "You could rehearse with us until the other musicians get here."

"Please?" Billy pleaded as he joined the group.

Nola looked at their eager faces. She had come to care for these young people so much. They were bright and talented and such fun to be around. They had helped her out when she'd needed them. Perhaps now it was time to repay the favor.

"I suppose I could . . ."

"Great! I'll go tell Starbuck." And before Nola could reconsider, Billy had headed back inside the clinic with the Kowalski sisters right behind.

"It's only a few times," Nola told Judy. "Just

until Harry can get the musicians he hired here."

"How can that help? Won't they need to learn the music?"

"No. Harry has sent them the music to learn in advance. He'll just need to coordinate the actors and the new musicians."

"And I suppose you'll have to get involved in that as well. That man . . ."

"I'm not doing this for him, Judy. I'm doing it for Ellie and Billy and the others." Nola was well aware that Judy had a soft spot in her heart for Billy and Jasper.

"You'll make sure that Billy or Jasper sees you back here every night after rehearsal?"

"Promise."

"And before you do anything else I want you to take those notes and show them to Reverend Diggs."

"Oh, Judy . . ."

Judy placed her hands firmly on her hips and the look she gave Nola stated more clearly than any words that this was not up for discussion. "I'll go and see Reverend Diggs," Nola agreed.

"And heed his advice even if he counsels staying away from Starbuck and his kind?"

"No. I will not be dictated to by someone too cowardly to discuss the matter with me directly. Harry's play is important. It could touch so many souls. How can I not be a part of that, given the opportunity?"

Judy untied her apron and reached for her hat. "Then if you won't listen to reason I'm going to the authorities," she said.

"No, wait. If we get the police involved think of how that might affect the tearoom. Our customers might decide it's too dangerous to be seen here. Let me speak with Reverend Diggs first."

"And you'll do as he counsels?"

Nola nodded and breathed a sigh of relief when Judy retied her apron.

"I'm sure it's nothing more than a prank," Nola told the minister as he read through each note. "In fact, originally I thought Mr. Starbuck was the author, but he wouldn't go to such lengths."

"More to the point, he would not make threats, Nola. No, this is someone who is becoming increasingly agitated by your continued association with Mr. Starbuck and his friends."

"That could be any number of people," Nola replied with a wry smile. "Perhaps some misguided soul is simply trying to frighten me."

"Still, one cannot be too careful, my dear. While Mr. Starbuck has been a generous and faithful supporter of this church and the community, there are those who persist in viewing his theatrical activities as being in questionable taste for a man of his position."

"Then why not send threatening notes to him?"

Reverend Diggs smiled. "Because, Nola, the sender of these notes may already view Mr. Starbuck as a lost cause while you — you are the innocent here, the one who must be warned and saved."

"You are saying that I should take this nonsense seriously?"

"Quite seriously."

"But to bow to anonymous threats," she protested.

"I am not suggesting you surrender, Nola. But certain precautions would be prudent."

"And what are you suggesting?"

The minister removed his glasses and leaned toward her. "I agree that the last thing you want to do is call attention to this matter. In my limited experience a person taking such drastic actions is seeking notoriety. However, you do need to keep the local authority apprised of the situation."

"I can't have my customers seeing a police officer coming and going, Reverend. Think what that would do to my business."

"I'm sure that Osgood Daniels can work behind the scenes, so to speak, so that no one is aware of his presence. But, Nola, he does need to be involved."

"I suppose," Nola reluctantly agreed.

The minister smiled. "I understand that the construction on the cabaret is a bit behind schedule."

"Yes. Rehearsals are being held in the hotel now."

"I see. Perhaps if you were to involve Oliver and Minnie Franks in this project? They are held in the highest esteem throughout the community and if they became a part of the preparation it just might be a way to break through this impasse that seems to have developed between the locals and the acting colony."

"But they have been — concerned."

"And what better way to allay those concerns than to bring the involved parties together? Besides, Oliver is an amateur composer himself."

"Well, if you really think Oliver and Minnie would consider it, then yes, Reverend. Thank you."

Reverend Diggs handed her back the notes and walked up the aisle with her. "I have to admit that I had some concerns myself when you first took the actors into your home and employ, Nola. I'm ashamed to admit that in the past I was inclined to view our summer theatrical residents as people whose spiritual needs were not my concern. But after observing the way you integrated Mrs. Chambliss and her peers into your business and then into your life even after they had moved out of your home and into the cottages, I decided to call upon them myself. I found most of them to be people not unlike the members of this congregation — people of solid faith."

"Oh, they are such good people, Reverend Diggs. I shall miss them terribly once the season ends."

"There is one other facet of this matter we need to consider, Nola dear," the minister said. "It is the matter of your feelings for Harry Starbuck."

Nola felt a flush of embarrassment creep up the sides of her neck, but then she stood tall and met his gaze directly. "Harry Starbuck and I have a somewhat complicated friendship. As you no doubt are aware, he hopes to buy me out. That is on the one hand."

"And on the other?"

I have feelings for him that are conflicting and yet thrilling at the same time. "He has given me such an incredible opportunity to be a part of his work on this production. It's so completely new for me — an experience I could never have imagined having."

"For what it's worth, Nola, I believe that he has your best interests at heart. Even his motives for buying your property seem to have become more complicated — and personal."

"In what way?"

Reverend Diggs smiled. "Now, my dear, you know I cannot reveal something that has been spoken to me in confidence. Suffice it to say that, in my opinion, you and Mr. Starbuck share a common trait — each of you cares deeply about the welfare of others."

Was the minister suggesting that Harry had come to care for her? "How kind of you to say so, Reverend Diggs. However, I do not deceive myself when it comes to Mr. Starbuck. He has shown that when he views something as an essential piece of whatever project he is working on, he will not stop until he has put that piece into its place."

The minister smiled. "And yet here it is August already and he appears to have completely lost interest in his initial plan to acquire your home and tearoom."

It was true that ever since the clambake, ever since the kiss, ever since she had agreed to work with him composing the music for his lyrics, there had been no mention of his buying her property. It simply had not come up. She turned her attention back to the minister. "There's still time for that. The construction of the inn is planned for next season. At the moment, his focus is on completing his play. I am well aware, however, that once he has completed that, we will have to face the other matter."

Reverend Diggs held the door open for her. "Nevertheless, when I refer to the matter of you and Mr. Starbuck, I am not speaking of your collaboration or of business, Nola. I am speaking of your heart."

"My heart is as sound as my mind," she replied quietly. "I know that there are those who see romance whenever circumstances throw a man and a woman together, but I am not one of those people. I am well aware that it is my talent for composition that has caught the attention of Mr. Starbuck."

"And you are all right with that?"

Nola smiled. "I am twenty-seven years old, Reverend. I know the line between romantic fantasy and reality. Working on this project has brought me an unexpected joy. I do not need Harry Starbuck's affection in the bargain."

Reverend Diggs took Nola's hand between

both of his. "He is a good man, Nola."

"Yes," she agreed.

"You have been good for him," he added. "Perhaps there is more at work here than you realize."

Nola opened her mouth to reply but could think of nothing to say. Was the elderly minister cautioning or encouraging her? When he had brought up the topic of her heart, Nola had been certain he was about to warn her of the possibility that Starbuck would break it. Instead he appeared to be giving them his blessing — as if there were anything to bless.

"Shall I speak with the Franks?"

"Yes. Thank you," Nola said and had to resist the urge to hug him as she had once hugged her own father. "And I'll tell Harry — Mr. Starbuck — of the change on my way through town."

"Perhaps allow me to handle that as well, Nola. Given these messages you've received it might be best if you and Harry . . ."

Nola felt her smile freeze. "I do not intend to sneak about. That will only provide more fodder for the gossip mill. Besides, whoever this prankster is, any sign that I have backed away or changed my routine will be a victory for that person."

"Just be careful, my dear," the minister

warned and his worried expression told Nola that he was far more concerned than he had first let on.

But this is 'Sconset, she reasoned as she walked through town. *Nothing ever happens in 'Sconset.*

Harry was in his office making the arrangements for the musicians he'd hired to arrive as soon as possible when he heard someone greet Nola on the street below. He replaced his pen and moved to the window.

Oliver Franks was huffing breathlessly as he caught up to Nola and hurried alongside her matching her long determined strides. He was gesturing dramatically and seemed to be trying to persuade Nola of something. Something she clearly was not taking to heart for she stopped just across from Harry's office and said something to Oliver that left him standing speechless for once while Nola wove her way through carriage and pedestrian traffic to Harry's side of the street. She looked up, saw him and smiled.

"Do you have a moment?" she called up to him.

"I'll come down," he replied. "Wait there."

Had she suffered another blow to her head? Surely that was the only credible explanation for why Nola Burns was standing below his office window in the middle of the afternoon and calling out to him for anyone to see or hear.

Harry reached for his jacket and hat and glanced out the window once more as he put them on. He certainly was not going to further raise eyebrows by keeping Nola waiting. Across the street, Oliver was still standing where Nola had left him only now he was greeting Mrs. Gillenwater and her usual entourage. Long a student of human body language and expression, Harry surmised that Oliver was sharing the details of his encounter with Nola with the old gossip and her friends.

Nola was waiting for him in the shade of the awning of the general store. These days whenever Nola Burns smiled at him as she was doing now, he had to look away until he'd had the chance to arm himself with his patented charming grin. The fact was that whatever his feelings for her might be, he was not her type and after the gala they would most certainly go their separate ways. On the other hand, he could not deny that without her ear for music, his script would never have been fit for a rough preview in 'Sconset much less a full production in New York.

"Miss Nola," he drawled.

"Now, Harry, I've just come from seeing Reverend Diggs and he has made this truly inspired suggestion regarding the play." In what seemed to be one long breath, she told him about the idea of asking the Franks to sit in on rehearsals and offer their suggestions. "It occurred to me that Oliver plays violin and the violin is the perfect instrument for Ellie's ballad just before the first act curtain."

"I thought Reverend Diggs agreed with half the congregation that you should not be involved in this."

"Not at all. He's just concerned, as are the others."

"And Oliver?"

Nola frowned. "That was unfortunate. Reverend Diggs had suggested he be the one to bring up the matter with Oliver but then when I saw him just now . . ."

"I take it he was not exactly delighted with the idea."

"He'll come around. I told him about the piece for violin and I could see that he was intrigued in spite of himself."

"And what about Mrs. Gillenwater?"

Nola blinked up at him. "What about her?"

From the moment Harry heard about the notes, it had amazed him that Nola had not once shown alarm. "You don't have to fill in for Ellie, Nola. I've just sent for the musicians I hired. They'll be here in plenty of time to put the final touches on the show."

"And until then?" Nola asked. "Besides, I want to do this. It's my opportunity to repay the company for everything they did for me."

Harry frowned. The truth was that the company needed all the rehearsal time he could give them. "There will be some rules," he said sternly.

Nola bristled. "I am perfectly capable —"

"Play by my rules, Nola, or the deal's off."

"Really, Starbuck, you are sometimes so full of yourself that you are quite impossible."

He arched an eyebrow.

"Very well, but you're being ridiculous."

Harry grinned. "Humor me."

"What rules?"

"We'll go over that later at rehearsal. I want to be sure that everyone — including Oliver and Minnie — are straight on how things will go until we find the person behind those notes."

CHAPTER FIFTEEN

Harry's rules were ironclad. Nola was not to ever be out alone after dark. He insisted that one or more of them would see her home, and more often than not he found a reason for that escort to be him. He even insisted on checking the entire property inside and out before leaving. Then he would stand on the front porch until he heard the click of the front door lock and her murmured "Good night, Harry."

After a few days, Nola was relieved that once again things seemed to have settled into a routine. Even the Franks seemed to have come around, especially once everyone in the cast raved about Oliver's violin rendition of Ellie's ballad.

"That's perfect, Oliver," Harry had told the choir director. And the entire cast had backed up his praise with their applause. Oliver had actually blushed and the disapproving expression that had seemed permanently engraved on Minnie's face for weeks now had softened just a bit.

But one night as Harry walked Nola home after leaving the rest of the actors at the turnoff to the cottages, she was having trouble concentrating on his lighthearted banter. And when he went about his usual tour of the downstairs rooms, she followed him, lingering in the doorway and watching as he checked each lock.

"You all right?" he asked.

She tried a smile but failed. "Yes . . . No."

"The notes have stopped, right?"

She wrestled with a possible lie and settled on the truth. "They had," she admitted. "Until this morning."

He held out his hand and she fished through her purse and produced the familiar blue envelope, then looked away while he pulled out the single sheet and read the note.

Nola Burns, you have been warned;
That man Starbuck, you must scorn.
Heed these words or pay the price;
Your life's too precious to sacrifice.

A friend

"Nola, this is a direct threat. When and how did you receive this?"

"Judy found it when she came to work this morning."

"Where?"

Nola swallowed and her lower lip began to quiver. "It was . . . She found it . . ." She felt the color drain from her cheeks. He took hold of her arm, clearly afraid that she might faint.

"Where?" he insisted.

"On the kitchen table."

The culprit had gotten inside?

"Come on," Harry said, heading back outside.

"Where are we going?"

"To the police. Enough is enough, Nola. This person has broken into your home — been in your kitchen." *Not ten yards from where you lay sleeping.*

As 'Sconset's sole officer of the law, Osgood Daniels's usual duties were little more than helping a tourist with directions. But once he'd heard Nola's story, the young policeman drew up a chair. His questions were so probing that they raised real concerns in Nola's mind. She began to consider the notes as the potential threats they were.

"Who might have something to gain by frightening you, Miss Nola?" Osgood asked.

"No one."

"Perhaps the perpetrator wants to see you

close up shop? Even leave the island altogether?"

Nola tried a laugh but the laughter stuck in her throat.

"In short, who are your enemies?"

"Enemies?" she replied. "In 'Sconset?"

Osgood leaned forward sympathetically. "Not necessarily. Perhaps this is coming from outside the community. Is there a vendor or supplier perhaps that you've locked horns with over time?"

She assured him that while she expected exceptional service, she could think of no one that she had ever dealt with who might resort to tactics such as sending threatening notes. "Anyway, how would someone off island be so knowledgeable about the people I choose to befriend?"

"Gossip is like a wildfire, Miss Nola. Doesn't discriminate between those in the know and those just curious. You take a vendor who calls on you and then goes on down the street to another business and hears folks talking . . ." He shrugged.

"Nevertheless, I am quite certain that what lies behind the notes has nothing to do with my business dealings, but rather with my association with the theater group. The notes are coming from someone who knows me — someone that I know."

"What about Mrs. Gillenwater?" Harry asked.

"I seriously doubt that she would have any idea of who might be . . ."

"Could she be sending the notes?"

The policeman cleared his throat. "Well, now, sir, a woman like that? It seems a bit of a long shot."

"It is impossible," Nola corrected. "Rose Gillenwater is always direct and to the point. She has told me more than once her feelings regarding my association with the acting troupe — and with you," she added.

Harry shrugged. "Exactly why in my view she's on the list. You have not heeded her advice, Nola. And we all know that she doesn't like that."

"It's not Rose," Nola insisted. "I refuse to believe such a thing."

She turned back to the officer. "Now, Osgood, I hope you understand that if it gets out that I've involved the authorities, my customers could become alarmed. It's imperative that you go about your investigation quietly and without fanfare."

"I understand, miss. I'll be discreet."

Later that evening he stopped by to make a full inspection of the property, especially the kitchen door.

"It's not the best of locks," he muttered.

"There's no sign of tampering but frankly anyone could have easily opened the lock without a key."

Nola assured him that Jonah would change the lock first thing the following morning.

"Might want to change all the locks while he's at it. Now don't you worry, Miss Nola, I'll be around but your customers won't even notice."

And true to his word Officer Daniels kept his distance from the tearoom during business hours although Nola had seen him watching patrons come and go and making notes with a stubby pencil in a dog-eared notepad he carried in his pocket. To her relief Nola also noticed that the policeman had increased the number of occasions he found to walk past her place, especially in the evenings. But when she heard footsteps on the front porch later, near midnight, Nola couldn't help herself. She was scared.

"Who's there?" she cried out.

"It's just me," Ellie Chambliss answered. "And Lancelot. Can we come in?"

"Of course." Nola ran to open the door and was surprised to see Ellie hauling the familiar large damask pillow where Lancelot slept along with a small suitcase. "What's happened?"

"We've come to stay the night," Ellie

replied. "Hopefully you haven't rented out my old room?"

"Of course not, but, Ellie . . ."

"Now, we won't take no for an answer, will we, Lancelot? We've missed you and I could never make a proper cup of tea and . . ." She stopped and gave Nola an apologetic smile. "Harry told me about the notes."

Nola relieved Ellie of the suitcase and pulled her into the foyer so they could close the door. "Bless you," she murmured, fighting the knot of tears in her throat.

"Are you kidding?" Ellie exclaimed in a voice that was a little too bright. "This place over that damp little cottage? No contest. Right, Lancelot?"

The dog gave a yap of approval and leaped from Ellie's arms to Nola's. He started licking Nola's face and she laughed. "You two get settled. I'll make us some tea."

As Ellie continued to nurse her sprained wrist, Nola continued attending rehearsals even after the professional musicians arrived. Although they had the music well in hand by the second night, the truth was that she was happy for the diversion. Even though there had been no further notes, Nola found herself looking at every vendor and delivery person, every neighbor or acquaintance she passed on the street as a potential suspect. Could Ian McAllister have sent the notes, she wondered as he bagged up her purchases. And if so, for what possible reason?

With Ellie once more living at Nola's it seemed natural that the entire cast would walk with Ellie and Nola to the tearoom before heading on down the lane to their cottages. Nola would invite them all inside and pull out leftovers for them to devour. It did not escape her notice that during these nightly sessions, Harry continued to move from room to room checking locks and windows.

"It's the city in us," the countess said one evening as she and Ellie sat with Nola in the parlor while the others cleaned up the kitchen and Harry checked outside to make sure no one was lurking about. "We tend to see villains even in picturesque 'Sconset."

"You know about the notes?" Nola asked.

Olga nodded. "Alistair — Mr. Gillenwater — mentioned it in passing. He's quite concerned."

"Olga, about Mr. Gillenwater . . ."

The actress straightened and her expression hardened. "That is none of anyone's business."

"I'm afraid it is. Mrs. Gillenwater is my friend — as are you. I'd hate to think that there was any basis for Rose's concerns."

Olga sighed dramatically. "It has always amazed me how you Americans find it so difficult to believe that a man and a woman might form a friendship without the usual romantic entanglements. Alistair — yes, *Alistair* — and I have found that we have common interests. Did you realize his ancestors on his mother's side were Russian?"

"No."

"Well, they are and he has always thought of traveling there — taking his precious Rose there."

"And how does that concern you?"

"It doesn't," Olga sighed. "It began with a simple comment I made to him before the clambake. He mentioned his heritage and desire to travel there in casual conversation. I said that I had a friend in Boston who specializes in tours to Russia. He asked me to write down the name and contact information since he was leaving for Boston that very afternoon. I did so and that is the end of the story."

"But Rose said that their sons . . ."

Olga waved her hand as if flicking away an annoying fly. "They saw their father take the information and then they saw him take

313

my hands in an expression of gratitude. That is what they saw. What they think they saw, and obviously reported to their mother, I can only imagine."

"Olga, I'm so sorry."

"For what?"

"Well, the gossip surrounding you has been cruel and unwarranted."

"No more than for you. These notes — the work of cowards."

Nola sighed. "I just wish we could all stop worrying about this and get back to our normal routines."

Olga reached over and took her hand. "As do we all, dear Nola. Thank you for refusing to join in judging me without first hearing me out. And thank you for believing me." She glanced toward the door where the others could be heard moving from room to room performing the nightly security check. "And now perhaps it is I who can help you."

"How?"

"I wonder, Nola," she said, lowering her voice. "Have you considered that perhaps Mr. Starbuck is someone who is clever enough to plot such a drama?"

"You mean his operetta? Well, of course, he's clever enough, Countess. Even you have had to admit that it's the most innovative . . ."

Again the glance toward the door and now Olga was almost whispering. "Not the play, Nola — these threats." She stood up quickly as the others crowded into the room.

"Ten o'clock and all is cleaned up in the kitchen," Jasper announced as everyone entered the parlor.

"Thank you all," Nola said. "Now go home. You need your rest. The opening is only a week away." She shepherded them all toward the front hall.

Billy kissed her cheek and whispered, "Sleep well, Miss Nola." Then the others took their turn kissing her lightly on the cheek and following Olga out to the porch. Only Harry and Ellie remained.

"I wonder, Ellie, would you give me a moment with Nola?" Harry said.

"Of course." Ellie leaned in and kissed Nola's cheek. "I'll be upstairs," she said.

When they were alone, Harry smiled down at Nola. "Everyone is looking out for you, Nola," he said. "You have won them over heart and mind."

And you? Nola thought as Olga's preposterous question rang in her ears. But instead of saying anything she led the way into the parlor. "You don't have to keep checking the house every night, Harry. The locksmith checked everything when he was here."

"Do you think I'm the one sending the notes, Nola?"

She was astounded at the question and yet, she could not deny that it had crossed her mind. "Not really. No."

"The countess has made no secret of her suspicions and I have to admit that I am the most likely culprit." He smiled wearily. "After all, the entire scenario has a certain dramatic flair."

"Melodramatic," she corrected. "Not at all your style."

"Nevertheless, I have something to show you."

He cleared his throat and Nola realized he was nervous.

"I had intended this as a show of appreciation for everything you've done, Nola. For the company, for the play — and for me. But perhaps it will serve a better purpose and set any doubts you may have about me and my motivations to rest." He pulled an envelope from his pocket and handed it to her.

"What's this?"

"It's the deed to the acreage just east of the cabaret. I'm going to build the inn there."

Nola opened the envelope and pulled out

the deed.

"It has a lovely setting — nothing like yours, of course. But I was able to acquire all of the land down to the shore so there's no chance someone will come along and build something to block the view," Harry said. "Guests will be near enough to the cabaret to bicycle or even walk between the two properties. It will be a kind of a compound with everything any city person could want right at hand."

Nola continued to stare at the deed, but the truth was her emotions were threatening to overwhelm her.

Harry sat next to her. "Say something, Nola."

"You did this for me?"

He grinned. "You give me far too much credit, Miss Nola. The truth is that you convinced me that 'Sconset would lose a great deal of the charm that makes the place so appealing without Miss Nola and her tearoom." He placed one finger under her chin and urged her to look at him. "Bad for business," he murmured.

"Oh, Harry, you didn't have to do this. The letters will stop and things will settle back to normal once we get through the gala. You'll see."

"Why, Miss Nola, are you saying you've

changed your mind about selling this place to me?"

"No, but . . ."

He leaned in and kissed her temple. "Thought not. You belong here, Nola."

Where else would she go? Nola thought and saw her future clearly. She — like Rachel Williams — would become something of an icon on the island. Well-known, even beloved. *And alone.*

"I have business in New York," Harry said. "I leave tomorrow for the week."

"But the rehearsals," Nola protested.

"The play is in good shape. Now that the conductor and musicians I hired are here, he and Ellie can handle rehearsals and I'll be back in time for the gala." He pulled the deed and its envelope from her fingers. "Good night, Miss Nola. Sleep well."

That night Nola begged off her usual tea and talk session with Ellie, protesting that she had let her paperwork pile up and needed to attend to some bills. She could see that Ellie didn't fully believe her, but the actress did not protest. Sleepless, Nola paced the first-floor rooms of her house.

She had won, she thought. This was her house — her business. And yet it didn't seem to belong exclusively to her these days. In seasons past she had grown used to her routine — a quiet supper alone or occasionally with a friend like Rachel Williams or Minnie Franks. Time spent making a detailed list of errands and chores for the following day. A few moments of quiet meditation and prayer after her nightly cup of tea. And then to bed.

But this summer had been so very different. These summer nights she often lay awake going over the events of her day — days that more often than not were filled with surprises. Some townsperson she had known all her life who had that day crossed to the other side of the street to keep from passing her and risking a conversation. The always sunny Kowalski girls whose giggles could be irresistible even when Nola didn't know the cause. Olga, who always maintained her distance, but who often showed surprising wisdom. And Ellie, dear Ellie, who by sharing her own joys and tragedies had gradually enticed Nola to talk about her grief over her lost youth, the parents gone far too soon, and her joy in the accomplishments of her siblings.

And in just a few short weeks it would all be over, she thought. The others would go back to New York or on to touring companies and once again the house would be as still as a winter's night on Nantucket. And

Nola would be left with what?

Dear Father, I don't know what will happen once the season ends. I don't yet know if I am living in some fantasy or if I am following the path You have set for me. All I know is that I have come to care deeply for them all and yet because of them I may have done irreparable damage to deeply held relationships here on the island. No, not because of them *— they have done nothing wrong. If it be Your will, please use Harry's play as an instrument to open closed minds and soften hardened hearts to the possibility that different is not the same as dangerous. And if that be Your will, then I will have been truly blessed. Amen.*

Nola leaned her forehead against the cool glass of her open window and closed her eyes. The air was heavy with the perfume of the roses that had come into full bloom. Below she could hear the always comforting rhythm of the tide rolling toward the shore. In the distance a foghorn burped its warning to ships at sea. And down the street she heard someone whistling the tune she had written for the closing song of the play.

Harry must have stopped at his office. And now there he goes pedaling home to his cottage. I shall miss hearing him whistle. Hearing him laugh. Nola turned her ear to the glass to catch the fading sounds of Harry's whistling. When this season ended it was the familiar presence of Harrison Starbuck bringing equal shares of frustration and delight to her life that she would miss most of all.

CHAPTER SIXTEEN

Harry could hardly believe his good fortune. The esteemed actress Lillian Russell was coming to 'Sconset for the opening of the cabaret. He sent off a telegram to Nola at once.

Held up here another two days STOP Back in time for opening STOP Bringing final act surprise STOP
H. Starbuck

Certain that Nola would share his cryptic message with the others, he couldn't help grinning as he imagined them all trying to puzzle out what the surprise might possibly be. In the meantime, he had work to do. Purchasing the land for his inn wasn't the only surprise he had in store for Nola. He glanced down at the copy of the script he'd brought for his investor meeting.

SIMPLE FAITH
An Operetta
Lyrics by Mr. Harrison Starbuck
Original Music by Miss Nola Burns

Of course, the businessmen who had already kept him waiting half an hour past his appointment would question that unfamiliar name. These chieftains of industry enjoyed being able to claim an investment in the arts, but they were less inclined to put their money into a production when they did not recognize the names on the script or marquee. Harry was already trying to sell them on the idea of the debut of Billy Andrews as the leading man. Adding an unknown composer to the mix might just be going too far. But Harry had not gotten where he was in the world of business without taking some risks — or convincing others to do the same.

"Mr. Starbuck?"

Harry glanced up. The secretary for the investment group was standing outside a pair of ornately carved double doors. "They are waiting, Mr. Starbuck," she said with just a hint of impatience.

"Well, then I guess that makes us even," Harry said with a grin as he passed her. "But this —" he nodded toward the script

"— will make the wait worthwhile for all of us."

With Harry away and rehearsals running smoothly, Nola tried to beg off going. She reminded Ellie that the threats had stopped and that with Officer Daniels still making his rounds, there simply was nothing to worry about.

"Or the person may simply be biding his time, waiting for you to let down your guard," Ellie argued. "Besides, what else have you got to occupy you? I mean, with Starbuck off on the mainland and all."

"You're a hopeless romantic," Nola sighed. "How many times must I tell you there is nothing between us? I don't deceive myself, Ellie. Harry's sole interest in me lies in what I can do for him. And speaking of business, have you seen my desk lately? Even now that the tearoom is finally fully staffed, I still have work here."

"And now that they are in place you have time to attend that during the day. Besides, you have this calming influence on everyone and you're as much a part of the company as anyone else."

So Nola continued to spend her evenings at rehearsal, right up to two days before the opening.

"I'm not going," she insisted. "I don't want to spoil the opening by seeing the dress rehearsal."

Even Ellie agreed this was for the best. "We're likely to be there most of the night," she told Nola. "The last act simply is not coming together properly."

"Perhaps everyone is nervous because of Harry's telegram," Nola guessed.

"That scoundrel," Ellie said, but she was laughing. "I wired him back to say we simply must know who he's bringing as the surprise guest. It affects the way we build the evening to its natural climax."

"And?"

Ellie shrugged. "You know Harry. His answer was a one-word wire, 'No.' "

"So what will you do?"

"Spend this evening rehearsing till the wee small hours of the morning," Ellie replied and gave Nola a quick kiss on her cheek. "I'll stay with Olga tonight in the cottage — that way I can sleep till noon and you can go on with business as usual here at the tearoom. Shall I leave Lancelot with you?"

"No. He just lies by the front door and whimpers when you're gone for more than an hour. I'll be fine. It's one night. Now go."

The truth was, Nola was glad of a night

alone. She loved spending time with Ellie and the others, but the cost of that was that she had neglected some of the work of running her business. Just that morning Judy had complained that she was running short of everything and if Nola expected her to make cones for the ice cream in addition to her regular baking she was going to need a greater supply of flour, sugar and other staples on hand.

"This isn't like you, Nola," Judy had said in a softer tone. "This place has always taken precedence over anything or anyone else. Are you feeling all right? That knock you took on the head was serious. Maybe you ought to see Dr. Wainwright just to be sure there are no aftereffects."

"I'm fine," Nola had assured her. "Just busy. You know how busy it gets this time of the year."

"That may be," Judy said. "But some are busier than ever with things other than getting this kitchen stocked or the place properly cleaned."

Judy had a point. Once the Cabbage Inn employees had arrived, Nola had been so focused on training them to serve customers and help with the baking and washing up that she had not yet taken the time to fill them in on other responsibilities. There was little time for Judy to attend to the house-keeping when she was overseeing the kitchen. Nola had tried training the Huff sisters to keep the public areas clean but more often than not they did only the bare necessities. Judy had complained that the Gillenwater boys were always hanging around flirting with the sisters and keeping them from completing their chores. It had been days since the front porch had been properly swept or the woodwork in the foyer even dusted much less polished.

Nola tapped her fingers on the stack of bills and orders she'd allowed to pile up on her desk in favor of attending rehearsals and staying up late to visit with Ellie.

And missing Harry Starbuck.

It was true. She missed him terribly. He'd only been gone a few days but it seemed more like weeks. What was she going to do once the season ended and he left for New York? He had wired her to say that his investors had agreed to back their operetta assuming they liked what they saw when they previewed it at the gala. That would mean that the cast would need to go into rehearsals in New York by the end of August. And that, of course, meant that Harry would leave as well. It would be months before they would see each other again.

"Oh, stop being so dramatic," she murmured aloud as she sat back down at her desk and opened the ledger. "New York is not the end of the earth. You can be there for the opening. And besides, what did you think was going to happen?"

She completed the supply order, updated her ledger and then went to the kitchen. There she tied on one of Judy's work aprons and gathered cleaning supplies — the broom, a feather duster, rags, furniture polish and a bucket of water mixed with white vinegar for cleaning the windows. By nine o'clock she had completed cleaning in the foyer and tearoom. She stood back to admire her work and to consider the front door.

The porch needed a good sweeping and the outside windows and woodwork needed cleaning as well. Still, she hesitated. While there had been no more notes, she could not help wondering if Ellie was right. Had the prankster given up or simply gone into hiding?

Was someone out there watching? Waiting?

"This is ridiculous." She pulled open the front door and moved her cleaning supplies onto the porch. With relief she saw that there was a full moon and a cluster of tourists had gathered on the footbridge to enjoy the starlit sky. With their chatter and laughter as background, Nola set to work.

As she washed and polished the etched glass panels of the door, she hummed some of the tunes she had composed for Harry's play. It gave her such pleasure to have contributed to that work.

"It's not professional enough," she had argued.

"It's simple and memorable," Harry told her. "It suits the play — simple music for *Simple Faith*."

She could not seem to stop thinking of ways they might further enhance the music with changes in tempo and rhythm. When Harry returned she would talk to him about her ideas. Perhaps he could use some of them for the New York opening.

When Harry returned . . .

One by one she pulled each of the white wicker rockers to one side of the porch and began sweeping the wide planked floor and steps. But she turned with a start when she heard the familiar squeak of the front gate.

"That you, Miss Burns?" Officer Daniels stepped into the light provided by the moon.

"Yes. Good evening," Nola called, ignoring the sense of pure relief she felt to see the uniformed man. "Lovely evening," she added.

"It's pretty late," he replied. "Past ten."

"Is it?" Nola realized that she'd gotten so caught up in her work that she'd failed to notice when the tourists had deserted the footbridge and left her alone. "I'm almost done here," she assured the officer.

"Maybe finish up in the morning," he suggested. "There was a little trouble down the way earlier. Some kids getting into mischief, setting off some firecrackers down by the actors' colony, but still . . ."

"Oh, there's nothing to do but sweep the side porch and put the rockers back in place."

"Let me help."

Nola could not deny that she was glad to have not only his help but his company. She'd never thought of 'Sconset as a place to fear but since the notes, she'd found herself jumping at shadows and watching over her shoulder on those rare occasions when she was out alone after dark.

"I'm guessing there have been no more notes delivered?" Osgood said as he lifted each rocker and set it into place.

"Not a one. I do so appreciate your concern, Officer Daniels. I expect it's your diligence that's made whoever was behind that decide to turn his attentions to other things."

"Still, can't be too careful," he warned. "You go on inside now and lock up. I'll just put these last planters back in place and be on my way."

"Thank you," Nola said and did as he suggested.

Inside, she turned the front door lock and then took the cleaning supplies back to the kitchen. By the time she'd put them away and returned to the foyer, Officer Daniels had gone. She stood in the darkened entrance inhaling the fragrances of her night's work and sighed. She was exhausted but Judy would be impressed — and reassured.

"Now, that's ever so much better and starting first thing tomorrow, I'll . . ."

She froze as behind her she heard the metal ping of the mail slot closing and the soft thud of something hitting the floor. As she felt her body tense, she heard footsteps moving down the front stairs, heard the front gate creak and close and she ran to the door and threw it open.

"Who's there?" she cried out.

A barking dog down the lane was her only answer as she watched two shadowy figures scurry soundlessly up the grass-covered street and turn down the lane that led to

Mr. Helton's cottages.

She stood for a moment trying to decide what to do. The fog was beginning to roll up the bluff and through the village. Nola shivered violently and ran back inside. This time she not only bolted the door, she pulled one of the heavy benches over to block it, then ran to the kitchen door and blocked that with sacks of flour and sugar from the pantry. And all the while she pointedly refused to acknowledge the presence on her foyer floor of a thick blue envelope.

It seemed all anyone in 'Sconset could talk about was the opening of the cabaret. The performance had sold out in a single afternoon at a cost of one dollar each. Visitors and locals alike barely blinked an eye at the price knowing they were about to enjoy the talents of performers who had made their reputations nationally and, in some cases, internationally. Performers who now spent their summers in 'Sconset basking in the mild weather. Older performers who enjoyed sharing memories of their days in the theater. Younger performers, like Billy, who had their entire careers ahead of them.

Word of Starbuck's surprise guest had spread through the village like a Nantucket fog with everyone guessing just who or what the surprise might be. And in spite of 'Sconset's well-deserved reputation as a place where nothing more than the most casual of clothing was required, Millie's notions shop was doing a booming business in laces, ribbons and other extravagant trims.

"What will you wear, Nola?" Ellie asked the day of the opening as she selected her costumes for moving to the dressing rooms at the cabaret.

"My gray silk, I suppose," Nola said absently as she took the gowns Ellie handed her and packed them into a steamer trunk. The truth was she had not been able to get the events of the last evening off her mind. The blue envelope lay unopened on her desk and she had not slept a wink.

"Forgive me, Nola, but gray is not your best color. Have you something else?"

"Oh, what does it matter what I am wearing," Nola said irritably. "No one will be looking at me."

"Except Harry," Ellie said softly.

"Ellie, I know you mean well, but you really must stop imagining that there is anything between Harry and myself. The truth is —"

"The truth is that you are in love with him and he with you. The only two people who don't seem to know that are you and Harry."

The actress burrowed through a second trunk and emerged with the most elegant ball gown Nola had ever seen. With something akin to reverence she took the gown from Ellie, allowing herself just a moment to enjoy the softness of the silk, the fine detail work of the delicate lace that framed the neckline and then cascaded into ruffles from the three-quarter sleeves and the hem of the skirt.

"Oh, Ellie, this is so lovely. Just look at this workmanship," she marveled as she examined the tiny silk flowers that formed garlands on the wide-ribbon straps, the large puffed sleeves, and the flared skirt.

"Try it on," Ellie said quietly.

"I couldn't," Nola protested.

"Couldn't or won't let yourself? There's a difference, Nola."

Nola thought suddenly of the note and the sleepless night and the long winter that would come when not only Harry would be gone, but Ellie, as well. "Why not?" she whispered and Ellie laughed.

"Why not, indeed. Here, let me help."

The gown fit as if it had been tailored to Nola's small frame. "It's perfect," Ellie announced as she fastened the pleated satin cummerbund into place.

Nola considered herself in the full-length

mirror. "I feel so . . . pretty," she whispered.

"You are beautiful and for once in his life Harry Starbuck will be speechless when he sees you."

"Oh, Ellie, I couldn't possibly. Mrs. Gillenwater will know immediately that I haven't anything so grand in my wardrobe and . . ."

"Let Mrs. Gillenwater worry about her own gown. I want you to accept this, Nola, as my gift. Without you this summer would have been a disaster. You not only took us all in and gave us work, but who would ever have guessed the talent for composing that lay dormant all this time."

"But you gave me so much more," Nola protested. "Your friendship and . . ."

"Will you wear the gown, Nola?"

Nola cast one more glance at her reflection and smiled. "Yes," she whispered and then she turned to embrace Ellie. "Yes. Thank you."

If it would have shortened the length of the trip, Harry would have personally turned the paddle wheel on the steamer as it made its way across the bay to Nantucket. He had handled all the arrangements for Miss Russell's trip to the island, although it had been her idea to travel in disguise as Harry's secretary. Her decision to put on a pair of eyeglasses and dress in a plain brown linen suit, a shirt with brown satin ribbon tie and a small straw split-brimmed hat had garnered her almost no notice on the trip.

The steamer was filled with guests from the mainland — businessmen, politicians and their wives — eager to reach the island, get settled in their hotels and get dressed for an evening that promised to be as grand as anything they had ever attended on Broadway. After landing Lillian Russell for the finale, Harry was quite certain they would not be disappointed.

But he was focused on one thing and one thing only — seeing Nola again. Although he had been away for only a few days, it felt more like weeks. She had haunted his dreams and more than once he had found himself prowling the streets of Manhattan after midnight as he tried to understand exactly where his relationship with Miss Burns was headed.

She's tied to the island, he reminded God nightly in his prayers. *That place is the only home she's ever known. The life I lead is so unsettled. How could she ever want that? Other than money — which she doesn't seem to care about — what can I offer her?*

He lost himself in the beat of his footsteps

on the deserted streets.

Love. Love. Love.

Harry knew the difference between a casual romance and abiding love. He'd known plenty of the former, but never the latter — until now. As much as he had tried to deny it, the truth of it was that he was in love with Nola. He simply could not imagine his life without her. These last few days had been testament to that and the very thought of being separated from her through the fall and winter while he produced his musical — their musical — had become increasingly unbearable.

Okay, I love her. Enough to go live with her on Nantucket? Shrink my dreams to managing local productions for the cabaret while I write plays for others to stage on the mainland?

"She would never ask that of me," he muttered.

And what would I ask of her?

"Ah, my sweet Nola, we could have it all — you and I — everything we could ever want."

But getting what a person wanted was not at all the same as getting what was needed. Starbuck had learned that when he had left the island to make his fortune. He had wanted success. He had wanted power. He had wanted money enough to live the life he chose. But even once he had achieved all of that, it had not been enough. He had needed to write plays, to tell stories that might touch hearts and change minds.

"And now what do you need?" he wondered aloud.

Nola.

Alistair Gillenwater joined Harry on deck as the steamer made its approach to Nantucket.

"I understand you bought the Sagan property," he said as he took some time to light his pipe in the wind.

"It'll be a good location for the inn."

"Better than the Burns place?"

"That property is no longer an option."

"Really?" Alistair puffed on his cigar as he digested this news. "And Miss Nola? Where does she fit on your agenda, Harrison?"

Harry leaned against the railing of the steamer as it sailed toward the dock in Nantucket Town. "Nola isn't on any business agenda," Harry replied, recalling the decision and purchase he'd made just before meeting Alistair at the docks. "Once we get through this opening, I hope to persuade her to be my wife."

Nola was planning the final details for the

reception she had offered to host following the opening performance, when she heard a familiar voice shouting her name.

"Nola?"

Heads turned in the tearoom as Starbuck bounded up the front steps and burst into the foyer. "Good afternoon, folks," he said as he swept off his hat and bowed. "Miss Nola?"

"What on earth?" Nola came rushing out from her office as Starbuck started down the hall toward the kitchen. When he turned and grinned at her, she had to restrain herself from the urge to rush into his arms and welcome him home. Instead she forced a frown. "Harrison Starbuck," she scolded under her breath as she settled for taking him by the arm and leading him into her office. "You seem to have forgotten that this is a place of business."

"I need your help," he said, then he grinned broadly and added, "and I missed you. Did you miss me, Miss Nola?"

Of course, she had.

"It seems as if you just left and now here you are back again. I've been so busy . . ." But then unable to keep up the ruse, she broke into a wide smile and nodded. "Have you been to the cabaret yet?"

"I came straight here."

Nola's heart skipped a beat.

"I need you to help me keep my surprise a surprise until tonight."

Oh. Her smile tightened against her disappointment that business had brought him to her.

Oblivious to the crests and valleys of her emotions, he led her over to the window and pointed to a woman seated in a carriage. "That's the actress, Lillian Russell," he whispered as if he might be overheard.

Nola looked at the woman in the wrinkled brown suit with frizzy wisps of hair escaping a haphazard bun at the nape of her neck. The woman glanced back and leaned a bit forward to peer up at the tearoom.

"No."

"Yes," Harry assured her. "And I need you to hide her here until tonight."

"Wouldn't she prefer the hotel?"

Harry chuckled. "She'd prefer the Ritz in Paris, but she owes me a favor and she'll go along with the plan. Actually I think she's rather enjoying all the subterfuge. Alistair completely ignored her on the way over — had no clue who she was."

"And what is the plan?"

"She is posing as my secretary. Since every other accommodation in town is booked, we'll say that you have agreed to rent her a room. She'll stay here until tonight at which time I will arrange for Jonah to collect the two of you and bring you to the cabaret."

"You're enjoying this, aren't you?"

Harry grinned. "It's fun and furthermore, everyone is going to be so surprised. Think of the pleasure they'll all have once they realize that the grand lady of the international stage herself has come to 'Sconset. Even those who have turned up their noses at you and Ellie and the others will come around when they see Miss Russell up on that stage."

"I don't know . . ."

"Trust me, Nola. Once the good people of 'Sconset have the opportunity to attend the opening of *their* cabaret and once they can tell visitors for years to come that they were in attendance the night Lillian Russell graced that very stage, all of the insults and snubs and warnings will be a thing of the past."

Nola glanced toward her desk where she could see the corner of the unopened blue envelope sticking out from beneath her ledger. "It might work at that," she admitted.

"Fantastic," Harry said and punctuated his joy by giving her a quick hug. "Wait right there. I'll go get Lillian."

Lillian played her part to perfection, even slouching a bit as she entered the foyer. Guests in the tearoom glanced up at the opening and closing of the tearoom door, but quickly dismissed the woman in the wrinkled brown suit and went back to their tea and conversation. Even Judy showed little curiosity as Nola led the woman up the stairs.

"I have a room just at the top of the stairs," Nola said. "I'm sure you'll be quite comfortable."

"Yes, miss," Lillian murmured as she followed Nola up the stairs. "Thank you, miss."

But the minute they were clear of an audience she straightened to her full height, pulled off the ridiculous oversize glasses and surveyed Nola from head to toe. "So you are the inimitable Miss Burns," she said. "I must say, my dear, that on the journey over I thought if I had to hear Harrison even mention your name, much less sing your praises, for one more moment, I would surely jump overboard."

"Mr. Starbuck has a tendency toward the overstatement," Nola said as she led the way into the largest bedroom and quickly bent to straighten a wrinkle in the bedspread.

"On the contrary. Harry has a keen eye for raw talent. If he says that you are a gifted composer, then you are. Oh, I suspect that his little operetta will improve under the hands of a more experienced lyricist and composer, but from what he showed me of your work, the basics are certainly there for him to once again be the toast of New York this season. I only wish I were available to play the lead."

"I'm sure if you told Harry — Mr. Star-buck — of your interest, he would . . ."

Lillian sat down at the dressing table and removed her gloves and hat. "I'll be performing in Europe this autumn. Perhaps sometime in the future, you and Harry can write something else for me."

The idea was preposterous, so much so that Nola smothered a smile. "I suspect this will be my first and only venture into composing for the stage, Miss Russell."

Lillian spun around. "Why on earth should that be? You're young and it seems to me that you have found the perfect place for composing." She gestured toward the open window. "The music of the sea accompanied by the breeze, and I assume there must be a foghorn somewhere close by. I know experienced composers who would be thrilled to find such perfect solitude in which to work."

Nola could see that once she had made

up her mind to something, Lillian Russell simply could not fathom there might be any stumbling blocks. *Like the need to earn a living and sustain the tearoom and . . .*

"Now, if you will excuse me, my dear, I really must lie down. It's been an exhausting day and one must be at one's very best for the public."

"Of course. Just let me know if there's anything you need," Nola said and backed her way out of the room, closing the door behind her.

Nola dressed for the evening with more care than she had lavished on herself in years. On her way through her parlor to await Jonah's arrival, she pulled out the unopened blue envelope. She had told no one about it and as she fingered the stiff blue paper, she wondered if perhaps she should read it or give it over to Officer Daniels or . . .

"No," she said firmly. "No more."

She took the thing by one corner, holding it as if it were some foul garbage, and walked to the kitchen. The fire in Judy's cookstove was no more than a pile of glowing embers until Nola dropped the envelope on top. She watched it catch fire, watched the corners of the envelope curl and blacken, saw the coward's words clipped from magazines turn to ash and firmly slid the cast-iron cover plate back into place. Then without a backward look, she walked back to the foyer to wait with Lillian for Jonah to bring the surrey around.

CHAPTER SEVENTEEN

Backstage, Harry had finally given in to Alistair's pleading and revealed his surprise. And when the actress arrived, still dressed in disguise, Alistair had practically been on his knees begging her forgiveness and insisting that she must allow him and his dear wife to host her during her visit.

"Why, Mr. Gillenwater, how very kind of you to ask. I had thought to hurry back to New York, but the truth is that I am quite charmed by your little village. A short respite would do me good, and I would be delighted to spend that time with you and Mrs. Gillenwater, but Harry tells me your daughter is betrothed to Charles Carrington. Surely Mrs. Gillenwater has her hands full planning the wedding?"

"Oh, but you must allow us the honor," Alistair insisted. "My wife would never forgive me if I allowed you to spend your holiday elsewhere. Besides, the Carringtons are staying with us, as well."

"Really? The elder Charles and his delightful wife are dear friends of mine. It will be lovely to see them again. I accept your most kind invitation with pleasure."

Once Lillian had agreed to spend at least one night in the Gillenwater mansion, Harry knew the evening was going to be even more successful than even he could have imagined. Rose Gillenwater might not care for theater people in general, but to play host to one of America's international stars as well as the renowned shipping magnate was something the matriarch would not be able to resist.

When Nola saw Harry step into the hall from backstage, she felt as if she could not breathe properly. He was dressed in black evening wear, set off by a brilliant white starched shirtfront and perfectly tied white silk tie. He had smoothed back his usually unruly hair so that his sharp cheekbones and strong jaw were even more prominent than usual. She saw him scan the room and when his eyes settled on her, it was as if all the other guests had simply disappeared.

He started across the room working his way through tangles of chattering guests, pausing briefly for acknowledgements or introductions, but all the while fixing his gaze back on Nola the moment he was free. And when he was still several feet away and Nola was inclined to step forward and meet him, Oliver and Minnie Franks appeared at her side.

"Ah, so the prodigal returns," Oliver joked. "Quite a crowd, wouldn't you say, Harry? You and your partners must be quite pleased."

"Indeed, it looks as if it's going to be quite an evening, Oliver, thanks to you and Minnie. I'm not sure you fully appreciate what you've both contributed to this production."

"Happy to help," Oliver assured him. "We appreciate the mention in the program."

At last he turned his attention to Nola. "Miss Nola, may I say that you are looking quite lovely this evening?"

"Thank you."

"I have to go backstage right away, but may I see you afterward?"

"Mrs. Lang and I must leave as soon as the final curtain comes down. I've offered to host a reception following the performance. Will you come?"

To her surprise, Harry frowned. "Of course. I'll look forward to it, but if you have a moment later, Nola, I have something to ask you."

Nola glanced up at him. His expression was so serious — his "business" face, Ellie had once called it. *So, here it was,* she realized. *We are business associates and nothing more. Oh, dear God, please give me the strength to put my fantasies aside and accept him for who he is and appreciate whatever he is willing to offer.*

She searched his eyes for something, anything, that might suggest more, but all she saw was that he was waiting for her answer so she forced a smile and nodded. And in that moment Nola knew that she had chosen. Once Harry and the others left — before the loneliness set in, she would close up the house and tearoom and then what? Perhaps go to visit her siblings? Yes, spend the holidays in England with her sister and the nieces and the nephew she had never seen.

She had earned his respect and that had given her the confidence she needed to move forward to whatever the next stage of her life might bring. Harry and the others had opened her eyes and her heart to a whole new world of possibilities beyond running the tearoom. When he had taken her talent for composing seriously, he had given her the confidence to explore that.

Surely, that was God's gift in bringing them together. *You have changed me,* she thought, but said, "I'll be waiting."

The grin he bathed her in was radiant and warm as he dashed to a side exit that would take him backstage.

Nola took her seat on the aisle and opened her program. Her name was there beneath Harry's — *Original compositions by Miss Nola Burns.* Her hand trembled as she closed the program and held it on her lap as if it were some precious jewel, and when she heard her music played by the small orchestra Harry had hired to accompany the actors, her heart skipped a beat. She immediately sent up a silent prayer begging forgiveness for the pride she couldn't seem to help but feel. But it was one thing to plunk out the notes of an original melody and scribble them onto a music grid, and quite another to hear the true intricacies of her compositions as played by multiple instruments. The moment Billy began singing Harry's lyrics to her melody, Nola knew that whatever else might happen that evening, this was a moment she would treasure for the rest of her life.

It wasn't long before she realized that the story unfolding on stage was not only touching her, it had captured the rapt attention of everyone in the theater. No one moved and it was that stillness that made Nola realize that a story about simple faith was everything Harry had ever imagined it might be. No one rustled a program. No woman fumbled with gloves or jewelry or gown. No man cleared his throat or shifted uncomfortably in his seat. It was as if people had been pulled into the drama playing out before them, and the effect was thrilling to behold.

As the curtain fell on the first act the audience took a split second to react but then they applauded loudly and a few people even cheered. Nola wished that she could be backstage with the others. How excited they must all be. Ellie had talked so much about how the actors onstage could always gauge an audience's reaction. "Sometimes we can feel them breathing," she'd said. "And when a performance is truly touching them, it's almost as if audience and performers have joined hands across the footlights. We are reaching their hearts and they are inspiring us to bring our best to the role."

How Nola wished she could share this moment with Harry. She could just imagine how excited he must be. And if only he could hear the praise being heaped upon him from those in the audience.

"I always knew that Harrison Starbuck was a gifted playwright, but choosing to present this latest work as an operetta is truly inspired," she heard one patron say as he escorted his wife back to their seats for the start of the second act. "It will be interesting to see how the production changes once he takes it to the New York stage."

"We should plan to attend the opening night performance," the woman replied.

Nola had to restrain herself from running backstage to tell Harry that people were already planning to see the production in New York. And then as the conductor tapped his baton on his podium and the musicians played the introduction to the second act opening, Nola realized that in just a few months, her music would be playing nightly on a New York stage. It might not be the concert halls she had dreamed of as a child, but it was a long way from a battered upright piano in the corner of a 'Sconset, Massachusetts tearoom.

By the second intermission, the audience was buzzing with excitement. It was as if they knew they were seeing something in its infancy that would one day be considered a classic of the American stage. And the atmosphere was positively electric when Harry stepped to the center of the stage before the final act. The applause that greeted him was thunderous. Nola watched him acknowledge the ovation with a slight bow and that boyish smile that would forever become her remembrance of this very special season.

"Bravo!" someone shouted and others took up the cry.

"Save your applause," he cautioned with a wider grin, "for you will need it to welcome our very special guest. A lady who certainly needs no introduction and who has come all the way from the stages of New York and Europe to take the role of the mother in this final act. Ladies and gentlemen, it is with great pleasure I present Miss Lillian Russell."

The gasp that swept through the hall immediately turned to cheers and whistles and applause as the audience rose to its feet and the grand lady took the stage. She played her part to perfection, in spite of the script she referred to from time to time. By the final number, several women in the audience were sobbing without apology and even some of the men were surreptitiously swiping at their eyes with the back of one hand.

Reluctantly Nola slipped out of her seat and hurried up the aisle to meet Judy in the lobby. They had decided they would have to skip the curtain calls in order to get back to the tearoom and have everything ready for the reception.

"I hope we have enough," Nola said as Jonah guided the carriage up the street to the tearoom.

"Well, it is what it is," Judy countered. "After all, I'll wager half the people who show up never intended to come at all but now that Harry's play is such a hit . . . What is that odor?" Judy said, sniffing the air as Jonah pulled the carriage to a halt. "Smells like rotten eggs."

Nola was still too caught up in the excitement of the evening to take much notice, but she could not deny that the odor got stronger as she and Judy unlatched the gate and started up the front walk.

"Oh, my," Judy whispered. She stopped and stared up at the grand old house.

Nola had been searching through her handbag for the key to the front door, but the distress in Judy's voice made her pause and look up as well.

The house — her lovely home — had been smeared and spattered with red paint and as Nola walked slowly up the front steps, she saw that the paint was not only fresh, it was still wet. The smell of rotten eggs was nearly overpowering as she stood on the edge of the porch and took in the broken shells and the liquid yolks and whites hardening on her windows.

"Who would do such a thing?" she whispered as she choked back tears.

"I'm going for Officer Daniels," Judy announced and started back down the walk. Then immediately spun around and came back. "No, I won't leave you alone. Jonah, go find Osgood now."

Nola reached for the doorknob, but Judy stopped her. "The culprits might be inside," she said. "Best we wait here or better, go back to the cabaret where we know you'll be safe." She took Nola's arm and led her from the porch but before they reached the gate, they could hear the laughter and excited chatter as their guests made their way through town by carriage or on foot from the cabaret to the tearoom.

As soon as the first carriage arrived, Judy took charge. "Officer Daniels is on his way here now," she stated. "Miss Nola's has been violated."

As word spread from carriage to carriage

and to those along the street, "Miss Nola's" became "Miss Nola" and by the time it reached Starbuck, the reports had Nola practically at death's door. Harry sprinted the rest of the distance from the cabaret to the tearoom and arrived panting and frantic to find Nola herself reassuring everyone.

"It's just a prank," she said.

"It's vandalism," Minnie Franks corrected her, "and as such should be punished to the full extent of the law."

"Officer Daniels is gathering the evidence he'll need to apprehend whoever is responsible for this. Now, please, everyone, just go home. I'm as disappointed as you are that we won't be able to celebrate this evening, but by tomorrow . . ."

Harry pushed his way through the crowd. "Are you all right?" he asked in a low voice as soon as he reached her.

"I'm fine," she said, but her voice shook and so did her hands and Harry just wanted to hold her against him until the shaking stopped. Until she knew she would always be safe with him. He also wanted to find whoever had done this and wallop the culprit, and he didn't for one second think God would punish him for either the thought or the actual deed if it came to that.

"Come here," he said and led her to the

side porch away from the others while Officer Daniels took charge.

"Harry, please tell them to go home," Nola whispered.

"No."

His refusal had the desired effect. Nola gathered her forces, eyes flashing with annoyance and stood her ground. "Well, they can hardly stay here," she argued.

"Whoever did this is hoping they have spoiled the evening for you and for everyone here. Well, let's not let them win, Nola. Let's have our party in spite of them."

Nola's mouth opened, then closed.

"Come on, Nola, you don't want all that food to go to waste and besides there's nothing more ravenous than a bunch of actors who have just given the performance of their young lives, right?"

"I wouldn't know," Nola said through gritted teeth.

"Well, I do. So, what do you say?"

"There is the slight problem of the smell of rotten eggs permeating the entire house by now," she pointed out.

Harry shrugged. "Easily remedied. Billy! Jasper! We need roses — armloads of roses. Go down the lane and cut them off the roofs of the cottages if you need to."

"Got it, boss," Billy replied.

"Besides, the smell won't be half as bad once we get everyone inside," he said, turning his attention back to Nola.

"I suppose we could . . ."

"That's my girl," he said and ran his finger along the curve of her jaw.

"You do know that you are impossible," she said, her voice as firm as it had been that first day she'd confronted him on this very porch.

"Very clear about that, Miss Nola." He tried looking chastised but instead broke into a grin. "I'll go in the back way and help Mrs. Lang in the kitchen."

"If we're doing this then you help me get everyone inside," Nola corrected. "Mrs. Lang has the Huff girls to help her."

Minutes later, the entire downstairs was crowded with theatergoers mingling with the performers. As he surveyed the scene, Harry had to admit it was a gathering he had never thought he would see. Not in 'Sconset. But the minute word filtered through town that Nola was in trouble, the town had banded together as one to come to her aid. He wondered if Nola had any idea how revered she was among her neighbors and friends.

Judy had insisted that Nola take a chair in the parlor. "If anybody out there needs to say something to you, then let them come to you for once. This is as much your night as it is Harry Starbuck's, so you just hold court right here."

Nola had not argued and that fact alone told Harry that she was more affected by the attack on her home than she was willing to let on.

"Miss Nola?"

Both Harry and Nola turned when Osgood ushered the Huff sisters into the room.

"What's going on?"

"These young ladies have something to tell you, miss. Meanwhile I'm going to arrest the real culprits."

The sisters kept their eyes on the floor as they nudged one another and muttered, "Tell her."

"*You* tell her."

"Girls, do you know who did this?" Nola asked.

"Yes, ma'am," they replied in unison.

The elder sister took a deep breath and met Nola's eyes directly. "We're really sorry, Miss Nola. We never thought they would go this far. We tried to stop them but, well, they just laughed at us."

"We thought they liked us," the other sister murmured. "Edgar said I was the sweetest girl he knew when I told him I'd put that envelope on the kitchen table to surprise you."

"Edgar?" Harry put the puzzle together at the same time Nola did. "The Gillenwater boys are responsible for this? For all the notes and the vandalism?"

Now the Huff girls looked worried. "We only know about tonight — and that one note," the elder one assured him.

"Well, I never. You girls just get yourselves back out to that kitchen and stay there," Judy ordered. "Before you get yourselves in any more trouble tonight."

The Huff sisters did not have to be asked twice. As they made their escape, Harry heard them casting blame on one another.

"If you hadn't . . ."

"Well, you were the one . . ."

Meanwhile Minnie and Oliver Franks assured others who had pressed into the doorway when they saw Osgood bring the two girls into the parlor that all was well. "Let's all step across the hall to the tearoom where we can sit and enjoy some of Mrs. Lang's delicious fruit punch."

The guests lingered for another hour, their low voices a sign that they were talking more about the real-life drama playing out in 'Sconset than they were reliving the operetta they had just seen onstage. As the clock chimed midnight, Nola heard Harry and Ellie assure the last of the departing guests that Miss Nola would be fine and yes, the tearoom would reopen in a few days, and of course, they could call on Nola to see if there was any way they might help.

When she felt Harry's hands on her shoulders, she had to resist the urge to turn to him and seek comfort in the strength of his embrace. "Has everyone gone?" she asked.

"For the most part. It's over, Nola. Osgood has the Gillenwater boys in custody," Harry assured her.

Nola started for the door. "Oh, dear. I wasn't even thinking. Poor Rose must be so devastated. I should go to her."

"She'll be fine," Harry soothed, urging her back into the chair. "I asked Dr. Wainwright to check on her and Alistair said the boys will be released tomorrow."

"They're in jail?"

"Alistair thought a night behind bars might do them some good. Give them some time to think about their actions."

Nola closed her eyes, then opened them immediately. "What about Miss Russell? Oh, Harry, you must go to her, explain what happened and offer her my deepest apologies."

"Tell her yourself," Harry said as the actress swept into the parlor.

"Well, Harrison," she said as he went to meet her and lead her to the unoccupied chair next to Nola, "you have always had a special flair for the dramatic but it seems this young lady has managed to outdo even you." She smiled at Nola.

"Oh, Miss Russell," Nola said. "I am so sorry . . ."

The actress dismissed any further comment with a wave of one lace-gloved hand. "Never apologize for the unavoidable, my dear. Harrison, it's been quite an evening. Thank you for this opportunity. I had forgotten how warm and appreciative audiences like this can be." She hid a yawn, then smiled. "And now, Nola dear, I am quite spent. Given the circumstances, I doubt the Gillenwaters need an extra houseguest this evening. Might I impose upon you to stay the night in your lovely guest room?"

"Of course, but I'm sure Harry could arrange a suite at the hotel now that everyone knows you're here."

Lillian smiled. "And therein lies the problem. I won't get a moment's sleep with people traipsing the halls trying to decide which room might be mine. No, I prefer your guest room if it's available."

"It's available anytime you wish to visit, Lillian," Nola assured her.

"Thank you, my dear. So I will say good-night." She tapped one forefinger against Harry's chest and smiled. "This little operetta of yours is going to take the critics' breath away, Harry. I only wish I were available to be a part of the cast. Perhaps next time you and Nola decide to collaborate, you'll keep me in mind for a role — a lead, of course?"

Nola fully expected Harry to laugh at the ridiculous notion that Nola might ever again pen a song worthy of a professional production. But as he took the actress's elbow and walked with her to the foyer, his reply shocked her. "Nola and I will definitely keep that in mind," he promised.

Once the famous actress had gone up to bed, Billy, Jasper, Olga and the Kowalski sisters took their leave, assuring Nola they would return the following day to help clean up the damage the Gillenwater boys had caused.

"Thank you," Nola said and the words caught in her throat as the enormity of support and friendship she'd seen this night hit her, making it impossible to say more.

"Nola, I'm just going to run back to the cabaret and get Lancelot," Ellie said as she wrapped a shawl around her shoulders. "Then I'll be back to stay the night."

"There's really no need," Nola protested. "Not now that . . ." Overcome by the emotional drama of the evening, Nola burst into tears.

"I'll stay," Harry said firmly.

"That would hardly be suitable, Mr. Starbuck," Rose Gillenwater announced. She stood in the doorway with Osgood Daniels, who had a firm grip on her two sons. "Nola, these boys have something they wish to say." She gave each boy a none-too-gentle shove toward Nola.

"Sorry," Edgar muttered.

"Yeah, sorry," Albert echoed.

Rose sighed. "That is hardly a proper apology. Now do this right or . . ."

"Sorry, Miss Nola," Edgar shouted, his fury apparent as he swung around to face his mother. "Was that better?"

"Young man, you will not speak to me in such tones."

"Why are you so mad at us?" he challenged.

Rose was absolutely sputtering as she attempted to find the words to address that question.

"Yeah, we did it for you," Albert added, taking courage from his brother. "You kept saying that you wished there were some way to get those actor people to leave Miss Nola alone and we thought if we sent her the notes . . ."

"You sent the notes as well?"

Nola thought Rose might faint, her face went so white.

"On your mother's notepaper," Harry guessed.

Albert nodded. "But it seemed like Miss Nola just ignored them. The one we left night before last . . ."

Harry shot Nola a look.

"I burned it without opening it," she admitted.

"Probably a good thing," Edgar grumbled. "We'd probably be getting sent away for ten years or something if . . ."

"You made at least one direct threat on Miss Burns's life," Harry said quietly. "That's a serious charge and unless Miss Nola burned all the notes, one still exists that proves my point, so I would be very careful what you say here."

Edgar and Albert refused to look at each other or anyone else. "You were the one who said we had to make each note more threatening," Albert accused his brother.

"Well, you were the one who thought smearing paint and rotten eggs all over —"

"Stop this right this minute," Rose ordered. "Officer Daniels, please escort these young men back to their cell. Their father and I will deal with them in the morning."

"But, Ma . . ." Albert whined.

Rose stood toe to toe with the boy who was already a good head taller than she was. "Now, you listen to me, young man. You boys may look like grown men but you are children and you have inserted yourselves — without permission — into a very adult issue here. If only you had come to me . . ." Her voice wavered slightly and then she grabbed each of her sons in turn, hugged him hard and then watched Osgood escort them from the room.

"There's no real harm," Nola said softly when Rose remained standing at the door long after they had all heard Osgood and the boys descend the front steps and move on down the street.

"Yes, there is," Rose murmured. Slowly she turned to face them. "It is always difficult to admit wrongdoing, but in this case I realize that I cannot avoid at least a part of the blame."

"Now, Mrs. Gillenwater," Harry began but she cut him off.

"Let me say this, Harrison." She gave him a wry smile and added, "You may never hear me apologize again for as everyone knows, I am seldom in the wrong."

Nola couldn't believe her ears. She had never once imagined that Rose Gillenwater might be hiding such a subtle and sly sense of humor. Harry chuckled and indicated with a sweep of his arm that she had center stage.

"Nola dear, the boys are quite within their rights to be confused. Over the last several weeks I have worried so about you and your entanglements with Harrison here and his band of minstrels that I'm afraid my concerns have quite dominated conversation in our home."

"You've always had my best interests at heart," Nola said.

"Be that as it may, I have led my boys astray. Without realizing it I have passed my personal prejudices on to them. Of course, what they did is a sign of their deep devotion to me and yet . . ."

"Mrs. Gillenwater," Harry interrupted when the older woman looked as if any moment she might dissolve into racking sobs, "may I make a suggestion?"

Rose pressed her fist to her tight-lipped mouth and nodded.

"Alistair's idea of a night in jail is a good lesson, but once the boys are back home . . ."

Rose wheeled around and faced Nola. "Don't you intend to press charges? They made threats and destroyed property and . . ."

"Let's hear Harry out," Nola suggested.

"As you may recall, Mrs. Gillenwater, I had some run-ins with authority figures when I was about your boys' age. The problem usually was one of having too much time on my hands."

"Edgar and Albert are often at loose ends," Rose admitted.

"So, let's put them to work. They can begin by repairing the damage they've caused here. They'll need to scrub down the walls and windows and then paint the entire exterior of the house."

"That's manual labor, Mr. Starbuck."

Harry shrugged. "Seems to me it beats jail time and teaches a far better lesson."

"They don't know the first thing about painting or window washing."

"Jonah Lang can teach them and keep an eye on them," Harry suggested.

Nola could see that Harry's idea was beginning to have an effect. "It would keep them busy and out of mischief, Rose."

"And if they happen to complete that work before they head back to boarding school in the fall, then I can use them backstage at the cabaret."

Rose stiffened. "My sons do not . . ."

Harry raised an eyebrow and Rose reconsidered.

"You won't allow them to appear on stage?" Rose bargained.

"No, ma'am," Harry assured her then added with his own wry smile, "not unless they prove to have more talent than the actors I already have in residence."

Rose sucked in her breath.

"Oh, Rose, Harry is just — well, being Harry. I'm quite sure there is no reason for Edgar and Albert to be in front of an audience."

"Of course, they are both quite gifted in the arts," Rose said. "Albert has a lovely tenor and Edgar . . ."

"Let's say that should I suddenly have the inspiration to use one or both of your sons in a production, I'll discuss it with you and Alistair first," Harry offered.

Rose took a moment to consider the proposal before her, then nodded. "Very well. I'll speak with their father and have him make the arrangements. Tell Jonah he can expect them as soon as they are out of jail — certainly no later than midmorning tomorrow."

"It's a good plan, Rose," Nola said as she took the older woman's hand between hers. "I can only imagine how hard it must have been for you to come here tonight. Please know that nothing the boys did has in any way changed my respect and admiration for you, Rose. You were always a good friend to my mother and you have been a loyal and protective friend to me. Nothing can change that."

Rose pulled her hand free and embraced Nola. "Sometimes it's difficult to keep up with changing times, Nola dear. Especially for those of us set in our ways. You've always been like another daughter to me, you know that."

"I do," Nola assured her. "Between you and Judy Lang I have been truly blessed to have not one but two wise women to take the place of my own dear mother."

Rose composed herself and turned to face Harry. "Violet tells me that had you not broken off your pursuit of her, she would have done so. These modern young women do have a way of asserting themselves." She glanced at Nola and then shook a finger at Harry. "You may wish to keep that in mind, Harrison."

"Yes, ma'am."

Rose glanced around the room as if to

satisfy herself that everything was in order. "Very well, then. I shall see you in the morning, Nola. And, Harry, be sure that Jonah Lang is here as well."

"Yes, ma'am," Harry repeated.

Rose made it as far as the door and turned. "Now, Nola, it occurs to me that those Huff girls should have some part in this. Perhaps they might take on washing the windows while Albert and Edgar get started on the housepainting."

"I'll make sure they're ready to work."

Rose cocked an eyebrow at Harry. "Are you coming, Harrison?"

"Not just yet," Nola replied before Harry had a chance to. "Mr. Starbuck has some business that he wishes to discuss with me, so I'll see you tomorrow, Rose."

As soon as Rose had left, Nola sat down at her desk. It felt more appropriate for a business discussion to take place in her office even at this late hour. She folded her hands and waited for him to speak. Instead, he paced the floor, his hands clasped behind his back, his tie loosened and shirt collar stud open.

"If this is about changing your mind regarding my property, Harry, you can have it," she said quietly. "All I ask is that you give me the remainder of the season to dispose of things — the furnishings and such." He had paused and was frowning down at her, obviously stunned that she had guessed what he was going to ask. "And there's the matter of Mrs. Lang," Nola continued. "I trust you will offer her employment in some facet of your business. Other than that . . ."

"Is that what you think this is about? A piece of property?"

"Oh, Harry," Nola said, smiling up at him, "wasn't that where this all began?"

"No. Yes, but —"

"But in the bargain we discovered something so much more precious. God gave us this opportunity to become friends, to combine our talents in a project that has brought us both such joy — a project that will bring that same hope and joy to audiences in theaters everywhere."

"Will you just stop talking for one minute and listen?" he said.

Surprised at his sudden foul mood when she was being so agreeable, Nola pressed her lips into the thin line that had once been her trademark when faced with a situation she could not control.

"Better," Harry said and resumed his pacing. "Now then, Miss Burns, I have had the occasion to spend some time here in this home, and while I have not yet been privileged to examine the upper floors, my acting friends report that the rooms are quite spacious and comfortable. It has occurred to me that the large bedroom overlooking the sea would make an excellent bridal suite. In time, Ellie tells me there's a smaller connecting room that could serve as a nursery. As more children come along, the other rooms would gradually fill up . . ."

"A nursery? What exactly is it that you are suggesting?" Nola asked, her confusion and curiosity getting the better of her determination to let him speak his piece.

Harry knelt so that their faces were at the same level. "I am not *suggesting* anything." He removed a blue velvet jeweler's box from his pocket and opened it. "I am on my knee pleading with you to become my wife so that together we can make this our summer home and raise our children here. I am imagining that we will take your bedroom here on the first floor and make it our library and music room where together we can work on our next play. Then we could turn the tearoom back to its original use as a dining room where we will entertain family and friends."

Nola watched as if she were in a dream as

he slipped the square-cut diamond ring onto her finger.

"I am saying that I love you, Nola, and if you will have me, I would like to spend the rest of my days with you. Will you do me the honor, Nola?"

A gasp and short bark from the foyer reminded them both that Ellie must have returned with Lancelot, so Nola raised her voice as she had seen her actor friends do when they wanted to be sure they were heard all the way to the back row. "Yes," she shouted as she wound her arms around Harry's neck. "Yes, I will marry you," she said as he lifted her and danced with her around the room and on out into the foyer where Judy came running from the kitchen. "Yes. Yes. Yes," she cried ecstatically as she punctuated each affirmation with a kiss to Harry's laughing face.

"Well, it's about time," Ellie announced and released Lancelot so he could join in their waltz. Then she took her place at the piano and pounded out the wedding march while Judy clapped her hands in time to the music and a startled Lillian Russell came running from her room to see what had caused such celebration.

EPILOGUE

Spring 1900

Nola reclined in one of the deck chairs of the ocean liner bound from London to New York and thought of all that had changed in her life in one short year. She glanced over at Harry who was dozing, the new straw hat she'd given him for Christmas tipped low over his eyes.

"My husband," she whispered just to feel the now familiar but joyous thrill of knowing they were wed.

As if hearing her, Harry smiled and reached over to take her hand, his eyes still hidden beneath the brim of his hat. "Happy?" he asked.

"Beside myself with joy," she replied.

"It's been quite a year," he mused. "The premiere of our first operetta on the New York stage."

"You *would* think of that first," Nola teased, then sighed dramatically. "Never fear, I am well aware that the theater will always be your one true love."

Harry tipped back his hat and gazed at her and the love that shone from those piercing blue eyes was so undeniable that it took her breath away. "If I never wrote, staged or saw another theatrical event, it would be no loss," he said. "But if anything were to happen to you . . ."

"Nothing is going to happen," she assured him, then she laughed. "Well, something will happen. Over the coming months I will get quite large I expect. My mother certainly did when she was pregnant and she was . . ."

Harry leaped from his chair and came to kneel next to her. "You're with child? What on earth are you doing sitting out here in the damp chill? Let's get you below and get you some hot broth and . . ." He scooped her high in his arms and headed below to their cabin.

"It's a baby, not a porcelain doll, Harry," Nola said, but she was laughing. She found that she laughed a lot these days.

"Our baby," Harry muttered. "How long have you known?"

"I suspected when we were with my sister — I think she did as well. With three children of her own and another on the way, she would certainly know the signs. This morning while you were wiring New York about the new cabaret season in 'Sconset, I went to see the ship's doctor and he confirmed it."

"Someone else will have to handle the summer season. We should stay in New York at least until the child is born so you can have the best of care."

"You're beginning to sound like Rose Gillenwater," Nola said, stifling a yawn as he laid her gently on her bunk. "And besides, who would manage the season? Who would run the rehearsals for our new production? Who would —"

She was interrupted by a light tap at the cabin door.

"Message for you and Mrs. Starbuck, sir. Just came over the wires," the steward said.

Harry tipped the young man and closed the door. "It's from Ellie," he added as he pulled the translated message free of its envelope.

"Read it aloud."

"Dear Nola and Harry,
Well, here we are at the start of an entire new century. Imagine the changes we'll witness! I can hardly wait to see the two of you. Everyone here in New York is already buzzing about your latest oper-

etta and jockeying for the opportunity to audition. You should think about staging a preview in 'Sconset again. It would be fun to get the whole gang together.

I have news as well. An old friend from Tennessee came backstage after one of my performances and we have been writing to each other ever since."

Nola pushed herself to a seated position on the bed and leaned forward. "Do you think that Ellie might have a new beau?"

"The guy's in Tennessee and she's in New York. She says 'old friend' — doesn't sound like romance to me."

Nola rolled her eyes. "Keep reading."

"He raises horses — racehorses. I'll tell you more when I see you. Oh, almost forgot, Alistair and Rose Gillenwater were in the city to visit friends and they invited me to dinner. Seems that their son, Edgar, caught the acting bug after working backstage last season and Rose is once again faced with a dilemma. She knows that she can no longer dictate the paths her children choose but she is intent on finding some way she can guide them. So why was I invited to dinner? She wants me to stay in their home for the summer and coach him. 'If he's going to pursue this idea, then I want him to be properly schooled in the classics.' Imagine that!

Well, my entrance cue is coming up so I'll end this. And so, my dear ones, safe voyage as you cross the Atlantic and much happiness as you set sail on this ship of matrimony. I shall hold you both in my heart and in my prayers until we are together again. Ellie."

"Oh, poor Rose. She must be beside herself," Nola said.

Harry stared out the porthole for a long moment. "Now, hear me out," he said as if she had interrupted some declaration. "If you promise to take care of yourself, perhaps we could put together a show or two for the season, but . . ."

"Yes," Nola said softly, reaching up to grasp his hand. "Let's go home to Nantucket and stage our new play at the cabaret with Ellie and Billy and the others if they're available."

"Of course, given your condition, it might be too much — and of course, there may still be those who . . ."

"I said, let's do it," Nola reminded him. "Your plays are a kind of ministry, Harry.

The lessons you bring to the stage touch people's hearts and renew their faith in God and their fellow man. It's important to continue such good work — to make full use of the talents God has given you."

Harry sat on the edge of the bunk and pulled her into his arms. "I love you, Mrs. Starbuck," he murmured. "How did I ever get so fortunate?"

"We had good people and God's eyes watching over us." She cradled her flat tummy. "And this little dear is going to have more godmothers and godfathers than she will know what to do with."

"She?" Harry raised one eyebrow. "What if it's a boy?"

Nola cuddled into the haven of his arms and closed her eyes. "Well, if he's anything like his father, I had best get as much rest as possible before he arrives."

Harry's laughter filled the cabin like music as he gathered her in his arms and the gentle rocking of the sea carried them home to Nantucket.

Dear Reader,

It's always a delight to return to Nantucket! And the tiny village of 'Sconset on the island's far eastern shore is a special place indeed. I must admit that when I first heard of rose-covered cottages, I thought it was perhaps the embellishment of an overzealous Chamber of Commerce brochure. But there they were! Quiet, peaceful lanes lined with small weathered gray cottages dressed in garlands of lovely, fragrant pink roses. Add in the history of theater people from Broadway summering there at the turn of the last century and well, it just had to become a setting for a book! One of the elements of living a life driven by faith and spirituality has always been to open my heart and mind to the possibility (rather than the threat) of broadening my personal world to embrace those who think, look or act different from me. In short, like many people, I have to rein in my normal human instincts to stereotype, to label and to judge. For me the "secret" has always been to remind myself that like everything else, diversity was also God's creation and the challenge becomes to find the "rose vines" that connect us all — even among the thorns of difference and disagreement. I'd

love to know your thoughts on this —
contact me via my Web site at *www.books
byanna.com* or by mail at P.O. Box 161,
Thiensville, WI, 53092.

Peace and blessings,
Anna Schmidt

QUESTIONS FOR DISCUSSION

1. What are your first impressions of Nola Burns? Of Harry Starbuck?

2. What are their first impressions of each other?

3. How do those first impressions (yours and theirs) change over the course of the story?

4. In what ways are characters in the book guilty of stereotyping others? Which characters and how do they stereotype?

5. Can you think of some examples of stereotyping that people engage in now?

6. When you see or hear someone engaged in stereotyping how do you react?

7. Nola has always had strong ties to the

town of 'Sconset. What is the basis of those ties and how valid are they for her future happiness and ability to live a full life?

8. Starbuck believes that theater can be used to reach people and lift their spirits in a positive way. What plays or films or television shows have you seen that you found spiritually uplifting?

9. What are some of the ways that you reach out to others as you live your faith?

10. In what ways were the parents and other townspeople responsible for the fact that the notes were sent and the vandalism followed?

11. In what ways was Starbuck's punishment of the culprits unique? And what impact do you think the punishment made on the culprits?

12. In many ways this is a story about labeling others. We all do it to some degree. What would be three positive steps you might take to be more open to and appreciative of the value that comes in know-

ing people of different cultures, races,
social groups, etc.?

ABOUT THE AUTHOR

Anna Schmidt is an award-winning author of more than twenty works of historical and contemporary fiction. She is a two-time finalist for the coveted RITA® Award from Romance Writers of America as well as three times a finalist for a *Romantic Times BOOKreviews* Reviewer's Choice Award. The most recent nomination was for her 2008 Love Inspired Historical novel, *Seaside Cinderella,* which is the first of a series of four historical novels set on the romantic island of Nantucket. Critics have called Anna "a natural writer, spinning tales reminiscent of old favorites like *Miracle on 34th Street.*" Her characters have been called "realistic" and "endearing" and one reviewer raved, "I love Anna Schmidt's style of writing!"

The employees of Thorndike Press hope you have enjoyed this Large Print book. All our Thorndike, Wheeler, and Kennebec Large Print titles are designed for easy reading, and all our books are made to last. Other Thorndike Press Large Print books are available at your library, through selected bookstores, or directly from us.

For information about titles, please call:
(800) 223-1244

or visit our Web site at:
http://gale.cengage.com/thorndike

To share your comments, please write:
Publisher
Thorndike Press
295 Kennedy Memorial Drive
Waterville, ME 04901